# The Frequency of Souls

## Mary Kay Zuravleff

Farrar, Straus and Giroux, New York

Library of Congress Cataloging-in-Publication Data
Zuravleff, Mary Kay.
The frequency of souls / Mary Kay Zuravleff.
p.    cm.
I. Title.
PS3576.U54F74    1996    813'.54—dc20    95-30232    CIP

The author is grateful to Iris DeMent
for permission to quote from her song
"Sweet Forgiveness," © 1992 by Songs
of Iris / Forerunner Music Inc.

*To Gary Zizka,*

*for much that goes unsaid*

*The Frequency of Souls*

Ever since he had built his first radio set from glass tubes and a spool of lead, George Mahoney remained convinced that the universe was soldered together with logic. That, in essence, was his philosophy, though there were corollaries, too: all supernatural phenomena, including what passed for miracles, were explicable; the dead were no longer among us; stars contained no truths for our future; and so on. This dogma had sustained him through such head trips as the Vietnam era, college during the early seventies, and sixteen years of marriage. Lately, however, in the slow afternoons when he was supposed to be advancing the cause of refrigerator design, George found himself watching his new office mate and reviewing his belief system.

Niagara Spense swiveled away from her computer and looked at George with an arched eyebrow that let him know he had been staring. For a number of reasons—her eyes, her size, her hearing aid—it was hard not to stare at the gangly girl scientist stationed at the next computer. Their assistant, Bev, had pointed out to George that Niagara sewed her own clothes, a dozen variations of a single prototype. Today she was wearing one in a gold paisley that was better suited to basement couches. George hadn't known women Niagara's age still sewed. It was a perfectly acceptable dress, maybe even one his wife, Judy, would wear. Short sleeves, no collar or buttons or belt. Each of the dresses had a tendency to slip off her left shoulder.

Before Niagara, George had only ever had one office mate, a bitter man with the personality of a snapping turtle. After forty winters on the project, the Veteran still said "icebox," and the one story he enjoyed telling, which George remembered like an earache, was how he had invented self-defrosting refrigerators to the surprise and betterment of the world. As the bells rang in 1992 and Coldpoint accounted for another slow year, the mean-spirited pioneer had been forced to resign amid talk of massive layoffs. Scarcely a week after the Veteran's retirement lunch, Niagara Spense was brought in to take his place.

This cloudy spring morning that was sure to end in scattered showers, Niagara extracted a filament of hair from the temple of her glasses, where broken strands often hung like fishing line, and returned George's stare with a personal question. "How did you come to be in Rockville, Maryland, designing refrigerators?"

George thought that if he told Niagara his story, she might be more chatty. Despite their sharing a fifteen-by-fifteen-foot windowless office, George knew little about her other than what he had gleaned from her personnel file. Even that was sparse. She was twenty-eight years old to his thirty-nine; her parents were concert pianists; while her Caltech transcript shone with A's, she had left without a doctorate. Shackelford, their boss, had interviewed her by phone. His notes consisted of "Smart kid" and "Nice voice," each underlined until the lead broke through the paper.

Still self-conscious in Niagara's presence, George fumbled with his clip-on tie, which was not nearly long enough for his six-foot-two-inch frame. George was bashful among homely women, perhaps because he had been a homely child who had come through adolescence transformed. He had grown into his once-bulging eyes, and as his body muscled up, his hair calmed down, settling into waves that drew compliments from his wife's friends. Through little effort on his part, he was tan and fit, and sometimes, when he saw a reflection of himself wrapped in his plush blue robe, pushing up his tortoiseshell glasses and leaning forward to shave the stubble at the square of his jaw, he could recognize himself as Magazine Man, a nickname his daughter had invented.

George had a theory that handsome people who start out unhandsome never quite get over those years spent avoiding eye contact. He raked a hand through the thickest part of his hair, watching all the while the muscle he made with this gesture.

How had he come to refrigerators? Any answer George gave would have to include Dino Park, off route I-75 outside Louisville. In George's life, Dino Park was like the wall in the laundry room where his children's heights were annually recorded, each gash a significant advance over the earlier marks.

"George," Niagara asked, "why engineering?"

George admired how Niagara reworded questions after he had let too much time pass. He hoped he would remember this trick the next time she didn't answer and he wasn't sure if her bulky hearing aid was turned on.

"It struck me that no one asks me that. I mean, people always ask Judy how she got into real estate." George thought it might be because she netted almost three times his salary selling houses.

Niagara said, "People ask me all the time, partly because of my parents."

"Physicists?" George tried to look as if he didn't know.

"Musicians."

"Really?" George said, setting his head to nodding. Her parents had been mentioned in her file, which he hadn't actually pilfered but had certainly helped himself to, having discovered it mislaid in the conference room. Afterward, George had run a computer search through the *Post*'s reviews. Her parents had twice filled every seat in the Kennedy Center, including the president's box; several concertos had been commissioned especially for Spense & Gignoux.

Niagara was holding on to the chain of her necklace. She closed her eyes and said, "Make a wish."

"Why?" George asked.

"That's what you do when the clasp touches the pendant. Don't you know a single thing?" Niagara fed the chain through the golden drop she always wore, until the fastener was under her hair. Then she lifted the neckline of her dress back onto her shoulder.

No amount of nervousness on George's part could compare with the fits and starts that possessed Niagara. Rather than be distracted, George was lulled by her quiet percussiveness, the tapping and flapping of her flyswatter hands accompanied by the jingling of her earrings.

In fact, one of the only places Niagara showed any variety in her wardrobe was in her choice of earrings. Mostly, they were large and pendulous, a noticeable violation of dress code. Nearly all of them jangled or clacked when she moved, which George thought would drive a person with a hearing aid nuts.

"What's it going to take?" Niagara asked. "Dripping water? Electrical shocks?"

"My story's not that interesting," he said. "What brought you to it?"

"Forget it," Niagara said. "I tell all, and then you say you don't remember. You're up."

George wished he could forget. He still dreamed about the long drive to Pershing Academy in the silent, spacious Impala. His mother's eyes baggy and sad as her ironing pile; his father coughing, trying to keep down his rage. Succumbing to Carol Greyson had required George to molt his suspicion, and free of that carapace, he had slithered and chirped, a young man animated by possibilities until exiled to military school.

But last week, when this nocturnal scene again unfolded, the picture he had carried in the hip pocket of his dreams was not of his high-school girlfriend. It was a portrait of Niagara Spense draped in black velvet, wearing nothing but the golden drop encircling her neck and that shoe-polish eyeliner he so adored. George might at least have conjured up the club's tennis pro, a redhead who had told Judy that underwear slowed down her serve. Niagara Spense had straight, cloth-brown hair, already bleached with gray. Her thick, wire-rimmed glasses magnified her eyes, and she was as broad-shouldered as George. With his night vision,

George was able to keep Niagara at a softening, flattering distance, just as directors shoot aging movie stars through out-of-focus lenses.

Stirring awake from the most recent screening of his recurring dream, George had tunneled under the covers toward Judy. A slight camphor odor from the foot cream she used lent an Arabian flavor to the stale air beneath the sheets; palm trees and oases were also present in the coconut-oil dressing she rubbed on the ends of her black hair, which was as slick as if it were laminated. George could see past Judy's knees to her muscled calves. Her silk slip of a nightgown flowed over her long thighs, and as she lay on her side, her stomach and smallish breasts (if he reached out, each would barely fill a cupped hand) sagged slightly toward the bed. George marveled at her unadorned clavicles, the bones nearly as visible as those on a skeleton.

He had licked the hollow above and between those clavicles hundreds of times. Judy's ability to keep herself, as well as their home, trim and focused had always elicited in George the release that precedes desire; now, her lack of voluptuousness diminished his appetite. Their lives seemed scrawny, lean to an unadmirable degree, and Niagara lingered in George's thoughts as a meaty veal flank for his subconscious to gnaw on.

Niagara began to shuffle through papers at her desk, from feathery scraps to computer-drawn schematics, slick as vellum. "If it's that traumatic, you don't have to tell me," she mumbled. "I was just curious."

George was embarrassed not to have answered yet. Dancing in his peripheral vision, Niagara was a blur of movement outside the rim of his corrected eyesight. She seemed bent on disorder as her flailing scattered papers of disparate sizes. The breezes she created carried the musky candle smell of a basement or it could have been her waxy lipstick, which she applied thickly, George imagined, to overcompensate for the thinness of her lips.

"Traumatic?" he said. "More like banal." Maybe when he and Niagara had worked side by side for fourteen years, George could explain how soldering a transistor into place had required the same concentration and nimble-fingered agility he had shown unhooking Carol's bra beneath her shirt and sweater. For now, he chose to focus on a time before Carol.

George removed his glasses before embarking on his tale. He had found that by clouding his vision and keeping his chair an office length from Niagara, he could simulate the effect of his dreams. Ten feet away and fuzzy, Niagara was more striking than odd, and with her desk lamp behind her, a blurry halo rose round her head.

In a low, lullaby voice more suited for Sheridan's bedtime story, George began. "Nearly every Saturday morning, my mother would scream at me for one thing or another, and my father would take me out on maneuvers." His intentions of telling a simple story had led him out on a personal limb, and he wasn't sure if it could hold his weight until he was finished.

"It wasn't what she said so much as the volume. That she could yell so loud at me hurt my feelings." Squinting, he could see Niagara was looking back and forth as if for an exit. Where was he going with this? All he had needed to say was that one good physics teacher had been his inspiration.

"Is that possible?" Niagara asked. "Sound would hurt your fillings?"

He was growing accustomed to Niagara mishearing him. *"Feelings,"* enunciated George, the last person in the world who would be expected to make that pronouncement.

"One Saturday, my dad took me to Dino Park." Usually it didn't matter where they went; the relief he felt in his father's company was enough of a treat for him. "Two years earlier, the attraction had been featured in the *Weekly Reader*, and our fourth-grade class made a pilgrimage there. That trip had required permission slips to ride the bus, parental volunteers, a buddy chain— one safety measure after another."

"Poor George," Niagara said, "so ready to be devoured."

George shrugged. "Why such precautions unless there was remarkable danger? It was as if we might break apart and be scattered to the four winds, spin off the earth. When Dad and I drove there, it only took a few minutes. We rolled the windows of the Impala down to the nub, and blasts of chives and honeysuckle were blowing in our faces. I was just enjoying the prospect of a long ride and we were there."

George didn't describe the park to Niagara; he thought the name said it all. He told her about how he and his father strolled from one wild-eyed, fanged monster to another.

"I don't get it," Niagara said. "Why were there monsters?"

"They looked like monsters to me," he confessed.

Then Niagara yelled, "Dinosaurs!" and George jumped. "I'm an idiot," she said. "Dino Park had dinosaurs, right?"

"Yes." George wondered if the words he thought he was speaking were different from what was actually spilling from his mouth.

"Dy-no Park," Niagara said, stretching out the syllables. "I thought Dyno was short for dynamos. I ask you why engineering drew you in, and you start telling me about some city park that, for all I know, featured generators through the ages."

In a huckster voice, George said, "See the turbines that powered Noah's ark. Marvel at transformers cast in iron by ancient Chinese scholars."

They laughed easily over the misunderstanding, chuckling as if they had a long history together. George was comfortable resorting to silliness, one of his chief parenting skills. When Niagara bared her wide teeth, she automatically reached up to cover her mouth. She wore no rings, though she had an oversized watch bound to her wrist with a strap the thickness of a belt.

"Welcome to Dyno Park," Niagara said, "where dynamos rule the earth."

While they were still amused, their boss marched in unannounced. The only black manager at Coldpoint, Shackelford had competed against the Veteran to get the position, and he rarely stopped by design after that. In fact, Niagara had reported to George that she had seen him only twice.

"Everything all right in here?" Shackelford said.

George wondered if his boss had ever heard laughter from the design office.

Niagara said, "George is telling me why he became an engineer."

"He won't be one for long if he doesn't get to work."

Niagara had decorated her corner with several cacti and a bushy plant whose long tendrils tumbled down the back of her desk. Shackelford pinched a waxy green leaf, surprising himself when he plucked it off. "This is real," he announced.

"Spider ivy," Niagara said. "It's good in offices because it actually absorbs toxins and reinvigorates the air with oxygen."

Shackelford scowled. "The Veteran never had plants."

George remembered how pitiful it had been watching the Veteran pack his single box of personal effects. Four decades in the same cinder-block building, and all they amounted to were a few posters of fighter planes, textbooks on refrigerator repair, a photograph of his wife and son that was taken around the time of the moon landing, and enough office supplies to open his own firm. That day, George had promised himself he would ask Judy for decorating advice, a vow he remembered whenever Niagara brought in another ornament. She had old tin toys and new plastic windups, including a refrigerator that waddled along on pink bun-iony feet. A dozen or more nineteenth-century photographs, each in an unusual frame, were hung on the wall. In a show of solid geometry, Niagara had pieced the odd frames together to form a circle. Comparing the two sides of their cubicle, George noticed that it looked as if Niagara had occupied her cozy corner for years and he were the newcomer.

Shackelford turned over an eggplant-shaped pitcher to look at the underside. "Is this a toy?" he growled.

"It's a pitcher," Niagara said.

"Looks like an eggplant," the boss remarked. Then he left without another word.

"Do we need to worry about that?" Niagara asked.

"God, no," George said with more confidence than he felt. He wondered why Shackelford had stepped in.

"OK, pal," Niagara finally said, "where were we?"

"Visiting the exclusive Dinah Shore Preserve," George bravely teased.

"The provocative Diane Sawyer Sanctuary," Niagara returned, further evidence that she could easily match wits with him.

George explained how his first trip to Dino Park had filled his imagination with talons and horned, rubbery faces leering through his bedroom window. So that he could get some sleep, George devoted his library period to dinosaurs. Not solely dinosaurs, for there were other items to be researched. Kevin Whitby had convinced George that the Mercury astronauts, their waste dumped out some space hatch, had orbited in formation with their own turds.

"I was tired of being the sucker," George said. His favorite book of that era was *Facts on File*, a cogent listing of brief truths that, bound together, weighed about as much as his head. By high school, research had become nearly an obsession. As U.S. troops sprayed Agent Orange in Asian jungles, George tried to defoliate the thicket behind his eyes, hoping that in weeding out the lies he would expose the snares and tiger traps set by wily classmates who gorged themselves on his ready embarrassment.

"Touring Dino Park with my father was a joy. I wanted the dinosaurs to be more realistic, even as I respected the owners' lack of conjecture. So much about the reptiles was unknown."

"Like whether or not they're reptiles," Niagara said.

"Exactly," George congratulated her, but he should have known better than to make that slip. He described to Niagara the focal point of the visit, a wide woman with a red bandanna on her head standing near what was then called a brontosaur. A crowd of people clapped and hooted. The woman wore faded dungarees and an embroidered work shirt, gold granny glasses, and strand after strand of beads and leather. She was part squaw, part weird aunt. George had never seen a woman his mother's age in this kind of getup. A star-shaped name tag on her chest identified her as Mrs. Harrison.

"Crowd on in, babies," she said, her Kentucky accent thicker than paste. "Don't leave any breathing room."

George's father ribbed him. He said, "From her size, I'd guess she's a bonbonivore."

George thought she looked absurdly graceful, gathering the

crowd close to her in a hug. On the small stage was an easel that held sheets of white poster board. Mrs. Harrison said, "Welcome to 'What's Wrong with This Picture?,' that Mesozoic game show y'all love to play." She flipped the piece of poster board, struggling with it in the drafty Kentucky spring.

The first picture was a drawing of a warty brontosaur sitting at a table elegantly set with a tablecloth and silver candelabra. A waiter stood at the elbow of the brontosaur, whose order was printed in a balloon above its head: "One hundred steaks, please."

"You, sir," Mrs. Harrison said to George's father, "what's wrong with this picture?"

"Dinosaurs aren't allowed in most restaurants," he said.

"Are you sure?" Mrs. Harrison asked. "I've never seen a 'No Dinosaurs' sign."

The group laughed. Guesses flew. The waiter was too short (he was drawn to scale), dinosaurs could not talk (only grunt and squeal, Mrs. Harrison instructed). George let the little kids have their say, but eventually the bad guesses beefed up his courage. "They didn't eat meat," he said. "Brontosaur was a herbivore."

Mrs. Harrison wiped her brow melodramatically. "Shwoo," she said. "I thought we'd never figure that out."

Next was a brontosaur throttling a tyrannosaur. George listened to a few wrong answers before he said, "They lived fifty million years apart."

After the third correct answer, Mrs. Harrison shook his hand and awarded him a plastic iguanodon. "If I were your mother," she said that memorable Saturday, "I'd be proud as punch."

"How did you know all that?" Niagara asked. Her head was cocked so that her good ear was closer to George.

"The herbivore thing was straight out of the pamphlet; the rest I remembered from my fourth-grade frenzy." George explained how memorizing the time lines and giving names to the plated creatures had eased his fears. Dipped in these facts, he had a shiny coat, a luster that dazzled. It was this protective shield, George told Niagara, that led him to delve into the factual world of science, first chemistry and then electronics.

He ended the story there, figuring why not close on a high

note. What he had left out was that after their Dino Park tour, his father compounded the day's events by allowing George a turn at the wheel on back roads home, where they were given a stony reception. George tried to stay out of his mother's line of sight, but his father bragged about how Georgio knew all the answers, even won a prize. When George dutifully held up the iguanodon, his mother said, "Aren't you a little old for that?" George recalled that her remark bounced off his armor, galvanized with factual prowess and some driving practice.

George made sure to fix on Niagara's rich brown eyes as he put his glasses back on; her eyes were one of the few features that improved with corrected vision. He hoped he hadn't given himself a headache by not wearing his glasses.

Niagara took a last loud sip from her china teacup. "There's more to that story, all right," she said. "If that were the whole story, you'd be a paleontologist, a children's book illustrator. There's something else."

Her intuitive powers unnerved George, especially considering how little attention she paid him. Of course, during the years he'd worked at the fiberglass menagerie, he had envisioned himself becoming a paleontologist. Hunting thigh bones the size of the family car, clearing up the mystery of the ancient reptiles' disappearance.

"George, George," his mother had said. "I see you as a surgeon in a crisp white coat; a pretty young nurse hands you clean instruments at your command." She had smiled at him as if he were a stranger. Then her smile hooked at the edge. "Honey," she said, "you don't want to be a grave robber." That was around the time George had learned that people could choose to have children, and he couldn't imagine why his mother had chosen to have him.

Niagara looked him over. She said, "You're off the hook for now."

"And you?" George asked.

"Why did I become an engineer?" Niagara drummed the fingers of both hands on her desk. "I don't seem to remember."

George's mouth dropped open in a guffaw.

"Relax, George. I'm kidding."

Once a sucker, always a sucker. He wasn't even that curious about what had led Niagara to engineering; for a bright girl with a talent for math and science, it was a good career. He wondered why she had left Caltech without her doctorate, how she had lost her hearing, why she did not buy herself a dress.

"Can I tell you later?" she asked. "I really will tell you, but I have to get some work done."

Niagara turned abruptly to her computer screen. Within seconds, she was squinting at some on-line catalog of refrigerator parts, her neck stretched forward like a snail's. She was not going to be his confidante; in fact, she had underwhelmed all his expectations. Trying not to take offense, George left his office, following the smell of boiled coffee and cigarette droppings down the green halls to the staff room.

The one-story building was shaped like a swastika, with four doglegs joined around a central entrance. George and Niagara's office was at the inside elbow of the southwest dogleg. Nearly everyone else who worked at a desk, rather than in the lab or on the line, had a private office, even if it meant building a wall down the center of shared space and punching another doorway into the hall. For years, George had expected his boss to announce that the design office would be halved, but it never happened.

Walking the corridor, George revisited his fantasies surrounding Niagara's arrival. Niagara had looked sensational on paper. She was a California girl, the daughter of famous pianists, graduate assistant to a Nobel laureate. In George's imagined scenario, Niagara, a tanned lovely in a sequined leotard, would wheel refrigerators in and open the various compartments, much the same way a magician's assistant shows off the box before stepping inside to be sawed in half. George would stand nearby in tux and top hat, bashful at the audience's wild reception, while Niagara unveiled the magic refrigerator they had together engineered. He remembered the disappointment he felt on meeting Niagara, when Shackelford had pushed them toward each other and said, "You two will be sharing this cell."

George saw a flash of lightning on his way to the staff room, and he instinctively counted the seconds until the matching thunderclap. George had passed the hub of the building and turned right down the southeast hallway; now he tacked left. When the rumble sounded, he estimated the storm at about seven miles south. From what he'd heard, it was coming their way.

## *The Match That Lit the Fire*

The pie case was nearly empty in the staff room. George picked out two fat donuts, crusty with sugar and age, and balanced one atop each coffee cup. Two donuts and two coffees, ninety and seventy-five cents apiece, respectively, plus eight percent tax— George had three dollars and fifty-six cents ready before the hair-netted cashier rang it up. He knew to wait for her to disclose the total; otherwise, she would harp about robots replacing people. Monday she had hissed, "I don't mess with your blessed refrigerators."

He pocketed four sweetener packets for Niagara, and when he approached his office, he turned sideways past Bev, like a dog with a stolen sock.

"What's that you've got?" Bev asked in the low-volume voice she had mastered for speaking out of the Veteran's earshot. She had tested the near-whisper recently and pronounced it inaudible to Niagara as well. "Sweets for the sweet? Pastries for the pasty?"

He didn't like Bev making fun of the pale rookie. The Veteran had practically demanded inhospitality; any attempts at niceties were shouted down. If anything, George thought, Niagara inspired the opposite. Maybe, hallway therapist that she was, Bev was offended that Niagara hadn't recognized her as the source of all information and asked for shortcuts or guidance. George was tempted to scold Bev, who was more like a sassy sister than his secretary.

George wanted to watch Niagara come to her own conclusions without a briefing from Bev. Neither was he interested in bringing Niagara home for dinner and having Judy find her a date from her stable of architects and carpenters. He wanted to keep Niagara to himself and get to know her at his own slow pace. He almost behaved as if she were invisible to everyone else.

Stepping carefully, George made it to his office without a mishap. Steam from the coffee rose up through the hole in the center of each donut, filling the air with an acrid cinnamon stench. Although George wouldn't take her bait, Bev got up from behind her desk and opened the door to his office. Even when she bowed and tiptoed backwards out the doorway, George did not acknowledge her sarcasm.

Niagara looked up from the catalog she was studying. She chose the larger donut, sloshed the coffee into her china teacup, and ripped open all four sweetener packets.

"Thank you," she said. "Does this mean we're engaged?"

Unlike with Bev, George basked in her mild teasing. Hearing a name like Niagara, he had pictured her with a cascade of foamy hair, the smile of a water nymph. Now her plainness tainted even his dreams.

George spent some moments every day speculating on what might be under Niagara's blanket of a dress. The fantasy was fueled by his observation that everything that was held close on Judy's body was splayed and dangling on Niagara's. Judy's earlobes, for instance, were tiny and attached to her jawline, whereas Niagara had long, loopy ears. His wife's breasts topped her torso like tight fists; George fantasized about Niagara's breasts spilling down to the lower half of her rib cage.

George pointed to the catalog. "What are they peddling?" he asked.

"Dishes," Niagara said.

"China?" He longed to see her coffee-brown eyes and their clear, creamy whites without the wire frames. Those eyes, he thought, would be wasted on a beautiful woman.

"Satellite dishes," Niagara said. "You have one?"

"No, we figure a hundred twenty channels would just triple the kids' arguments."

Niagara said, "May I ask you something?"

"Be my guest." George was prepared to teach her all he knew about refrigerators: what had been attempted; what had been, until now, only a vision.

"Do you like actual engineering more than theory? Is that why you're in industry rather than the university?"

Later, he realized she could probably have used a pep talk —one day the star of Caltech and the next a refrigerator designer without an authorized key card to the lab—but at the time the question seemed pointed at his inertia.

"I only have a bachelor's degree," he said. "You didn't need a master's when I started. The Veteran didn't even have a degree."

"Don't panic," Niagara said. "I meant it as a compliment. You seem so content."

"Medication," George said, knowing it was a weak joke but wanting never to hear another compliment of that order. You make such a good paperweight, George. You seem so happy with your limited intelligence and ambition. He wished she had met him in his icemaker days, when he had been at the top of his form.

Niagara gripped the handle of her china cup between her knobby index finger and thumb. No doubt, her finger would not loop through the slender ear of the delicate cup. "It's refreshing to finally be with people making things rather than up in the tower doing pure research."

"That's not why I'm here," George said. "Too much hot air in academia," he said. "Too political."

"Too political?" Niagara repeated.

"Sure. Why you get funding, who gets tenure."

"George," she spoke his name with disappointment, then she gathered her stringy hair into a thin tail. "Why don't you have a private office?"

"I don't know." He sounded like his chubby son being asked about the remains of a pie.

"Why were you saddled with the Veteran? Why do you have to train the new girl? Why, though no one around here seems aware of it, do we need to stop using chlorofluorocarbons?"

"Politics?" he asked.

"Of course." Her lips rode high above her teeth in a grin. Though George could tell she wasn't being malicious, it still needled him; like most engineers, he enjoyed a laugh at someone else's expense. They went back to their respective computers, but for George, the day was ruined. When were they going to have that session in which Niagara sat at his feet and begged for the story behind the first icemaker, chilled water dispensers in the door? Maybe all he could teach her was how to hang on until retirement making minuscule design changes.

George thought about the clinical term Judy had coined for him. When she was angriest about his inability to express or even recognize his needs, she called him a textbook passive-passive. Her invented definition was that a passive-passive was someone who does nothing in the cause of self-interest and holds it against no one when he is ignored.

George had always considered the label a little severe. In reality, what did it matter if he wanted steak and Judy wanted chicken? He would live to eat steak another day. She had such strong, clear urges, he felt it would give him as much pleasure letting her have her way as he would get imposing his will on her, just to even a score he was not keeping. Traits Judy had branded apathetic he credited as easygoing. It was Niagara calling him content that had him scrambling for counterevidence and recognizing for the first time the ramifications of Judy's tag. Today he could see that if you leave a car parked long enough, the tires go flat and the battery won't hold a charge.

George had always imagined that if something came up that

he felt strongly about, he would fight for it. Sitting at his desk, he felt strongly about Niagara not dismissing him, and so George suggested they get a hamburger for lunch. He tried to imitate the confidence displayed on a tintype near the center of Niagara's circle of photographs: a man costumed in western garb, complete with rifle and a lariat draped across his chest, was staring down the camera as if it were prey. Just making the invitation was more assertiveness than George had shown in years, and it sped up the pulse at his temples.

"Off campus?" Niagara asked, and she clenched her fists in anticipation. "I'd be delighted."

Her ready acceptance left George with an hour to occupy. His butter softener was almost ready for the monthly meeting on Friday. He had no idea what an extra computer chip with timer and temperature control would cost; neither could he think of an instance when the butter had been excessively hard. Still, what was left for a refrigerator to do? Judy wanted him to devise a way for the box itself to flag food that was going bad. Frankly, the task seemed too complicated for a design project.

George toyed with Niagara's stats. He surmised that she was just shy of six feet tall, say seventy-one point seven five inches. He converted her height into centimeters, doing the pyramid of multiplication by hand on a scratch pad. He guessed her weight at 160 pounds, 72.58 kilograms, or, because he always liked an excuse to multiply, 2,560 ounces. If Judy was a woman, Niagara was a woman and a half.

George was reminded of his past again, when kids in junior high had taunted him about being outside looking in. When he would show up with a ball and glove, the other guys were already sweaty and starving. Perhaps the only time he had felt in the thick of things was when Carol Greyson was clamping her mouth around his penis; he was conscious then of thinking, This is what happens to sixteen-year-olds. He had read it in books, seen movies where teenagers groped in the back of souped-up cars, but Carol's conduct was the first indication he'd had that those stories might have been more than wishes.

Exiled from Carol, George went back to feeling like a spectator of fun, or worse, like someone whose presence chased fun and spontaneity away. In college, he always wanted to sit in the section at a concert where people clapped in rhythmic unity, where girls in gauze twirled in the aisles and the singer told secret stories the rest of the audience was not privy to. George had often watched the fun from the mezzanine or balcony, which was too wide a gap for the spark to cross. But if he sat in the front section, the action would flare up in the stands, as a tangle of folks formed a samba line to dance up and down the balcony stairs.

George remembered how Carol rose to the challenge of showing him the inner circle. Her presence inspired people to turn off the TV and start a round of strip poker. Or someone would begin playing truth or dare, and they would all get a buzz from the rush of telling secrets.

Maybe engineering had attracted him because, as a group, his coworkers neither incited riotous behavior nor understood what the fuss was all about. The dress code was a good example. Because the engineers ostensibly visited the factory line, they could not wear clothing that might catch in drill presses or automatic lathes. They had to wear ties that would detach from their necks if grabbed by a steel roller, and their shirts had to be short-sleeved, so that the evil machinery would be less likely to get hold of them. Eyeglasses had to be fitted with safety lenses, which meant the frames were thicker than most, and traction demanded that shoes be crepe- or waffle-soled. The shreds of personal vanity George had acquired through the years had brought him to detest the dress code. His colleagues, however, never complained, and their appearance outside the office indicated that they regarded their work uniform as a guideline to their private wardrobe as well. They seemed to prize their nerdy ways. As Frank in quality control often said, "I'd rather be called a geek than a lawyer."

For George, meeting Judy in college had been a case of two twigs rubbing against each other, creating first warmth and then their own kind of fire. Not passionless fire, either; in fact, finding someone else who felt out of sync but who had the humor and beauty of Judy imbued in George a long-lasting desire for them to be out of sync together. Judy pretended to treasure her distinction as a raven-haired beauty amid her pale Southern sisters. "Make a fist in Georgia," she would say, "and you get a handful of blond hair." But she had also told George that every Christmas she used to ask Santa for freckles.

There were still roles in their life where they were neither fish nor fowl, and yet they had company in each other. Judy and George lived on Newark Street, NW, in Cleveland Park, an affluent neighborhood named for Grover Cleveland's summer home. It made sense for Judy, as a D.C. realtor, to live in a D.C. house, especially one that had been built in 1886 by Cleveland's second vice president. Except for Bev, everyone at Coldpoint was apprehensive about George's address: Aren't you afraid you'll be murdered? How can you live right up against everyone in the city? Isn't the traffic horrible? What they didn't realize was that from his six-thousand-square-foot house, George could walk to the post office, coffee and chocolate shops, Italian and Greek delis, and the Metro; sitting on the back deck, which overlooked a ravine of trees down to a little stream, he could hear the change ringing in the bell tower of the National Cathedral.

Minutes before noon, Niagara began coming out of her trance. She saved her work, backed it up on disk, and even exited to the network menu, as if the world might end over lunch. There was no reason for George to mimic her, as he would lose nothing if the computers crashed. He unhooked his raincoat from the back of their door and then removed Niagara's as well, uncertain for a moment whether to help her into it or not. Was he coworker, elder statesman, suitor, buddy, or artifact? With exaggerated gallantry, he held Niagara's coat by the lapels.

"Everyone's always offering to help me get dressed," she said, slipping into her coat. "What I need is some encouragement to get undressed."

George cleared his throat and grabbed his keys from the desk. He pretended he was the one hard of hearing.

Walking down the hallway on their way to lunch, George and Niagara ran into the factory foreman.

"The dynamic duo," Emilio said. "The design department is charged up, no?" He winked at Niagara.

George said, "We're on our way out."

"I come also." To George, he said, "Maybe we call your wife and double-date."

George did not back down. "We have design work to talk about."

Emilio took Niagara's elbow. She stood five or six inches taller than he. "Business lunch?" he asked. "Is better—then my lunch is paid for. I'm free."

"Design business," George said. He sounded like Harris again, whining that Sheridan was bothering him.

"That's why I come looking for you," Emilio said to Niagara. "I like your idea."

She said, "It's still very rough."

With his free hand, Emilio reached up to put his finger to Niagara's lips. "Shh," he said. "Is perfect. All the years I been here, is the same thing: make them crush ice, make them talk. Nobody say make them smell good, make the doors see-through. I want that you make them lighter. You have any ideas for that?"

"George and I, we have to go eat. But maybe we can talk tomorrow."

Emilio let go of her arm. "I ask George, but he would design a fridge that walk from corner to corner."

Niagara's complicity was pure betrayal. George's eye twitched as his nerves and impulses cross-circuited through his body. In fact, George had attempted to make refrigerators smell better, an experiment that had failed pathetically. He tried to remember the last truly useful option he had appended to the box.

Emilio, standing on his toes, whispered something to Niagara and dodged down the hall.

With the boldness of another man, George asked, "What did he say?"

"George," Niagara scolded, "it might be personal."

"Of course," he said. He watched his and Niagara's feet slap against the checkerboard linoleum.

"Then again," Niagara said, "it might not be. I have no idea—my hearing aid was off."

Sharing a good broad chuckle almost made up for the fact that Niagara had shown her design to manufacturing first. George never previewed his ideas to the guys on "the other side," so-called because manufacturing was on the opposite end of the plant but also because their chore of having to implement every design change, be it silly or significant, put them on the other side of many decisions.

Niagara and George left the building, and their walk broke into a canter as the sprinkles started landing faster and heavier. Running past empty parking spaces, George could smell the puddles of oil and antifreeze, the scents renewed by the rain. Niagara ran just in front of him. The raindrops hitting her coat intensified its garage-sale sheen, though neither was very wet when they reached George's car.

The diner was a modern facsimile, with all of the chrome and none of the greasy buildup that old restaurants accumulate. There were only two or three tables empty. "Smoking?" the hostess asked, and George remembered with a smile Harris's Quote for the Day. Harris read the *Post* and skimmed the *Times* each morning, adopting one odd sentence as his Quote for the Day. Today's *Times* had a story about a fight between Staten Island neighbors—shots were exchanged because one guy's Doberman relieved itself on his neighbor's boxwood. Harris picked a quote from the cop on duty, who allegedly said, "The match that lit the fire was the dog urinating."

Niagara and George were shown to the nonsmoking section. George was grateful for the corner spot. He scanned the crowd for coworkers, guilt-ridden that he had actually left the office and driven to a restaurant with a woman not his wife. Of course, his colleagues were all in the Coldpoint staff room, eating various fried foods and smoking between bites.

From parties, George knew that Judy's real-estate associates drank herbal teas and sparkling waters; few smoked. Tended by interior designers, personal trainers, nutritionists, and even motivational counselors, they were in touch with their houses, bodies, and minds. It wasn't accurate to say that none of the guys at the plant were worried about their guts, let alone their psyches or surroundings. Good intentions surfaced around New Year's and rippled through the plant after someone suffered a double or greater bypass. A group from the mechanical division might announce that they intended to substitute pinochle for lunch. Within a week, somebody would bring chips, then bean dip, then pork rinds and salted nuts to the game.

Seated at their sliver of a table, George and Niagara talked about the storm outside. Niagara had a flash-flood story; George contributed one about a twister. The waitress kept forgetting they existed, a problem George had experienced before. It took earthquakes and lightning for them to get water, falling trees and roofs lost to high winds to finally place their order. Niagara removed the sugar dispenser lid and screwed it back on. George was glad she had not packed tools or she would probably have dismembered their tableside jukebox, which was out of order.

George's BLT arrived just as he and Niagara were starting to sound like the Weather Channel. George turned his attention to his sandwich. He had never been so mindful of a lunch. The toast was striped brown, with a frill of lettuce immodestly showing under the straight bread, and the pickle and potato chips in pale green and gold, respectively, were luminous against the thick white plate.

George bit and chewed and swallowed. Periodically, he squinted slightly to study his lunch date. They were too close here with only the tiny diner table between them. Niagara looked out of scale, not ugly really, just too large. George preferred the distance from his desk to hers. One thing he could see more clearly from this range was Niagara's jewelry. George had thought that the drop she wore around her neck was yellowish orange quartz or plastic. Up close, he could see it was amber, petrified tree sap, with a gnat or mosquito lodged inside.

Amber was popular that spring because of a blockbuster

science-fiction movie that George was avoiding. George could not abide the genre, because he hated anyone mixing science and fiction. A year or two before the movie was out, he had read the facts in *Science Times*. Basically, a few guys from Berkeley had successfully extracted the DNA from the blood of bugs petrified in amber. Postulating that a forty-million-year-old mosquito had sucked dinosaur blood, they figured that the bug's blood might still contain some dinosaur DNA. With inordinate amounts of luck, they hoped to isolate the DNA, replicate it thousands of times over, inject an alligator with their mix, and hatch a little tyrannosaur.

George also used this opportunity to get a good look at Niagara's earrings. Today's were uncharacteristically quiet. Shaped like kites, the red-and-gold collages appeared to be made of paper, and each had a small gold tab sticking out one side.

"Like them?" Niagara asked.

George was startled. It was as if he thought her hearing problem had dulled all her senses and that she would not notice if he stared at her.

"Very unusual," he said. "They're nice."

"Don't overexert yourself, George," Niagara said smugly. She took off the right one and pulled the tab, lengthening a thin strip of paper that had been folded accordion-style and tucked into the earring. "Fortune earrings," she said. "Care to hear your fortune as told by an earring?"

"Sure," George said.

She read from the wrinkled paper, " 'You will do foolish things, but you will do them with enthusiasm.' Hmm, maybe that's mine."

George almost asked why she thought it was an inappropriate fortune for him, but he supposed he knew. "I want that one," he said. "What's yours?"

She wadded the fortune back into the right earring and looped it through her weighty lobe. "You'd think I'd remember," she said. She disconnected the left earring and read solemnly, " 'Trust everyone, but always cut the cards.' Oh, that's good. One of my grandfather's sayings."

"Did you make those?" George asked with new admiration. They seemed so fashionable and witty. Maybe out of her work uniform, she wrapped bracelets round her bony ankles, drove to the grocery store wearing a jacket with fringe.

"In grad school," Niagara said. "I had a sidewalk stand in Santa Monica." She shrugged her magnificently wide shoulders in a modest dismissal of her talents. "It paid for circuit boards and supplies."

Passing the time with Niagara, George remembered how he used to be wary of small talk, suspicious that someone would lull him into a position of ease and then trick him or ask him the only question about dinosaurs or Louisville he had failed to research. Linguists argue over the invention of speech; was talk first necessary to express pleasure or pain, pain or the location of prey? Tucked in across from Niagara, George would have guessed that speech had been invented for mutual comfort, to share small talk about the weather or each other's health.

In a bold quest for personal details, George asked Niagara, "Why electricity?"

She swallowed a generous bite of burger. "I'm used to being alone," she said. Reaching under the bun, Niagara extricated two serrated pickle slices, and she pulled several miniature napkins out of the dispenser.

"You want me to go?" George asked, puzzled.

"No," Niagara said. "God, no. I mean, I spent hours by myself as a kid."

"Only child?"

"One brother," Niagara said, "who went to boarding school when I was three. My parents wanted me around, but they were either on the road performing or they were practicing seven hours a day."

"It must have been tough," George said, parroting a line he had heard Judy use on a troubled friend.

"I invented ways to comfort myself. I would follow my parents around the house, memorizing every magazine or armrest they touched before they left. Then when I'd cry, I would touch those things again and again. Pitiful enough?"

"Your fillings hurt," George said to make her smile.

Niagara waved away his remark. "Sometimes I traveled with them. They always had the illusion that they would take a few extra days in Rome or New York. But I think because there were two of them, one never wanted the other to think that work wasn't important. Every city where we were scheduled for a holiday, they would find a studio and settle in for more practice."

George looked away from Niagara's smudged glasses to her hands, which overlapped around the hamburger bun. Those hands couldn't possibly pick their way across a concert grand; Niagara's knuckly fingers weren't even the hands of an usher. "Did they expect you to play?"

"When was a piano available?" Niagara replied. "The two we had were either being played, tuned, or rested."

"So where were you?" George asked.

"Ordering room service," she said. "My parents pretended I was their glamorous child who was too advanced to mix with grubby kids, but, really, I was a nerdy little girl with thick glasses and a hearing aid, terrified of anyone my age."

George was in over his head here. Was he supposed to assure her that glasses made any girl look nerdy, that her hearing aid was barely noticeable, that she was probably as glamorous as her parents presumed? He asked again, "Why electricity?"

"Right," Niagara said. "All my toys, they had to do something. I loved winding, spinning, setting them in motion. My all-time favorite was Larry the Lion; he had a soft plastic muzzle and a barrel-shaped body covered in the thinnest of plush."

George could picture her nuzzling the pathetic stuffed lion.

"You pulled Larry's string," Niagara said, "and he talked." She opened her mouth wide in a roar and then, in a cartoon voice, she said, " 'Oh, I scared myself.' Anyway, one morning the string broke, and I assumed Larry was choking. No one was around—not my mother or father, not my tutor, not even the goddamn cook—so I went to the utility drawer and got a pair of scissors. I spread newspapers on the kitchen table and opened him up, fully expecting blood and body parts."

"How old were you?"

"Eight," she said. "I didn't think stuffed toys were real, but this one talked, for heaven's sake, and I figured he had a throat or lungs."

George imagined Niagara eviscerating the worn-out toy. A snip of the scissors and sawdust would spill out, much to her astonishment.

"The operation," Niagara said, "was a success. I have no idea how I knew to do what I did; the only comparison I can come up with is playing by ear. I cleaned the parts and reassembled them, threaded a new piece of string through the voice box, and sewed him up." She looked at her watch, with its face the size of a desk clock. As if yawning in response to seeing a yawn, George checked his watch as well. They had been gone for an hour and a half, longer than any lunch except for the Veteran's banquet, which may have been the longest three hours of George's life.

"OK, OK," Niagara said, speeding herself along. "So then I started taking my hearing aids apart. It became an obsession with me, this machine resting on my ear. I would resist for five or six weeks until I had to break it open."

Niagara had twisted the little napkins, three of them, stained with mustard, into knots. She lined them up now between her and George.

"Aren't hearing aids all the same?" George asked.

"I stopped when I discovered that. Then outlets started to haunt me. Behind that plug was an unseen current that mysteriously animated things. This life force was saved up in batteries, it ran through the walls of our house or hotel. I was hooked."

To George, electricity was about as mysterious as a hammer. He saw it as a tool that slightly advanced man learned to use thousands of years after sharpening flints against a rock. Electricity had been harnessed, like mules or water power, to perform useful chores. He liked that it was invisible, too, but it was no miracle.

At Pershing, once it was clear that Carol was not going to answer any of the love letters he had sent to the Little Flower Home, George devoted himself to a celibate study in cause and effect. He mixed chemicals and tested free-fall formulae, experiments that resulted in locker explosions and more than one dead rodent. Enhancing soil with coffee, with eggshells, with nut-studded chocolate bars, he grew butter beans. But when he pressed the telegraph key, thus completing a circuit and sounding the dit and dah that are the atoms of words, he knew electricity —unseen yet predictable—was to be his chosen field.

The check came, and George was relieved to see it was correct. Not that he would have caused a scene, but one thing he was brave about was correcting others' arithmetic. He had taken on the mortgage company, the IRS, and a good supply of waiters and waitresses.

In the car on the way back, George was conscious of his profile, the way Niagara's breathing clouded the windshield, the family trash scattered about Niagara's feet. Rain fell faster than the wipers could clear; George had to hunker down in his seat to see between smeared arcs. Contrary as a magnet, George was both strongly repulsed by and attracted to Niagara's cabalistic streak. Here was a woman who knew more about electrical fields than what was in her purse, yet she acted as if every time someone flipped a switch and a light came on, a tiny miracle had occurred.

George tried to recall where he had heard people espousing Niagara's kind of job-related mysticism. His memory was jogged by the sight of Congressional Mall, one of a dozen strip shopping plazas they drove by on the way back to the plant. Niagara's reverence had the same tone of devotion as that of the Congress junkies who swarmed at the Cleveland Park block party. Not the former and present legislators in the neighborhood—from the last Democratic vice president to the freshman congressman from Nebraska, they kept up their end of the recycling and zone parking conversations. It was the press agents and legislative aides, the men Judy referred to as "by-products," who admired each other for absurd shows of loyalty such as going without a honeymoon or missing a son's graduation, as if devoting one's life to the intricacies of the Commerce Committee were a sacred calling. These men fed on subcommittee hearings like a teenager on scorn, eventually believing that every event was part of a delicate chain of politically motivated decisions. If this was the difference between a calling and a job, George thought, he definitely had a job.

George's afternoon crept by. There was no window in the large cubicle. From the clouds he had seen at lunch, he deduced that it was raining intermittently; if the rain had cleared up, Judy would be out showing houses and Harris would have called to read George the notes Judy had written to the two of them.

As of last fall, Harris had persuaded his parents to let him stay home alone the occasional afternoons that Judy was out. Judy would schedule a play date for Sheridan or bring her along, and she would leave Harris written instructions and phone numbers for every conceivable problem. Reading Judy's notes was a comic ritual between him and his son. Harris's note would outline appropriate and off-limits snacks, and it always ended with, "Call your father and read him his note." Harris would rip paper and blow into the telephone, pretending George's note had been pulled from an envelope bearing the name of the next Nobel Prize winner. "Sweetheart," George's note always began, and Harris had taken to making up endearments. "Sweet-and-Sour Heart," he would read, or "My Dearest Taco Pie." George's note enumerated Judy's itinerary and estimated time of arrival, as well as any grocery or errand requests for George.

He called home, but the answering machine was on.

At five, when the log-out message flashed across their computer screens, neither George nor Niagara made a move to comply. George couldn't say why Niagara lingered; George himself felt reluctant to start over as strangers in the morning. Until Niagara arrived, George's most daring fantasies had been brainstorming with a partner, preparing refrigerators to enter the twenty-first century.

Niagara was winding a chunk of her hair around her index finger as she stared at her satellite catalog. She let go of her hair, which did not for a second remain coiled, and pointed to an industrial dish that was airport- or television-station-size. She whispered, "I'm saving up for this one." It was the cost of a half dozen luxury cars. She flipped the pages back to a dish the height of a two-story house, which was pictured by the dish's side. Someone had enhanced the photograph with jagged lines meant to suggest television programs seeking out the enormous ear. Niagara said, "Here's what I have now."

"You have room for that in your yard?" George asked.

"No," she said, "I have a lab site in Gaithersburg."

She had been in town less than two months; how and why would she have set up a lab and a dish that fast? Just last week, George had read about some backyard scientists who claimed to have found a new galaxy. They had yet to discern whether they were, in fact, listening to the noise of undiscovered stars or errant signals from neighborhood garage-door openers.

Niagara closed the catalog and began putting the computer to bed for the night. She said, "Do you and I meet before Friday?"

"If you want," George answered, eager to rehearse for the design meeting if only to hear her plan. He had not seen her print out any schematics, crunch any numbers. "For your first one you can just give ideas."

Niagara looked insulted. "I'm almost done," she said. "I'll have sketches tomorrow."

Curious as he was about her design, he so wanted them to leave on a personal note. "What are you doing with the dish?"

"I'm listening," she said.

George asked again.

"I'm listening," she repeated.

He was about to ask a third time when he realized that she was answering his question. If she had left Caltech with a doctorate, she wouldn't be here. He hoped she hadn't classified him as a relic, just as he had judged the Veteran backward and slow. He told her about the people who might have found a galaxy to show her that he followed at least the science news in the *Times*.

"Amateurs," she said. "Can't hear the difference between stars and garage-door picker-uppers."

"What are you listening for?" George asked.

"George, George, George," she said, "you don't want to hear it. You'll be sorry if you know."

Later, George thought there ought to be a sign that people were required to flash when they told you something that would change your life. Although even if Niagara had given him some signal, he would have pressed on.

"Tell me," he said. Thrill me. Fill me.

In a parental tone, Niagara asked, "What do we say?"

"Tell me, please." He expected the news to affect him the way gossip affected Bev. The suspense alone was a sensation he hadn't felt in a long while.

"You were warned," Niagara said. She closed their office door, though no one ever stayed late. Like a sentry in front of George, she stood tall, with her arms crossed and her feet apart. "I am listening for the dead," she said.

There was no teasing in her voice or her stance, both of which challenged George. He felt like a balloon let loose before being knotted: his thrill deflated quickly and he ricocheted from elation to intrigue to flat suspicion. Finally, he asked, "What do you mean by dead?"

Niagara pulled her chair in close and sat down. She said, "Whispers of bodiless voices on a faraway frequency hungry for an audience."

Just like at lunch, George was winging it. It was rare for him to have to improvise at all, let alone twice in one day. "You mean the spirit world and Tarot-card stuff?"

"It's all energy to me. You were talking about Dino Park— well, it was fossils that led people to a life before ours. Why can't there be audible fossils of our ancestors?"

"Why should there be?" George managed to ask. What he was thinking was, Once, they burned your kind at the stake.

Niagara shook her head. "Nothing is lost," she said. "It only changes form. First law of thermodynamics."

She rolled her chair back to her catalog, systematically folding down the top right corner of specific pages. George didn't know if he should preserve the silence or not. The mind tucked behind Niagara's rich brown eyes made him feel reckless, as if gravity existed only when she said so. Everything George believed in told him not to accept her science fiction. For a tingly second, George thought about how he had censored himself that morning, fearful that she would think him strange.

Niagara looked up suddenly, and George suspected his thoughts were printed across his forehead as clear as type on a computer screen. She was neither defensive nor embarrassed. She pushed the bangs back from her face, a nervous habit that did nothing to keep the hair out of her eyes. "You were a budding paleontologist," she said to him. "So look at it this way. I'm listening for the bones of souls."

Try as he might, he could not wrap his mind around that. "You're listening on the radio?" he asked.

"Mostly," she said. "My theory is that lives extinguished are smoldering on some frequency. It's kind of like that old joke where the little kid loses a quarter in the grass, and then his big brother sees him looking for it in a parking lot. You know that one?"

"No," George said.

"The big brother asks him why he's looking in the parking lot and the little kid says, 'It's brighter here.' "

George presumed her reasons were better than that. He was aware that all satellite communications reach earth by radio, though he didn't know the details involved in turning the radio waves back into television programs or spy photos.

"At Caltech, I got time on the radio telescopes, but they're a little steep for home use."

George felt himself formulating a thousand questions, experiencing a burning curiosity that had not flared in some twenty years. It was as if, by lighting on electricity as his chosen field, he had shorted out his ability to wonder and to doubt. Sure, a circuit was a thing of beauty and a comfort to him as early as high school, but where had his urgency to know and discover gone?

George saw his once-prized reams of facts as so much brittle paper, leaving crumbs of useless knowledge in the cuff of his pants, the pocket of his short-sleeved shirts. Maybe what Niagara Spense knew would fill the next volume. Maybe she would write her theories across his back, along his hairline.

"I can't hear dog whistles," Niagara said, "but they make noise. Can you live with that?"

At that instant, George thought, he couldn't live without it.

## ~~~~~*Daniel Boone Was Buried Somewhere*

Traffic heading back to the city was barely moving, and George lurched home alongside the gunmetal Saabs and Jaguars that served as offices on wheels for men with expensive haircuts. These men, double-breasted and starched, in boxes, talked on the phone as they drove, their hood ornaments announcing their heraldry slightly ahead of their arrival. Meanwhile, George hoped the Oldsmobile wouldn't overheat on the slow march south.

George was too self-conscious to pay for a good briefcase, let alone a luxury sedan. His philosophy was something like, "Just because you can afford it doesn't mean you deserve it," while Judy's was more along the lines of, "They developed this product with people like me in mind."

He did have to confess to an expensive haircut, though. The whole family was trimmed by Henri; George had first gone to give Sheridan courage and because he suspected that Judy wasn't just flattering him when she said his dark, wavy hair deserved the touch of a professional. Of course, she had been right, and he had to admit it was a relief to get a haircut that matched the current decade.

In the first few miles away from the plant, George shed his engineering skin, a ritual that began with him pinching both sides of the knot on his clip-on tie. From years of practice, he knew just where to press so that the elongated jaws snapped open and released their hold on his collar. It was a gesture that predated Coldpoint, a tweak George had perfected prying snapping turtles loose from sticks that he and Kevin Whitby had poked around in the murky cow pond beyond their subdivision.

George draped the clip-on tie over the rearview mirror, behind the parking pass, then he worked the vinyl pouch holding his calculator and mechanical pencils out of his left shirt pocket. He unbuttoned his collar two notches. Checking to see if he could change lanes, he caught a glimpse of his grass-green eyes and high, wide cheekbones in the mirror. Though he felt the same as he had in college, he was beginning to carry his mother's bags under his eyes.

Rush-hour radio chattered until George switched off the commercials for waterbeds and imported beer. He had been hoping to hear a weather report; now he could read it off the clouds. Thunderheads building in the southeast, a bruised sky of such yellow and blue that it might possibly carry some hail. The wind smeared his car with signs of tree sex: pollen stuck to the spermy raindrops on the windows, and maple seeds, sent out into the world on lusty puffs of air, clogged the tear ducts of his windshield-washer fluid.

George went over Niagara's news again, feeling a fatherly embarrassment toward her electronic grave robbing. He couldn't bring himself to buy a new car, yet she planned to spend six times that for her farfetched hobby. That was a lot of box tops for a giant decoder ring. What made her think she could talk to the dead? It's not that he felt she was haughty; he meant, what had made her *think* of it? At Coldpoint, George had added bell upon whistle in new refrigerator options, an accomplishment that amounted to keeping his head in an icebox for fourteen years. Why hadn't he thought to step back, close the door, walk around the machine, or at least look down on it from above?

George took the left exit off the bump and grind of Wisconsin Avenue onto the beltway and two miles later exited south on Connecticut Avenue. Crossing the D.C. city limits, he traveled backwards through the alphabet of three-syllable followed by two-syllable streets. Newark Street was midway through the second progression. There were no one-syllable street names in the plan; after the set that included Newark came the letter streets, W through A if you were traveling south toward the Capitol.

Moving to Washington, George had immediately loved the way D.C. radiated outward from its political center, the tiers of alphabetical streets like the circles of blame constructed within every governmental enterprise of the city. George read with interest about the swamp that had been plowed under for L'Enfant's plan, and he speculated on what had flourished there earlier.

Back in Louisville, highway crews mostly uncovered arrowheads and coal, except for a few major finds like on the Harrisons' farm. George remembered when he wished fossils could talk, when he wanted to wring their stories from a thigh or tail bone. Did they have any inkling that the world was changing faster than they could adapt? If it was sudden, could they sense the asteroid hurtling toward them, the heat more intense than the boiling volcanoes whose sulphur belches scented the air?

Two visits to Dino Park were just the beginning. The Monday after his quiz-show success, he had wanted to be with people who credited him with knowing something, a longing that inspired him to pedal over to Dino Park. Because of the stretch along the gravel emergency lane of I-75, it was a fairly dangerous bike ride; his mother would surely have forbade it had he asked permission. As George scaled the final hill, some truck driver hugging the shoulder let go a long blast on his horn, and George's flinch wrenched the handlebars hard to the left. In a cloud of dust and ground stone, George found himself off his banana seat with the stingray bike on top of him.

When he finally arrived at the front gate and Mrs. Harrison told him admission was sixty-five cents, George said, "I was here Saturday."

Mrs. Harrison said, "I'm afraid it's sixty-five cents every day."

George routed through his pockets to retrieve the iguanodon, which he offered up to her. "I won 'What's Wrong with This Picture?' "

Mrs. Harrison held on to George's wrist, surveying the damage from his bicycle spill. His shirtsleeve was shredded at the elbow, and blood covered his arm. "Baby," Mrs. Harrison said, "you're all torn up."

That's when George started crying. Mrs. Harrison abandoned the admission booth to tweeze out stones and to disinfect the wide abrasion. She insisted on calling his mother to tell her where George was. George expected Mrs. Harrison to hold the phone away from her ear while his mother carried on, but Mrs. Harrison neither winced nor changed her chatty tone of voice. Afterward she said, "Your mother was happy to hear from us."

Because it was a school day, only one or two families were visiting, and so Mr. Harrison invited George to go on Dino Park rounds with him on his tractor. Mr. Harrison had long hair for a man and more wrinkles than a mummy. He took George to the spot where, digging a foundation for new stables years earlier, he had unearthed a small hypsibema, a specimen that had previously been found only in North Carolina and Missouri. Mr. Harrison had roped off the site, which he covered with a tidy shelter made from corrugated steel. Waves of afternoon sun wriggled around the silver roof, making the site look like someone's dream on TV.

"Everyone out for a drive, looking for a bathroom," Mr. Harrison yelled over the tractor, "mistaking the pitched shelter I built for a comfort station. Me and Mrs. Harrison figure if that many people need a bathroom, then they probably need a reason to drive and gas to drive with."

Mr. Harrison paved the pasture, installed gas and diesel pumps, and built scaffoldings in the shapes of monsters. The next spring, rather than trimming hooves and watching for colts, he was lathing joint compound onto the dinosaur skeletons, molding fiberglass skins, and carefully setting their glass eyes within sockets. "Herbivores' eyes I aim to the horizon," Mr. Harrison explained. "But the carnivores, they have to watch the ground for prey." George found Mr. Harrison's practical concerns laden with wisdom.

In the trapezoid marked off by Lexington, Louisville, Nashville, and Knoxville, Dino Park had plenty of competition. There were caves near the Tennessee border, and their formations were said to resemble Man o' War or Deborah Kerr. Daniel Boone and Davy Crockett unwittingly lent their names to wax museums and trading posts, filled with the dull reflections off fringed vinyl deerskin jackets next to bins of plastic tomahawks. To the Harrisons' credit, the creatures at Dino Park didn't rhythmically thrash their tails, challenging visitors to putt through. Neither were slides built into their scaly butts—Dino Park was not a playground. And it seemed entirely appropriate that the park was funded by the purchase of gasoline, the rich fuel resulting from dinosaur compost.

At the end of the afternoon, Mr. Harrison hoisted George's bike into the back of their yellow Ford. Mrs. Harrison had crowned the old truck with a stegosaur, perhaps the most simpleminded creature ever to walk the earth. George's mother was too shocked by the sight of the Harrisons to be anything but numbingly polite. George tried to see the couple through his mother's eyes: an overweight woman dressed like a hillbilly and her older, gnarled husband. Long after the stegosaur was out of sight, George waved to the truck, something he hadn't done since both his grandparents were still alive.

After that, George would bring Mrs. Harrison a pear frugally saved from lunch or a ring he had made from telephone cable strewn around the new housing development, and she would wave him in. Sometimes other boys would tag along, but for a variety of reasons George was usually alone to ride his bike in circles around the -saurs and -dactyls. First, Mrs. Harrison didn't like to make a precedent of letting kids in free; second, and more difficult to take, was that the other twelve-year-olds did not seem to understand the privilege being extended to them. Kevin Whitby offered Mrs. Harrison a piece of chalk stolen from homeroom, and using sticks or a sharp piece of gravel, he tried to carve dirty words into the wrinkly knees of the ankylosaur. Even George's friend Bobby put crinkled cans of Mountain Dew into the camptosaur's jaws.

George could not explain his devotion to the tacky roadside

attraction. It had something to do with discovering that dinosaurs were real—not, of course, the camouflage-colored models in Dino Park—and that a few of them had actually walked the streets of his Kentucky home.

As a little kid, George had staged sandbox battles with triceratops and sergeant brontosaur commanding a troop of plastic World War II army men wielding flamethrowers. Both privates and dinosaurs were bathed in army green from head to toe. They rode in dump trucks and fire engines, fighting a band of Sioux who had formed an uneasy alliance with various troll dolls kidnapped from little sisters on the block.

At that time, someone could have told George that World War II was just a story, and he would have accepted it. But as he became devoted to facts, he wanted to know: what actually happened before he was born? Daniel Boone, for example, had a TV show, but he was also in George's history book. Daniel had been in Pennsylvania, had found the door through the mountains into Kentucky, had been captured by and escaped from the Shawnees. James Bond, George learned, was invented, but Daniel Boone was buried somewhere and trees he had carved messages into still lived. Dinosaurs had also left traces; many of them had managed to drop dead in well-preserved bogs, their ribs lined up like the keys on a piano. That a giant bone uncovered in 1676 belonged not to a human casualty of the Great Flood but to an extinct species was deduced in 1825, five years after the death of Daniel Boone. George used to marvel at the thought that although dinosaurs were closer to Daniel Boone on the universal time line, Daniel could not have been aware of their existence.

On George's thirteenth birthday, the Harrisons offered him a job. For three years, George patched prehistoric torsos, hosed down spikes, and restocked Dino Park pamphlets. George convinced the Harrisons to rope off a site near the hypsibema, and when Mr. Harrison told him to take a break he would scrape the earth with teaspoons, using toothbrushes to dust off boulders in hopes of finding mastodon molars. During this era, paleontologists were arguing whether Earl Douglass, digging through a dinosaur burial ground in Utah in the summer of 1910, had inadvertently placed a camarasaur head on an apatosaur body and invented the brontosaur. Mr. Harrison was convinced that he had and that the actual skull looked less like a bulldog's and more like an ugly collie's. It wasn't until 1979 that the name of the thunder lizard officially reverted to apatosaur, "deceptive lizard"; however, years before, George had shot out a new label with the label gun and helped Mr. Harrison mold a faithful cranium for the beast. He had broken a hacksaw decapitating the hybrid.

Pedaling for hours on his new three-speed and spending afternoons climbing onto the backs of multistoried lizards, George became well-muscled and tan as buckskin. Bright sun or a stroke of luck likewise spared him disfiguring acne, and Mrs. Harrison would smooth down his hair and call him "my good-looking Seminole."

Carol Greyson was calling George, too. Whenever he came home from work or a bike ride, his mother waved the rainbow-colored message pad at him. "Doesn't she know a lady never calls a gentleman?"

"She's not a lady," George would correct his mother.

George welcomed Carol's calls. He would never have had the nerve to summon her forth except in his fertile dreams, with their promises of globe-shaped breasts and silky red pubic hair. Though he would have sworn to Niagara that clairvoyance did not exist, George remembered how Carol's body had been exactly as he had imagined.

Still, there were surprises. He had not suspected that breasts could look so different from one moment to the next: thin and droopy in the warmth of the sun, filling and rising with his touch or the chilly caress of a breeze, the flesh bumpy as reptile hide. Carol would pull into Dino Park at the end of George's shift, open her trunk to his bicycle, offer George a ride home and more.

Carol Greyson had a lot to offer, beginning with no mother. Notorious for his lack of discipline, Carol's father let her drive one of his rusted heaps as soon as she finished seventh grade. Her older brothers and sisters, who were in and out of detention centers, told dirty jokes that she and George would try to figure out. They puzzled over punch lines like "All I know is, I'm a pint low." George thought a dipstick was a synonym for dork.

George would have liked to thank Niagara for rekindling his Dino Park days, though he suspected he was entering the phase of his life that was more memory than action. He had always felt a touch of contempt for the Veteran's advancing age and experience. The Veteran's years had not brought wisdom and insight; rather, they had rendered his mind inflexible, brittle as the hips of an old lady. In a three-legged-race with the aging engineer, George knew that his youth and strength had kept them from tumbling. But now that the girl wonder had appeared, George feared her vast expanse of vision might be the asteroid that threatened his lumbering ability to lead or just keep up. Was he becoming the dim-witted stegosaur, thundering through the forest in search of succulent treetops, while Niagara learned the principles of flight? Was he the slide rule to her calculator, the building-sized computer to her silicon chip?

Just today, Niagara had mentioned the urgency behind a chlorofluorocarbon substitute that was not ozone-depleting. If the current legislation held, they had three years to find a new solution, yet within the plant the topic never came up. Were the research-and-development people working on the problem? George doubted it. The two R&D engineers were obsessed with installing an object reader into the box. Shoppers would feed their grocery receipts through a scanner, and as they removed food, they would enter the code in the refrigerator's computer. This computer would aid the consumer in a variety of ways. Say you couldn't remember how long the eggplant had been languishing in the vegetable bin—the computer would know. Or you could request a dinner menu and, based on the contents of your refrigerator (you might have to answer some basic questions, such as "Do you have paprika?" "Would you prefer Mexican or Thai cuisine?"), the computer could suggest six or seven of some five thousand recipes.

Pulling into his narrow Cleveland Park driveway, George automatically hit the garage-door opener, and then he pictured Niagara, sitting in bad light at a radio set, headphones on, listening to the door-opening mechanism call across space to the switch inside the garage. "Open says-a-me," the electrical impulse would chirp, or perhaps, "Incoming."

When George came in through the garage, Judy was leisurely pouring herself a glass of iced tea. George looked his wife up and down. Judy's tanned, hairless legs stretched prettily down to her tiny penny loafers. At five-five, she was just on the short side of average. She was wearing white pants that ended below the knee (what his mother used to call pedal pushers) and a starched yellow shirt; for Judy, a Georgia brand of Southern belle, these were her play clothes. Before she opened her arms to George, his wife set her glass on the kitchen island and shook her head slowly from side to side. George admired the way her blue-black mane grazed her shoulders. Judy's hair was full and had the slight, ripply wave of a lasagna noodle.

"How's my Main Squeeze?" she asked.

"Fine," George said. He bent down so that Judy could kiss him on the nose. When George held her hand, he noticed, as he did most days, that their skin color was an exact match. They had the complexion of tennis players or weekend sailors, although neither of them spent much time in the sun.

Judy's shirt was buttoned to the neck; across the top button she wore a wooden pin in the shape of a dog. "Is that new?" George asked.

"It's by one of Sharon's Santa Fe artists." When Judy smiled, her lips shone bronze against her white teeth, which would have been even but for her raised incisors.

Bluegrass music twanged through the kitchen. George concentrated for a second until he identified the tune. It was an old gospel song, "The Time Has Come for Him to Come Again."

"I have been beside myself all afternoon," Judy said. "What if the rain blows down the cherry blossoms? I'll lose at least one of my spring sales."

Judy always made it sound as if they had to pay a commission each day she didn't sell a house, though her goal was only six properties annually. Two of Judy's commissions added together were the down payment on their house, which was the same price as the renovation of the Kentucky state capitol undertaken during George's childhood. She bought items George suspected were closer to priceless than pricey, like the antiques in the master bedroom, which duplicated her childhood dollhouse. Sleeping in a maple sleigh bed crafted by slave carpenters for the "big house," George found himself surrounded by heavy blocks of wood with a disturbing history.

The weather had forced Judy to reschedule her appointments; she had learned long ago that no one buys an expensive house on a rainy day. Their own kitchen counters, gleaming marble empty of any appliances or stray dishes, resembled a show home's. No signs of inhabitance were evident except for the refrigerator door, every family's minigallery of drawings, schedules, and plastic-food magnets.

What kind of icebox dwells within the home of a refrigerator designer? With his daily twinge of remorse, George approached the family cooler. It was a late-model side-by-side, white, with ice dispenser in the door (crushed or orange-slice-shaped cubes), extra-deep door storage (designed for gallon milk jugs and family-size ketchup bottles), and an experimental aerator system that was meant to refresh the inside of the fridge by periodically replacing the refrigerator air with kitchen air. This last feature, an idea of George's, was a continual reminder of his limitations. Ultimately, a box of baking soda was more effective than the aerator system. Instead of eliminating the odors of stale onions and wilted lettuce on the way to becoming slimy, the machine basically vented them into the kitchen, so if the box wasn't kept relatively clean, the entire room smelled like the inside of the refrigerator.

"Did you see the lightning?" Judy asked. "And it came down again around two. I can't have an open house if there are branches down."

George said, "I got caught in the two o'clock storm." He reached into the refrigerator for a beer, conscious of keeping his voice and reach smooth. "Niagara and I went out for lunch."

In the refrigerator, there were homemade ravioli and some chicken breasts in marinade. George selected a beer and closed the door.

"You have the manners of a debutante," Judy said. She grinned at her husband. "Does anyone else talk to that poor girl?"

Judy thought Niagara was wholly out of place at the plant. She had actually heard of her performing parents, and, like George, she had formed her own vision based on Niagara's name and the résumé George had told her about. Judy cast her as spacey and spoiled, using Niagara rather than her real name (Judy predicted Gretchen) and following the Grateful Dead around California, much to her parents' chagrin.

George smiled now at Judy's forecast. In fact, Niagara did follow the dead around California, but instead of wearing tie-dye and dancing like a goofball to some guitar bridge, she sat alone in a Quonset hut, headphones on her good and bad ear, hoping to catch the echoes of ancestors.

George said, "She and Emilio seem to be pals." He consulted the menu on the refrigerator door. He hoped Judy wouldn't be offended by his reticence to dissect Niagara on the kitchen table.

The posted menu had him down as tonight's cook.

| | |
|---|---|
| *Mon* | *leftovers from Friday* |
| *Tues* | *spinach pie—Judy* |
| *Wed* | *chicken—George* |
| | *grocery shopping* |
| *Thurs* | *leftovers from Sunday* |
| *Fri* | *ravioli—Judy* |
| *Sat* | *fish—Judy* |
| *Sun* | *chili—George* |

George suppressed an urge to ask Judy, "What's for dinner?" He reckoned he could grill the chicken outside before any more rain fell. "Where are the kidlings?" he asked.

Judy mocked a look of horror. "Don't you have them?" she said. George searched his shirt pocket, and they laughed together.

"Let's see," Judy said, "Harris is at Daniel's house, and Sheridan's with Victoria and Dominique at Dominique's."

"Soccer tonight?" George asked tentatively.

Judy bowed her head. "I give up," she said. "If he wants to

quit, that's his decision." She rubbed George's back down to his backside. "Rough day, sweetie?"

"Kind of interesting," George said. "When's dinner?" He wondered what was passing for a meal at Niagara's house.

Judy said, "I told them to be back by six."

George looked at his watch. Five-thirty. He kissed Judy on the top of her head and studied the sky. The clouds out the back window gave him about forty-five minutes before the next storm. If he skimped on charcoal, he could have a hot fire in fifteen minutes, dinner in thirty. Soccer would probably be canceled anyway.

George used to love the Washington spring—frost one day, eighty degrees the next, interspersed with shouting thunderstorms. The incredible fluctuations justified the attention of a weather buff like himself. Also, in a city not known for its sense of humor, spring weather provided the natives with plenty of amusement. The annual cherry-blossom parade was sometimes held when the only white frilly presence was snow on confused buds. Other years, the trees had peaked as many as two weeks early, or frost and rain together robbed them of blooms. Tourists rained on the city as well in spring, and George had always thought that one reason they wore so much D.C. memorabilia—knit caps and Redskins jackets or Hoyas T-shirts—was that they had packed for the wrong season or that the season shifted midday. Already, the yeasty warmth of this afternoon was turning to a cold damp, and George changed from his work clothes into a medium-weight Georgia Tech sweat suit.

The weather humor George used to enjoy waned shortly after he and Judy bought their first home. It was one thing to watch a deluge from a sixth-floor apartment and another to smell it creeping into the basement. The last laugh was sounded when Judy began selling real estate. Flowering shrubs sold many an unsightly bungalow, and Judy worried over the ups and downs of D.C.'s yo-yo spring more than any farmer.

George climbed down to the deck the back way, from the stairs off the master bedroom balcony. Scraping the lever back and forth beneath the Weber, he sifted out some ash, then he refilled the kettle with charcoal and set some fancy wood chips to soaking in water. He plugged in the fire starter. Judy had bought the trendy varieties of aromatic wood, which George liked to use because it made the fire reek. Soon, the smell of burning that conveyed warmth and danger and dinner smoked out of the kettle. Once George got himself organized, the flames had subsided, allowing him to scrape off the grill with a wire brush before he laid the batch of chicken over the coals.

Because he was an electrical engineer, George worked no more, no less than forty hours each week, practically a part-time schedule in his neighborhood of lawyers and legislative disciples. In the early evening, George was the only man out playing catch with his son, the only father helping his daughter capture ants for her ant farm. He was comfortable being a dad on the Street of Mothers, determined as he was not to experience the outside-looking-in phenomenon as a parent. He wanted to cook for his children, hear about their new friends, their scrapes, their victories.

On the weekend, grills all over the neighborhood would be fired up. Judy called this area the Steak Belt; whenever she had a businessman who had come ahead of his family to buy a home, she scheduled the showing for dinner hour in the Steak Belt. George understood how the smell of a backyard grill could sell a house. A good meal cooked outdoors—did all men enjoy starting a fire as much as he did?—eaten with the hands, juice dripping down the chins of your six- and twelve-year-old.

The screen door rattled, and Sheridan ran out, hurling herself at George's knees. She yelled, "Daddy! Daddy's home!"

The weimaraner next door started a barking frenzy. George swooped Sheridan up into the air and away from the spitting grill, giving her an exaggerated kiss on the cheek. They walked over to the fence so she could pet Bobo, whose gray head bobbed like a puppet above the fence line. George tipped Sheridan barely over the top of the fence, and Bobo, stretching up to his full height, licked her face. George was happy to see that the grass in his neighbor's lawn was in worse shape than his own.

"What did you do today, pumpkin?"

Sheridan petted the velvety dog. Then George took her back so he could keep an eye on the chicken. "We got wet," she said, "and then Mrs. Hayes had us read a play, and guess what?"

George said, "You were the princess?"

"Better."

"You were the frog?" he asked.

She laughed her high, tinkly laugh. "I was the puppy," she said. "Rowf! Rowf, rowf!"

Bobo barked in response. George put Sheridan down, and she went over to the fence to talk to the dog through a knothole. Harris came home, too, but when the family sat down to dinner, he didn't have much of an appetite.

"Harris," Judy asked, "did you and Daniel eat all afternoon?"

Harris's fleshy cheeks splotched red.

George intervened. "You need to stay hungry for dinner."

Judy said, "My mother used to say, 'Always leave the table hungry.' Do you understand what that means?"

Harris said, "Don't be a pig."

Sheridan laughed. Before he realized that he was just exchanging one awkward topic for another, George asked Harris about his history quiz.

"I can't win," Harris said. "If I say the Austro-Hungarian Empire, she wants Germany and vice versa."

Harris's latest method for giving his teachers grief was to provide answers with more accuracy than they desired. George and Judy tried to discern whether he was being a clown or an overachiever. Harris seemed sincerely hurt that his answers were not wrong but not right either, actually too right.

Judy said, "We have to figure out maneuvers for tomorrow."

George volunteered to take Harris. It was a challenge to get the boy out the door on time, but George thought he'd spare his son one of Judy's early-morning lectures.

Judy smoothed Sheridan's glossy black hair. "Pumpkin, stay at school until Mommy comes to get you." To George she said, "I'll take her to my afternoon house."

"That Woodley Road place?" George asked.

"The Bremenhoffers.'" Judy crossed her fingers. "Third showing. I meant to tell you, the refrigerator in that house has an emergency generator for power failures. It's attached to a solar collector out the kitchen window."

"Japanese?" George asked.

"Swedish, I think."

"Damn." He begrudgingly credited the Japanese with pushing the edge of the refrigerator envelope, but he didn't like to think Coldpoint was losing ground to the whole world.

"If there was a storm," Harris said, "there wouldn't be any sun. They might as well stick all the food outside."

George feigned pride that his twelve-year-old had noticed the design flaw first; he put out his palm, which Harris gave a victory slap.

"I thought of that, too," Judy said, "but they said that in Sweden, there's plenty of sun after snowstorms."

"Not in the winter," Harris said.

"Good point," Judy concurred.

George half expected Sheridan to say she had also noticed that the solar collector was more a gimmick than a useful option, making George the only person at the table who had felt envy at the neat trick. How did his own family view the gadgetry he perpetually devised?

"Can I have an Oh Boy while you're at the store?" Harris asked.

Everyone looked at Harris's plate, where half a chicken breast waited to be eaten. He had cut it up and moved it around, but no one was fooled.

Sheridan said, "Can't have dessert unless you finish your dinner."

"Spoken like a true parrot," Harris muttered.

If Sheridan realized her teasing was causing family tension, she would overturn her milk or worse, touch something hot or sharp. George said, "We'll have popcorn later if we get hungry."

Judy stayed with him. "If I sell that house, we might buy your father a new car."

"Cool," Harris said. "Can I pick it out?"

"My car is a collector's item," George said, feigning haugh-
tiness. "Do you see any other Oldsmobiles on the street? A little
credit for stepping out of the mainstream, please."

Sheridan said, "Baby Agatha rides in a pink car."

"We're not getting pink," Harris said. "Mom, Dad and I are
not riding in a pink car."

"Pink's out then," Judy said with a smile to George. "Store
orders?"

"Fruit leather," Sheridan sang out.

"Fudge Man," Harris requested.

After dinner, Judy went grocery shopping alone. This was
part of her system. After evaluating prices, produce, crowds, and
time spent in line at various stores, Judy had chosen her supermarket. Then she entered foodstuffs into the computer, listing the
items in the order they appeared on the shelves. In about an hour
and a half, Judy could prepare an inventory for two weeks of
groceries, shop, and have the food put away. Between her trips,
they needed only to restock milk and fish. On the weekends, they
bought produce and fresh bread from a farm truck parked on the
other side of Reno Road.

While Judy was out, Sheridan watched an animated movie,
singing loudly along with the earthworm and the petunia. Harris
and George played a few rounds of rummy. George popped corn
with the air popper, but he let Harris put butter and cheese sprinkles on the kernels in his bowl. In George's opinion, Harris was
not fat. Still, George recognized that undermining Judy was no
solution to her leaning on Harris.

George knew that left on his own, it took him an hour to
pick out a cereal for the kids, and he ran up the food bill with
specialty cookies and smoked fish. Judy did not clip coupons, she
bought few things in bulk, and still she managed to keep their
food bills below par. George was amused by her strategies and
her conspiracy theories.

To hear Judy tell it, coupons were evil. They encouraged
people to buy sugary cereals, trendy snacks, and sprays that
cleaned no better than vinegar but were environmentally toxic.
Saving forty cents could not be worth sorting through and cutting

up those advertisements, printed on paper that wasn't even re-cyclable. People tried applying them to the wrong size or brand name, or they attempted to pass them off after their expiration date, all of which added to everyone's wait. Judy thought she should get an across-the-board discount for not using coupons.

The virtue of buying in bulk was another myth she debunked. If she stocked up on a dozen bars of soap for the family, one of the children would develop a rash. Sheridan and Harris would get fixated on dragon-shaped fruit chewies, but when Judy bought a case, that would be the day they stopped eating them. Overnight, only goobers had dragon chewies in their lunch. Judy had deduced that children want food to be a luxury; anything in abundance must be common or overly healthy. Before each shopping trip, she allowed them one request. She said it was worth not taking them along to be tempted by a supermarket of choices.

Before Judy returned, George had put Sheridan to bed, and he was quizzing Harris on his history questions.

"What happened," George asked, "at the end of 1941 be-tween Germany and Russia?"

Harris said, "Moscow and Leningrad were under siege, but Hitler had to retreat."

"Good," George praised him. He tried to look at Harris ob-jectively. True, there was no unused space in his extra-large boy's T-shirt. He had a roll of stomach over the top of his jeans, which Judy had bought in chubby size. His features weren't distended with fat-boy jowls; however, along the inside of his thighs, the legs of his pants rode up as he walked. He was heavy, what George's father would have called stocky, like all his mother's sisters.

Harris said, "Russia's two classic assets, Generals Winter and Space, saved their butt."

George flipped a few pages. "That's not here."

Harris said, *"Columbia History of the World."* His smile pushed his cheeks up under his golden eyes. Harris would look practically like Judy if his face were thinner.

"Cool, huh?" Harris asked. "At first I thought they were talk-ing about real generals, and then I got it. Winter. Space."

George said, "That is amazing." He was proud of Harris's

curiosity, and although he knew the dangers of taking credit for his children's talents, he still attributed Harris's desire to know more to genetics. He also worried about his boy. George himself had been saved from excessive strangeness by the Harrisons, who had inspired his son's name. Who would save Harris? Or were Harris's intelligence and imagination such that he should be pushed to his limit?

George maintained that even if kids didn't want to fit in, they wanted to know how. "I'm impressed," he told Harris, "but you may want to leave that off your exam."

"Mrs. Briggs told me not to read ahead," Harris said, "and now you're telling me not to read outside of class?"

"I'm not saying that," George said. Harris was a sensitive kid, and George dreaded the whining in his son's voice when he thought he was being criticized. "I'm saying you might want to read for your own sake and not for Mrs. Briggs'." He stroked Harris's arm and Harris let himself be stroked. "It's not a plot," George told his son. "It probably seems like one, but it's not."

Harris was unconvinced. "They don't want me to learn what really happened."

"Next year," George said, "they'll tell you more, and the year after that, even more."

"But they might be wrong," Harris whined. "How do you know what to believe?"

"You pick and choose," George answered, aware of how lame that sounded. Truth was, he was revisiting that question himself.

"Dad," Harris's voice sounded like a siren. "You guys act like I'm doing stuff on purpose, but I am clueless."

George heard Judy's car humming to a stop in the garage. Harris heard it too, and his eyes widened. George hoped Harris was not going to start dreading Judy, as he had his own mother at Harris's age. Because she always insisted on dragging the groceries in alone, they did not go downstairs. George could hear her open all the cabinets and begin her high-speed shelving.

"It's easy for her," Harris said softly. "She doesn't like junk food."

So they were going to talk about Judy. "She doesn't like junk food," George said, "because she knows it's unhealthy. She makes herself not like it."

"Daniel's mother says growing boys need sugar."

Daniel was a string bean, but George couldn't say that. He was already starting to feel guilty that they were talking about Judy, as if she could control even their thoughts. But wasn't this part of his role as a father? The truth was that George himself was lately irritated by Judy's compulsive tendencies. Her dogged ways had made George's life quite comfortable for sixteen years; in fact, her systems had allowed George to let go of many worries that had crippled other couples. There were no arguments over what programs the kids watched, who cooked, or even what to cook. Judy welcomed his input, but if George didn't offer any, domestic decisions were made quickly and ruthlessly.

Niagara's mystical plainness inspired a desire in George to let things play out naturally, to be led, as he had been in his days with Carol Greyson, by instinct rather than by obligation.

"I think you're wonderful," he said to Harris. It was something he had read in one of Judy's magazines while he was sitting on the toilet, and it sounded store-bought. Harris detected only his father's sincerity, and he grinned as he ducked his head.

George liked seeing his gestures copied by his kids. He told Harris, "The secret is not to become a specialist in anything on the syllabus. It makes everyone nervous."

It took another twenty minutes for George to convince Harris to turn off the lights and go to sleep. He felt bad for his son. After a dozen years of swallowing whatever cockamamy story is fed you, one day you want to throw the plate across the room. That day happens in sixth grade. It's not a willing emotion; probably, George thought, it's boy hormones asserting themselves. Sixth grade was when it had needled George that most knowledge came from a variety of unreliable sources: teachers, parents, twelve-year-olds, even books. Not only that, the sources regularly contradicted each other. Depending on whom you trusted, Daniel Boone habitually or never wore a coonskin cap; he shot every Indian who came within rifle range or he shot only the ones who he knew meant him harm.

Maybe for boys, sixth grade is the beginning of self-awareness and paranoia. Suddenly there seems little evidence to support most of what is taught. And further reading reveals how people once possessed knowledge and then lost it, like the ability to construct a democracy or plumb homes for running water. Of course, in sixth grade George read large-print, illustrated biographies and grade-school books about science; Harris was memorizing the *Columbia History of the World.*

In the master bedroom, Judy was also reading. George crooked his neck to see the title on the ragged library book: *How to Raise Your Daughter to Be Financially Independent, Emotionally Secure.*

George said, "Harris is all wound up."

Judy put down her book. "When he wouldn't eat that chicken, I wanted to pump his stomach, just so I could see what kind of crap he had been stuffing himself with."

"I saw you bite your lip," George said.

"I just want to shake him. He's getting so fat and all he eats is junk."

"He is not fat," George said. "Stop saying that."

Judy placed her tasseled bookmark in the paperback. George should probably have skimmed refrigerator articles in the weekly clipping file, but he would rather watch his wife. Most nights he sincerely intended to read up on other innovations, especially on new ideas for coolants. But after a family dinner and putting the kids to bed, all he wanted to do was listen to the weather and watch Judy perform her evening rites.

Judy was perched on the edge of the bed, and her brown shoulders and distinct collarbone stood out beneath a lavender silk gown. She sat up straight and began brushing out her dark mane, brushing so hard George cringed.

"It's stimulating," Judy said.

The club of a brush had rigid wire bristles; George could not see how that vigorous a stroke could be anything but painful. Was the point to move the hair into place or to teach it a lesson, show it that flyaway strands would not be tolerated?

"Did you hear the Quote for the Day?" George asked. He

could still remember the whole quote, which he recited to Judy: "'The match that lit the fire was the dog urinating.'"

Judy laughed. "He's a piece of work, our boy."

George flipped the TV on to catch the weather report. His timing was just right, though he could have done without the inane chuckling that marked the transition from news to meteorological conditions. The satellite map swirled and churned, showing both of today's storms. High of seventy-five degrees, too hot for March. And then they introduced the year's cumulative temperature, an even 3,600 degrees. This was a new statistic. The weatherman acted as if it were an exclusive report of his station, as if any clown weren't able to add up the high temperature for ninety days in a row. Even though he knew the statistic was low-tech and useless, George was drawn to it.

When a beer commercial came on, George switched off the TV. He said, "Maybe if junk food weren't taboo, it would lose its appeal."

"I didn't tell you what he said after school."

"What?" George asked.

Judy had finished the hair torture and cleaning the clumps of dark hair out of her brush. Sitting on the edge of the bed, she raised her arms perpendicular to her body, like a scarecrow. She would hold this position for five minutes. "I offered him some carrot and zucchini sticks with yogurt dip—"

"'I'd rather have Oreos,'" George predicted.

"Worse," Judy said. "Very politely he told me, 'No thanks, I'm trying to get large enough to create my own weather.'"

George was amazed. Was his child a genius or a nut? "Where did he get that?" he asked. It clearly aggravated Judy that he thought Harris's remark was anything but smart-ass.

"He knows how you love the weather."

"Please," George said, "I am not encouraging him to become Mount McKinley." George would not let her put this in his lap. He found Harris's quips an untroubling source of amusement.

Judy said, "His counselor thinks he should take the SAT."

"He's twelve," George said.

"They have that gifted program. Let's find out if he's abnormally smart or just smart-mouthed."

"He's twelve," George repeated. "Twelve-year-olds shouldn't take college-admission tests."

Judy said, "Then tell me your plan." She narrowed her eyes and forced her shoulders farther from her ears. She was puffing a little bit. "That child is unhappy. Look at what he reads, what he eats—he's turning himself into a freak."

George resisted the temptation to call attention to Judy's reading habits. He wanted her to enjoy Harris more, let him unfold to whatever shape he might take rather than practice parental origami on him. "Maybe we could just observe him for a month or two. You have to admit, he's an interesting kid."

Judy's arms were trembling a little, but they stayed firmly at nine-fifteen. Finally, she exhaled them down to her side. "You always act like goals are for simpletons, but we have got to get him on track."

George said, "He's a motivated boy. Why can't he make his own plans?"

"It's true that men are allowed more drift. Before I got a real-estate license, my only offers were secretarial."

George was annoyed that she had brought the conversation around to her. "You have a degree in psychology."

Judy said, "I have a college education. You think every man who majors in psychology starts out as a secretary? If women don't have plans, they get nothing."

"Who are we," George asked, "to plan his life?"

Judy started kneading George's thick palm, while George tried not to let down his guard. "Honey," she said, "that's what parents do."

He knew she couldn't help it. Her brain raced ahead to the next unscheduled moment and began listing the options, the itinerary, the budget, the savings plan. They should have started this discussion when Harris was nine and had gone to Nationals with his science-fair project. It certainly stood out among the baking-soda volcanoes and the patterns of iron filings. Harris had made a scale model of a clay Hiroshima the instant it was hit by the atom bomb. Flour sprinkles outlined the remains of vaporized villagers; a motorized *Enola Gay* flew high above the mushroom cloud.

As George waited to hear Judy out, he remembered an Indian documentary he had recently happened upon. The film explained how Hindu women decorate their homes with rice-paste paintings in hopes of persuading the goddess of wealth and prosperity to stop by. In one particular region, a woman begins her daily routine by painting an intricate design in front of her house, sketching a path from there up to her door, and drawing in the actual footsteps for the goddess to follow. Where most viewers might have been moved to reflect on the nature of rituals and devotion, George involuntarily pointed at the television and said, "Judy!" recognizing his wife's third-world double. You must prepare your house to welcome wealth and prosperity; in fact, it couldn't hurt to show the goddess just where she might want to place one foot and then the other.

Judy finished massaging George's right hand, and as she moved his left thumb in a wide circle, she said, "I was just thinking . . ."

"Let's hear every step," George said.

"We could go as a family to Nantucket, rent that same house, or, if Harris gets into the gifted camp, you and Sheridan and I could drive him there and then have our own campy experience—go to Niagara Falls or the Adirondacks."

"Niagara Falls?" George asked, just wanting to say it out loud. Niagara falls, it sounded so appealing. "Is the gifted camp fun or school?"

Judy said, "He doesn't have to go," which made George pretty sure that the place was an intensive study course. "But don't forget," Judy said, "if he doesn't pass history, then we're stuck here all summer."

If George wanted to irritate his wife, he would cook without a recipe or flip the channels aimlessly, sampling a football game, a nature documentary, and a telethon. Most of the time, it never occurred to him to make a list—his only goal, at which he had proven triumphant, had been to outlive his mother. George knew as well as Judy that five years could slip by without him noticeably evolving.

"I feel guilty," she said, "telling you what your options are. But if I didn't do this, would we even take a vacation?"

"Probably not," George said tenderly. He knew she could never enjoy some slapped-together jaunt he might come up with; her trips included elaborate picnic lunches to be eaten in the gondola of a hot-air balloon.

George asked, "What do you think happens after you die?"

Judy said, "You find a younger wife, do whatever you want."

"I mean, what happens to everyone," George said.

"Oh," Judy said. "Not much. Buried. Dug up in a million years like your dinosaurs. Scientists will say, 'The boy ate seven to ten Oh Boys a day. Obviously, the women of his tribe did not act as mothers to their young.' "

George hadn't expected his wife to mention God or eternal life. Judy believed that just as you were dealt a family, so you were given a religion. Judy was an Episcopalian by birth. And while she felt a responsibility to take what she could from the experience, she did not feel compelled to profess her faith as a convert might.

It wasn't as superficial as it sounded. George, for one, loved the gospel music of his native Kentucky, although he did not share the faith that spawned the songs. He considered his passion for the hokey verses a regionalism, a concept that also explained Judy's attachment to the Episcopal church.

Judy reached behind her neck and fanned her thick hair out around her head. George was propped up on one elbow; he stroked Judy's blue-black mane and looked for silver strands. Then he perched over his wife and slowly kissed the hollow dip in the center of her collarbone. For a fleeting second he wondered who had given Niagara the amber drop she wore there.

"Dinosaurs," he said, "had clavicles."

"I find that hard to swallow," Judy said. She smiled a willing grin. "Did they have sternums?"

George kissed her breastbone, which was slightly arched.

"Sternums," he said. "Stomachs," he said, kissing lower. He raised the silk gown up over her thighs, above her navel. "Scars," he said, kissing the entire width of her dotted cesarean line.

Carol Greyson used to recite selections from the Dino Park pamphlet as she and George messed around, kissing in the shade of the triceratops' shield. " 'Except for the color of their hides, absolutely no imagination was used in constructing the creatures' accurate massiveness.' " At fifteen, Carol dwelled on "the color of their hides," allowing George to cup and sometimes suck a wondrous breast. George devoted himself to uncovering the mysteries of Carol Greyson's body, more compelling than anything under the dirt. By the time they were sixteen and she was stuck on "constructing the creatures' accurate massiveness," she was apparently two months pregnant and they were both too dumb to know it.

It was George's mother who bore the news. His father sat at the kitchen table, his head bowed, while George's mother wept and screamed and wrung the sash of her gingham housedress.

"Is this the way we taught you to behave?" she asked. "What did she make you do?"

It was amazing that the clot hadn't burst then. Maybe it hadn't formed yet, because ten years later, when the blood gushed into her brain, she had been yelling at George's father about something as mundane as taking out the trash.

As his mother berated George—the point of her outstretched finger white hot and dangerous as a blacksmith's poker—George had a flash of insight. You *could* choose to have a child, but sometimes the choice was made for you. Performing her antifertility dance, his mother tore paper into shreds and wailed; meanwhile, George wondered what exactly caused pregnancy. George had learned about sex empirically rather than from his parents or the boys in his class. He figured if anyone knew they were getting close to danger, it would be Carol. George had kissed her strawberry pubic hair; Carol had stroked his aching cock until it burst between her breasts, her legs, between her tongue and the roof of her mouth. Later that day, his father showed him a condom and talked to him about responsibility. George had seen boys fingering the cellophane pillows; he had thought the ring in a square packet had something to do with jerking off.

On his last day at Dino Park, hosing down an allosaur with a soapy jet stream, George marveled at his lack of choices. After enjoying a daily allotment of passion, he was being exiled to Pershing Academy, though the alternatives weren't any more savory. The Harrisons suggested he marry Carol, add on bumper cars, maybe a petting zoo behind Dino Park. Either marry Carol, be a seventeen-year-old father, and deface Dino Park with kiddie rides, or leave home, the Harrisons, and his honey to attend a military school: that was the dilemma that woke George now with a shudder in the night.

George ran through the facts to calm his pounding heart. It was the storm that had jolted him awake. The storm, he reasoned, with its siren wind banging the downspout against the front of the house and the claps of thunder rattling the French doors in the master bedroom. The Pershing dorm, reeking of cigarette smoke and boys' feet, was ancient history, his mother was thirteen years dead and buried, he was in his six-bedroom, four-bath, shingled estate five hundred miles east of Louisville. It was only thunder.

George tucked himself around Judy's body, not quite touching her back with his chest, lest his heart wake her. His legs folded neatly under hers, and her sweet rump sat in his lap. He cupped his left hand over her rounded stomach, remembering when first Harris and then Sheridan had filled her belly out to arm's reach.

It was during Judy's first pregnancy that George noticed her tendency to develop an unswerving routine. To combat morning sickness, to nourish the fetus, to maximize breast milk: Judy was practically superstitious about her prenatal care. Certainly George had seen glimmers of this behavior before in Judy. But when she asked him to help her get up at five-thirty each morning to eat a bowl of cereal, he saw that her patterns were her way of staving off evil spirits.

Associating with Niagara and watching Harris struggle to map out his own future, George was beginning to yearn for some new paths, and he even recognized it was his turn to forge them.

Judy's hand on his shoulder—"Right this way"—felt more like an order than a courtesy. This need to sidestep his wife reminded him unpleasantly of his childhood alliance with his father against his mother, whose fits of temper and silence were to be avoided at all costs. George had weird fantasies of Niagara, Sheridan, Harris, and himself driving along in an old jalopy to some rickety amusement park, the children's faces smeared with chocolate and cotton candy, Niagara's lipstick blurred at the corners. Why couldn't that day trip take place with Judy in the front seat?

And it wasn't only that. As in the months after Sheridan was born, when Judy went through an uncharacteristic depression, George found himself wondering about Carol Greyson and the child they had made. Now he had to update his musings. What would their child be like as a twenty-two-year-old? He had always visualized Carol choosing young parents with a van and a loose-limbed vitality, that is, if anyone gave a sixteen-year-old unwed mother a choice about her child's destiny. George hoped his kid had enjoyed a delightful childhood, and that during his or her adolescence had shown the spirit of the lively woman who had birthed him or her. George wondered, for perhaps the eight thousandth time, why Carol had written no letters in return. Now that their kid was grown, could George ask the Little Flower Home to contact his lost child?

Niagara was really nothing like Carol Greyson. For one thing, she was damn smart, a quality that, if Carol possessed it, she kept well hidden. And Niagara was awkward and big and not conventionally attractive. Not only that, she wasn't exactly courting George. Carol had been voluptuous and forward and brassy. Their common link—except for Niagara's high-school outfits and makeup—was simply George's desire for them.

George held fast to his trim wife, recalling how just a few hours earlier, she had bucked and swayed with a well-practiced rhythm. Just the thought of taking a step away from her scared and inspired him.

~~~~~~~~~~~~~~~~~~*Getting the Wall to Talk Back*

Even though he and Harris were running late, George stopped at the donut shop. Harris picked out an eclair, and George carefully selected a half dozen donuts. He motioned to a booth, figuring he had about three minutes to talk to his son.

"Quote for the Day?" George asked.

"It's excellent," Harris said, his speech muffled by a mouthful of eclair. He took a swig of milk. "These guys, they think that every sound wave somehow gets embedded in the objects it has to pass through. So, like, what I'm saying now is being absorbed into the booth. Got it?"

"I think so," George said.

"OK, the Quote for the Day is what one of the guys says to the *Post*. He says, 'People have been talking to the wall for years—we're just getting the wall to talk back.'" Harris's eyes were wide with wonder.

"That is a good one," George agreed. He loved how his son revered experts. He would have liked to hear Harris paraphrase the whole story—for a sixth grader, he comprehended an astonishing amount—but he needed to talk to him about Judy's plan.

"What do you want to do this summer?" George asked.

"Mom's sending me to fat camp, isn't she?"

"What?" George said.

"I know she made an appointment with my counselor to talk about camps. She wants me to go to Weight Watchers camp or something." Harris was chewing his eclair as his eyes started to fester with tears.

"No," George said. He reached across the table and put his hand on Harris's pudgy arm. "She wants you to go to gifted camp, but to be honest, it sounds like year-round school."

Harris wiped his nose with the back of his hand. "Gifted like smart?" he asked. "You think I could get in?"

"I'm sure you could," George said, "but that's not a good reason to go. You'd be away from your mother and me and your little sister, and there would be classes and labs most of the day. I would miss you a lot."

Harris looked down at his remaining bite. He was so cute when he was complimented; George couldn't understand why Judy wasn't tempted, as he was, to give him constant praise.

"Tell me what you really want," he said to his son. "If you apply to this camp, you have to take the SAT and be away from home for six weeks. That's most of the summer."

"Which part of summer?"

"Starting Fourth of July."

"Then I couldn't go to Nationals," Harris said.

"National what?" George had no idea what he was talking about.

"Science fair. Nationals are at Disney World this year."

George had forgotten that spring was science-fair season, Harris's favorite school-year event. Harris had not sought help from George, who feared he was outliving his usefulness as a father as well as an engineer. "What are you working on?" George asked.

"It's a surprise," Harris said, both proud and embarrassed.

"Come on," George said, "I can keep a secret." He hadn't seen any suspicious construction or hazardous materials in Harris's room. It occurred to George that he hadn't been in the attic lately.

"No," Harris said firmly. He had a wide grin on his face. "It's a surprise for you."

"For me?" George asked.

"It's a combination surprise and science-fair project," Harris said. "You'll find out next Wednesday." Then he waved his hands in front of him parallel to the table. "No more questions, please. Press conference over."

On the drive to school, Harris jabbered away about his classmates and their silly pranks with an animation George hadn't heard in months. George wanted to know more about the science-fair project, but he kept his curiosity under control. In front of the school, he said, "Pay attention to the questions," by way of wishing Harris luck on the history test.

"Got it bagged," Harris said. He opened the car door before George came to a complete stop.

It was about eight-fifteen by the time George arrived at work. He vowed to start waking Harris earlier, knowing how obsessive people at the plant got about punctuality. The engineers could not have kept more regular hours if they were forced to punch a clock.

Bev waved her paperback mystery at George when he was still a long way down the hall. From her perch she took in more than most. Bev had a knack for speculating which of the looks exchanged in the corridor might be followed by phone numbers or even keys. She was so sharp she could often detect Shackelford's mood with enough lead time to buzz George on the intercom.

"Morning," Bev said. "Keeping banker's hours?" She quit smirking when she saw the box of donuts. George had pegged Bev for a lemon, so when she reached for a custard, he was glad he had bought two.

Bev asked, "Why wasn't Harris at soccer last night?"

"He begged us to let him quit," George said. "Did they play in the rain?"

"Just long enough to get soaked. You don't mind that he quit?"

George shrugged and picked up the photograph on Bev's desk. "New picture," he said. He hadn't noticed the snapshot

"Don't worry," Bev said. "Massoud got it on tape. Anyway, I'm amazed Judy let Harris quit."

"Me, too," George agreed.

"It must be so hard to be a fat kid."

"He's not fat."

"He's overweight," Bev said. "Judy says so all the time."

Bev aimed her bluntness equally at everyone. George nodded toward the closed door of his office. Bev whispered, "She's in there all right." With the hush of a TV golf announcer, Bev filed her report. "This morning, she's wearing a lovely whisper of a dress, organza tea-length, with a grosgrain sash."

George flapped his fake tie at her, "Like you and I are such fashion plates."

Inside, Niagara sat military-school straight at her computer. Refrigerators hovered across the screen, each one exposing a different mechanical element: coils, condenser, insulation, door assembly. Niagara did not look up. From where she sat, the office door was on her right. Although she had normal hearing in her left ear, George usually had to announce himself; for six weeks, he had been debating the protocol of this presentation.

"Hello, hello," George said. For some reason, he thought the second hello added a personal touch.

Niagara looked up, and she switched on her hearing aid. "Hey, George," she said, just a hint of California in her voice.

George could see by their shingled look that she had trimmed her bangs again. A few little hairs coated the lenses of her glasses. Today was the day of the solid red dress that looked like a raincoat liner—it crept down her shoulder, past a frayed black strap.

George asked, "Did you go to Catholic school?"

"No," she said.

"I thought maybe you grew up in uniforms."

"Is that a question?" Niagara asked. "Because you know each question costs one donut." Niagara looked down at her unadorned chest. "Actually," she said, "I grew up in an array of little-girl dresses. Lace, chiffon, organza."

That was two times in as many minutes that someone had mentioned organza. Might Niagara have heard Bev's commentary through a nearly closed door? George could not recall, or perhaps he had never known, if organza would feel stiff or silky between his fingers. The thought of Niagara's frilly girlhood practically sent him into a trance.

Niagara pointed to a plump, powdered donut. "Bavarian cream?" she asked. "Or is it just white-filled?"

"Custard," George said. "And chocolate-covered custard, and almond paste with chocolate icing, lemon, and a cinnamon-sugar for me."

Niagara lifted the shoulder of her dress back into place. "I will talk," she said. She stood up and nearly shut the door on Bev's head. Then she opened the door again and asked Bev, with a strictness George had not heard her use before, to answer the phones because they were having a meeting.

Niagara took hold of a puffy custard donut, which gave up its filling on the first bite. "What do you want to know?" she asked. "Why refrigerators? How I plan to spend spring break?"

George was bewildered by his choices. He wished he were a racehorse, so he could take a practice lap around the track. What terrible accident had cost Niagara her hearing? Did she wear those clothes because of frugality or factory rules? Why wasn't she sharing notes with other geniuses, searching to find a unified field theory rather than a modified butter softener? What force had delivered her to his side?

George said, "Start with your work."

Looking to the left and then to the right, Niagara let a few seconds pass. As if she were trying to hush herself up, she put her hand in front of her mouth and spoke very quietly. "While I was at Caltech," she said, "I heard about a Dr. Hanszen who had managed to record a message from a dead physicist. This guy started talking about what properties of physics he understood now that he was dead, but the communication was incomplete and Dr. Hanszen couldn't duplicate the conditions."

"You're working with Dr. Hanszen?" George asked.

"Actually, he's dead. But I've got his notes."

George recoiled. When he was faced with theories like this,

his way was to let people express their views without responding. He was mostly embarrassed for anyone who professed a wide-eyed faith; however, it was a measure of how seriously George took Niagara that he felt he owed her the courtesy of a rebuttal. "Why do electrical impulses housed in the body have to go anywhere?" he asked. "Maybe we're like batteries—finite storehouses—trickling down our charge until we're spent."

Niagara dropped her head in shame. "Please, George. Do you think a baby chokes on a raisin because her battery is dead? That an angel taps a drunk driver on the shoulder and says, 'The van in the other lane—they're all out of juice.'"

How had he become the object of ridicule? He, who believed so little on the cosmic scale. Whether he had chosen engineering or engineering had chosen him, the whole question of existence seemed pretty binary. You're on or you're not on. Flip a switch and there's one less circuit sucking at the source. No, even that was overstating it, because he credited no source.

"I'm not asking you to agree with me," Niagara said. "I'm just answering your questions."

"Another donut?" George offered.

Niagara acknowledged his bribe for peace. "Algernon Hanszen was skeptical at first. No university wants to fund this, and he had more evidence than those Big Bangers."

Her tone was remarkably like Harris's when he revealed the Quote for the Day. In fact, today's quote shared a premise with Niagara's childhood comfort rituals, in which she ran around stroking objects that her parents had touched, thereby connecting with them via the transitive property of equality. Despite himself, George wondered if a sofa armrest could possibly preserve a parent's caress. Rather than deride her gullibility, George found himself admiring Niagara's capacity for belief.

"Is this your dissertation?" George asked.

"This," Niagara said, "is why there will be no dissertation." As deftly as a musician might sound a violin string, she plucked another donut from the box. She laid the pastry on her saucer and pushed her glasses back in place, leaving a spot of powdered sugar on the bridge of her frames.

George longed to remove her glasses and clean off the hairs and smudges. He took his own off, sprayed them with lens polisher, and wiped them dry, the way you might grab a toothpick if the guy across from you has food between his teeth. George was sitting close enough to see Niagara's black eyeliner, her clumpy eyelashes.

"There will be no dissertation because Hanszen died?"

"No," Niagara said, and now she covered her mouth with three fingers. "They wouldn't buy it, George. I couldn't get any faculty support, not to mention grants."

"Do you have Hanszen's tape?"

"It was lost before I could even hear it. I know that looks bad."

George thought that looked worse than bad. "Don't get sucked into some magic act."

"Prolong the freshness of your food," Niagara spoke with the cadence of a carnival barker. "Have ice in the dog days of summer with the help of our clean white box."

George found her sarcasm unattractive, though he supposed that if he were working a century ago, he would be designing better ways to stack blocks of ice beneath the sawdust. He had always been awed by the shift in thinking that preceded refrigeration. From packing in ice, people began to consider the concept of heat exchange—instead of putting ice on the box, make the box cold by taking heat out of it.

George was somewhat reluctant to know whether Niagara was making strides in her hobby. "Are you getting anywhere?"

"I can tell they're out there," she said. "Who knows? Maybe one of your dearly departed will tell me the George Mahoney story."

"You find my dead relatives," George threatened, "and I may have to join them."

Niagara looked sharply at George's phone, and George heard his buzzer. It seemed to him she had looked before the sound. George picked up the receiver.

Bev said, "I know you're having some big powwow, but Shackelford wants you."

"Coming," George said. He hung up the phone. To Niagara he said, "Shackelford."

"Don't tell him about my lab work, OK? Mr. Shackelford's distrustful enough as it is."

"He must love it when you call him mister." He patted Niagara's arm. "I wish I didn't know about your lab work," he said, which he instantly regretted.

Bev had no idea why Shackelford had requested George. "He's been pretty tame lately," she said. The boss was part of Bev's euchre club, and Bev used the Friday-night card game as a weekly forecast of Shackelford's crankiness. "Last Friday, he yelled at Manning once," she said. "Nearly snubbed out Cushing's wife in the nacho dip."

George regretted not asking Niagara about her plans for a new feature, in case Shackelford wanted a progress report. Frankly, he wasn't sure if he was supposed to be supervising Niagara or just sharing a cubicle with her.

Shackelford's office was near the center of the plant, and George stepped lively to get there. There were three vice presidents, each stationed at the head of his corridor like guard dogs. The president, or rather the president's empty office, for he was usually in Singapore or Taiwan making labor deals, capped the southeastern corridor, which comprised conference rooms, the mainframe computer, and the staff room. Sales and marketing were located in the northwest corridor; manufacturing in the northeast. Shackelford was king of the southwest dogleg, home of research and development, quality control, and design. Design had always called manufacturing "the guys on the other side," an attribute that took on new meanings as George thought about Niagara's work.

As often as he had walked the stretch from his office to Shackelford's, George today felt he was taking in the view through an unfamiliar lens. Niagara's arrival was responsible for the effect; her presence refocused the way he viewed Judy, Harris, the past, and the standard operating procedures of the plant. In design, anyone who suggested starting over was derided for reinventing the wheel. Here was a perfectly good cold box, why struggle?

Chlorofluorocarbons were leaking, so they designed false walls to contain the gases; the boxes were so heavy they were nearly immovable, so designers came up with an internal hydraulic lift, which actually added to the weight. George pictured them unveiling the '93 refrigerator, only to watch the behemoth splinter the kitchen floor and fall through to the basement.

Shackelford, standing behind his wide burgundy desk, was occupied with a slender cigarette filter pinched between two of his thick fingers. The boss was George's height, with another hundred pounds in his legs, arms, and gut. Nearly bald, making up in girth what he lacked in hair, he looked equal parts imperious and comical. In personality he was that way as well, like a tyrant with a weakness for chicken jokes.

"You buzzed?" George asked.

"No, but I'm trying." Shackelford shook the cigarette and laughed at his joke.

"Serves you right," George rashly teased.

The boss quit smiling and sat down. "I got some news for you," he said. He tried to take a puff from his cigarette. If there had been any loose papers on the expansive desk, he would have sucked them up with his effort; nevertheless, the tip of his cigarette barely glowed. "Son of a bitch. What the fuck is this, a block of wood?" His slack cheeks grew hollow as he tried to pull in a smoke.

Shackelford's temper had broken braver men than George. One engineer had transferred to air conditioners just to avoid seeing the boss through another divorce or attempt to quit smoking. George had once witnessed Shackelford chew an entire pack of nicotine gum, an account his coworkers renounced, as a body's tolerance would have to be superhuman in order to chew that much nicotine without seizing up.

"Is it supposed to be such an effort?" George asked.

"Supposed to be a breeze," Shackelford said. "Made by those fucking water-filter people." Finally, in his deep, rough voice, he said, "I'm the one to tell you, George. I'm not even sure how to say it, what with your history and all."

Shackelford checked the connection between the cigarette

and the filter. He held a lighter up to the cigarette, even though a thin jet trail wafted from the end. Stumped, he picked up the box as if to review the instructions on the back.

Usually, Shackelford couldn't wait to get George in and out of his office. George began to worry that the Veteran's retirement was the beginning of a housecleaning. He wished he had brought a pad of paper with him or, better yet, a graph. George relied on his ability to stay motionless under attack, a trick he had devised to shorten his mother's rages.

The hulking smoker tried to take another drag, and then, with a "Motherfucker," he yanked the cigarette free of the holder and sank the filter in the metal trash can, where it rang like a clapper. The noise reverberated in George's temples with the unpleasant resonance he recognized as an early migraine warning.

Automatically, George began a silent litany of figures, a habit he practiced to stave off the headaches that plagued him more and more frequently. Start with the mortgage plus utilities plus the credit cards (had they paid off the balance recently?), Judy's car payment, the car insurance . . . Shackelford was staring at him, and he suspected he might have closed his eyes for a few seconds. George forced himself to stop the infernal summing in his head and focus on his boss.

"Bad news?" he asked.

Shackelford clamped his lips around the tobacco stick as if it were oxygen in an air crash. He took the second of two long drags. "Hard to know," he said. "Well, son of a bitch, of course it's bad. Bad fucking news. And I'm the one to tell you."

"Ready and waiting," George said, wishing he kept a joke or two in his head. A thought almost as worrisome as his own demise occurred to him: what if Niagara's work had been discovered? If Shackelford could get away with changing nothing on the refrigerator from year to year, he would gladly do it. The man did not applaud innovation, and his favorite ideas were new names for old options. George could not predict how Shackelford might react to rumors regarding Niagara's necromantic hobby.

Shackelford's nostrils were still smoking. "I just never know how to read you, Mahoney."

George said, "Bad news is bad news."

"God damn it," Shackelford said. "That's what I mean."

George sensed this was getting personal. He wondered if his headache would stop at pins and needles.

"I'm the one to tell you," Shackelford repeated. "It's the Veteran, the motherfucker. He had himself a stroke this morning."

"No shit?" George heard himself say. He put his right hand alongside his face, fingers on his eyebrow, to mask the twitching from his boss. He wasn't in trouble after all, and Niagara wasn't in trouble either. It was a terrific blow, but a blow for his old office mate, not for George.

So the Veteran had been felled by a stroke. All this time the old man's spitefulness was keeping something at bay, like salt ground into meat so it doesn't become rancid. "Some early retirement," George said. The tingling in his head was wearing off; in its place was the hook of a dental pick in a ripe cavity.

"Know how I found out?" Shackelford asked. "His woman calls me at home—five a.m.—screaming. Get this, George. She says the man loved this place, loved his job."

George said, "Loved to tell me I didn't know beans."

Shackelford said, "Loved to tell me to go to the grass and chew hay."

In just six weeks, George had practically forgotten all the ways the Veteran would tell them to go to hell.

"That bitch of his," Shackelford said, "that bitch tried to tell me the man lived for work."

George didn't mind Shackelford calling the Veteran any name he could think of, but he didn't want him smearing Ruth. On any given day in his and the Veteran's cubicle, George would register a silent, empathetic moment of pity for her.

Shackelford exhaled, graying the air around his head. "Forty years, I told her, the man deserved a break."

"So now he's broken," George said. He didn't know why he was mad at Shackelford, except that his boss had been more concerned with getting another milliliter of nicotine into his own lungs than with either George's peace of mind or the Veteran's health. Also, in light of Harris's Quote for the Day, George found himself reluctant to bad-mouth the Veteran, as if every word he spoke would be absorbed into the spongy ceiling tiles, allowing for a skilled snoop to wring his remarks from the porous panels.

"Don't pull my fucking chain, Mahoney," Shackelford said. "You never begged me to keep him."

"He wasn't much of a partner." George wondered if the Veteran had enjoyed a rich inner life, one that ran so deep beneath the surface as to be virtually undetectable.

Would it be insincere for Shackelford to show some pity? George had been raised in the South, where consideration outranked wealth in reckoning community standing, and so he was consistently stunned that most engineers were oblivious to giving offense. Any one of them might point out that the goal your daughter missed cost the basketball game, that you were losing your hair, had paid too much for your car. George felt he was surrounded by men who were all brains and no heart.

In their belief that they saw more clearly than the rest, the number crunchers and techies often tuned themselves, ironically, to the pitch of the zealot. The Veteran had been an extreme case, deriding intellectuals and liberals most because he perceived them as too fainthearted to face facts.

George was trying to manufacture some sympathy for the constricted soul, when Shackelford lit a new cigarette off the old one and said, "I got to tell you, the last good idea that bastard had was just after you arrived."

Hadn't anyone ever told Shackelford the magnetic door latch was Judy's idea? Judy had thought of the simple modification to save kids from getting trapped inside; the Veteran ran off with the idea and the credit.

"His last week," George said, "he sat there studying maps of Europe as if they were schematics. I asked him where he wanted to go, and he said, 'I don't want to go anywhere, blockhead.'"

"Well, he may be going to Shadyside."

Shackelford finished the cigarette and immediately started patting his pockets, looking for something else that would take a match. He found a cigar inside his suit coat, and with a single bite ripped through the plastic and topped it. When Shackelford opened his desk drawer, George saw that instead of spent mechanical pencils or the odd service pin, his boss had an entire drawer of matchboxes and lighters.

Now that the news was out and Shackelford had gotten his fix, George was anxious to ask him something. "Clarence," George said, wishing he had used Shackelford's first name more often.

"Mr. Mahoney," Shackelford said.

George looked down at the red-and-white stripes on his tie, wishing as he did every morning that clip-on ties came in more modern patterns. Say it, say it, his head coached with its throbbing. Say it, say it now. Talking to his own shirt front, George asked, "Why don't I have a private office?"

"You really want to know?" Shackelford sputtered, as if he had been keeping the joke from George all these years. "Because you never fucking asked." He leaned back in his broad chair, and his belly rose like the sun.

"Your girlfriend," Shackelford said, "she bothering you, George? She distracting you with her ugliness?"

"No," George said. "I just wondered why I had to be with the Veteran for so long."

Shackelford returned to level. "You sure it's not the girl?" He shook his head. "Tough on the eyes," he said. "She is one ugly white chick. I'm the one to tell you, she looks like a weasel."

"She's fine," George said.

"Mahoney," Shackelford roared. "You going to tell me that when you go home to that nice piece of yours, mother of your children and fresh to boot, your head isn't pounding from looking at Niagara Spense all day?"

"I'm going to tell you that." His head was certainly pounding, but it wasn't from ogling Niagara. George was sitting up straight now, his arms at his sides, as if he were on the stand; he spoke without hesitation as some kind of character witness on Niagara's behalf. One of the axioms George had learned from marriage was that no one else can ever fully understand your attraction to your mate.

"I fucked up," Shackelford growled. "I interviewed her by phone and now I'm paying the price. You know what they're going to find out? You know what someone's going to unearth?"

Shackelford was capable of weaving a whole paranoid background for Niagara, more sinister than anything George or Judy might have put forth.

"She's pretty private," George said.

"That's what they'll say in the *Post*," Shackelford said, tapping a gray ash onto a plate on his desk. It remained a squat cylinder standing on its end. "Two words," Shackelford said. "Dead men."

"What?" George asked softly. Now the nerves in his teeth were setting off alarms in each ear. He hoped he would be able to walk out of Shackelford's office upright. Niagara herself had requested that George avoid mentioning dead men to Shackelford, so it had to be a lucky guess. Was she really that spooky to everyone? George found her ninth-grade makeup so endearing, found the way her glasses magnified her eyes so sweet, that he had forgotten how people avoided her.

"I think she knits," George said. "She makes quilts or something."

"I'm the one to tell you, I bet she left behind an apartment of body parts. Invited the poor bastards in for tea, maybe a bourbon."

In addition to a migraine, Shackelford was giving George the creeps, which was the effect he had on many people. George said, "She's new, you know. Maybe she seems a little strange."

The boss blew a foul wisp of smoke into the airspace just over their heads. George visualized the fumes drifting outside to mingle with the fugitive chlorofluorocarbons escaping in Coldpoint's very exhalations. Which way to the ozone hole? The toxins would unite in their mission to expand the earth's bald spot.

"Dead men," the boss repeated. "Like that cannibal in Milwaukee." With a smile of satisfaction, he said, "Face it, Mahoney, your girlfriend is a weasel."

# *You May Be Troubled by*

# *Silent Radio Waves*

B ev said, "Couldn't happen to a more deserving fellow. I mean, how is he?"

"Coma," George said.

She exhaled snidely. "How can they tell?"

George was sitting on what had been the Veteran's desk, and Bev and Niagara had wheeled their chairs around in front of him. Another time, George would have welcomed this gathering, but right now he was suffering a rare bout of emotional turmoil, enhanced by two startlingly fast painkillers Bev had dug up from the bottom of her purse. Once the shock of not being on the hot seat had waned, George began to resent Shackelford for taking his own sweet time with the news. He hoped everything he had heard about the power of nicotine addiction was true, or else their boss was one sadistic bastard.

What had Shackelford meant about reading George? Surely he didn't think George would leap out a window because the Veteran had been struck down. Maybe he feared that George would up and quit, throw Judy and the kids into a camper, tour New Mexico. George couldn't fathom being mistaken for someone who could buck the system and live off the cuff; he didn't know anyone anymore who even pretended he might go this route.

Then there was the confusion and unexpected remorse for the Veteran's state. The Veteran talked only to complain or to brag about what his pension was worth after forty years of "unalleviated boredom among fools." He was a human fossil, ossified by routine, neck-deep in a bog of bitterness. When Shackelford had let the Veteran go, George had experienced only relief, so why did he feel culpable now?

A dozen years ago, when Bev and Massoud became new parents, their colicky son, Mike, seemed to share the Veteran's personality. Harris had just been born, too, but from the start, eating brought him all the satisfaction and stimulation he needed. Frustrated, Bev had noted, "It's just like being at work. I keep thinking, If only he would speak to me, and then the instant he opens his mouth, I think, If only he would shut up."

Not that George or Niagara would be chosen as Dinner Companion of the Year, but even for an engineer, the Veteran was laconic.

"He's too young for a stroke," Niagara said. "George, are you going to go see him?"

George appreciated her humane response. "Maybe I'll call his wife."

"Right," Bev scoffed, "and get an earful from her? Who needs it?"

"We could all go to the hospital," Niagara suggested.

Bev and Niagara locked glares. Might Niagara think that the Veteran had retired gladly, satisfied with four decades of refrigerator enhancement?

"He had a stroke," Bev said to George, "now she wants to give the guy a heart attack."

Bev studied her nails, pointed and pink. She was George's age, eleven years older than Niagara, but where Niagara's getup made her look like a schoolgirl who had been held back a grade, Bev's ensemble resembled a Miami retiree's. She had a permanent tan and frosted hair, and today she was covered with what looked like Necco wafers on her T-shirt, ears, and wrist.

Bev eyed them over the top of her red-and-purple glasses. "Break time," she said, "and I got a date with a *schvartze*." She got ready to meet Massoud. "Listen, you two," she said to George and Niagara, "if you're going to close the door, make sure you each keep one foot on the ground."

With his face heating up, George donned the cloak of authority. "Shackelford wanted to know how your project was going." He was going to have to hold his fantasies a little closer to his chest if he wanted to avoid Bev's scrutiny.

"He creeps me out," Niagara said. "Always looking at me like I'm the ugliest woman on the planet."

"He barely knows you," George said by way of comfort. From his perch, he could see the clunky, bandage-colored hearing aid sitting atop Niagara's right ear. He envisioned the circuitry inside and the damaged eardrum beyond that. He wondered what Bev had undergone to warrant the pills she had given him.

Niagara busied herself with her sleeve, brushing at some spot. She said, "I'll tell you about my project today, but it's still really rough."

George promised to be encouraging.

She looked up at him. "He worked here most of his adult life," she said.

"He wasn't a hostage."

"Jesus, George. No one said you were responsible."

But he did feel responsible. Or maybe he felt doomed. Would whatever was visited upon the Veteran rain down upon his head? Did he have—did he want—twenty-five more years of refrigerators? He figured he should pay a dutiful visit to the Veteran, though he was in no shape to drive. George's altered mind began to thrill at the idea of being alone in a car with Niagara.

"We could both go," George suggested.

Niagara swept herself up out of her chair and grabbed the vinyl trash bag she called a purse. "Let's," she said. "I'll drive."

George consulted his watch. Ten-thirty. He couldn't imagine what else he was supposed to be doing. Niagara had left her coat behind, so George took only his blazer.

In the parking lot, George began to fixate on the Veteran. Here was a man who was partial to jokes that humiliated or stained. He had called Bev "the Jew," Massoud "the colored,"

Shackelford "the a-hole." The only people the Veteran hated more than the rich were the poor. George straightened his mouth into a neutral expression, neither condoning nor critical, the expression he used to wear at work every hour but lunch.

Niagara had not yet asked George for electrical guidance; in fact, George was beginning to suspect that in a design competition she would pummel him. But she jangled her keys now with a mock festiveness, and George knew she expected him to be, as Bev would say, a mensch. A colleague is wounded, his electrical synapses firing slowly, perhaps not at all. The one who was a pioneer has been made obsolete, and he is suffering. George strapped himself into Niagara's plain gray Buick, which, except for the tape deck, had all the options of a car equipped for an Amish family. An open hole of a glove compartment, no discernible heating or air conditioning, black, sticky seat covers. It had the melting-vinyl smell of an old car in the sun.

The Veteran was a mean-spirited jerk who had inspired afternoons of heartburn and facial tics. That and his medical condition were flooding George with the same blend of guilt and hopefulness he had experienced driving to the Louisville Methodist Hospital a third of a lifetime ago. "Georgio," his father had said when George answered the phone, "your mother's had an accident." Apparently she was yelling at George's father about his incorrect use of the trash-bag twist tie when her face released into a serene, blameless expression and she fell face down to the floor, a result of an aneurysm bursting in her brain.

George had felt a relaxation of unmeetable standards, a surge of self-acceptance as he and his father kept a dutiful vigil by his mother's bedside. George had pledged to outlive her, which is not the same as hoping she would die.

"May-belle," his father had said, stroking her exposed and punctured arm. "May-belle, Georgio and I are here with you now. We just went to catch a bite at Ollie's. I had myself a burger and some pepper fries, Georgio the same."

It would have seemed as if she were mad at them for eternity, her silence swallowing all their news, except that her face was still. Her lips were not pursed; they were a thin, flat ribbon. She had broken her nose in the fall, so both eyes were bruised, giving her the look of a woman in a silent movie. While she lay motionless, George tried to remember if she had just once looked at him with blankness rather than disappointment, openness as opposed to anguish. Another revelation during that ordeal was the delicate way George's father treated him, despite the fact that George was already out of school and married. He spoke to George as if George were a fragile, emotional child. Wasn't he just the opposite? Hadn't he been hardened by his mother's harangues? Perhaps, George thought now, his father understood the guilt caused by having your wishes granted.

George remembered nodding in agreement with his father as the old man told the doctor to disconnect the life support. "Absolutely," George had repeated, "she would not have wanted this," as if he had ever had any idea of what his mother had wanted.

There was no battle; the doctor shook their hands and left the room. The nurse held George's father's arm as she described to them how May-belle's breathing would become irregular and eventually stop. She asked them if they wanted any time alone. When they said no, she turned off the many wheezing machines, and then she actually pulled the plug—two plugs—from a wall socket.

George heard the familiar childhood refrain in his head, "You're going to get in trouble," but then his mother slowly stopped breathing and she died. George embraced his father, who had always been tortured by his affection for his wife versus his allegiance to his son.

His mother's only child, George presumed he would pay dearly in the future, but the only emotion he could discern at the time was a deep weariness. He felt as if a jagged, rusty trap had finally released his leg, a leg that the trap itself had somehow brought into existence.

George had little opportunity to enjoy his father free from the tug of his mother. First, the house got dangerously sloppy and then his mind, as if without his wife around to keep him taut, the old man had relaxed into a puddle. He was still quite young, not even sixty, yet he lived in a nursing home run by the machinists' union. When George visited, he talked only about the Triple Crown of 1948 and a shredded pork sandwich on a hamburger bun.

Aglow with painkillers, George was remembering the pleasure of his dad's company more than the loss of it. Niagara's luxury car, a relic of the days of cheap gas, rode relatively smoothly over Rockville Pike. As they stopped at the light in front of Georgetown Prep, George could see budding trees and new leaves along the well-groomed hills of the private school. His headache remained at bay.

Every year he stayed in Washington, George understood more about privilege and entitlement. At Pershing Academy, George's fellow desperadoes were constantly reminded that the world owed them nothing and that they were going to have to keep their boots and noses clean just to stay out of reform school, the next stop if military school failed. And if military school succeeded, the next stop for many was worse, a customary tour of duty in Vietnam. George was one of maybe six boys who let the draft lottery and college applications decide their fate. As it was, a quarter of the senior class had died in the war or as a result of it.

George felt he was observing not so much another generation as another caste. The Georgetown Prep boys had their own golf course; girls at the Madeira School had horse stables and private riding lessons. These children were not responsible for cleaning out the stables or weeding the grounds even as disciplinary actions. High school for them was a series of once-in-a-lifetime opportunities—audiences with the president, prime ministers, the pope. They were American royalty; for them, stepping in front of a door triggered it to open automatically. The closest everyone else came to that feeling was at the grocery store.

Two cars behind them honked when Niagara cautiously stopped, missing the opportunity to turn left in the incremental opening after the light had switched to red. The noise brought George back to his surroundings, which he was determined to relish. In the featureless Buick, the lidless glove box contained motivational tapes titled "Intuition Pays" and "How to Get Respect in Your Field." George read aloud from the label on the second tape: "Will you be present when your luck changes? Your ship comes in? When what you've been waiting for finally happens?"

"Spare me," Niagara said. "It sounds so dumb when someone else reads it."

"Is it helpful?" George was trying to sound open-minded.

"I'll save you twenty bucks," she said. "Basically it says you can't depend on anyone else to bring you excitement or success."

George wondered why she needed a tape for that; more than most people, she generated her own excitement. Beneath the tapes were a seriously compromised Old Testament and a mimeographed flier. George picked up the bluish page, instinctively bringing it to his nose for a whiff of grade school, but it was past smelling. Capital letters proclaimed at the top of the flier, "YOU MAY BE TROUBLED BY SILENT RADIO WAVES."

"You'll like that," Niagara predicted.

George read aloud. " 'The silent radio was invented in 1953. At first, only one-tenth of one percent were affected, but now experts predict that eighty-five percent of the population hear a silent radio, which sounds the same as thoughts in their heads. Everyone is having a field day with these sad, innocent people. If you or someone you know has told a lie, fought with his mother-in-law, or bounced a ruinous number of checks, you or they might be guinea pigs in mind-control experiments.' "

Niagara said, "That soldier at Dupont Circle, he gave it to me."

George had seen the guy. His pulpit was a beat-up recliner he had lugged to the north exit of the Dupont Circle Metro, and in all weather he was there in full fatigues, chatting himself up.

"Read the last line," Niagara said.

George skimmed the essay about TV cameras in light bulbs and the author's appeal to the ACLU, where the staff kept denying they knew anything about mind control by silent radio. George read the final line aloud: " 'It has become a tough world for the electronic hearing citizen.' "

"Spooky, huh?" Niagara said. "Like it was written for me, in a way. Maybe if the soldier handed you a piece of paper, it would be about the dangers facing green-eyed men."

"Mistaken for cats," George said. He felt cheered by her reference to his eyes. It reminded him of Mrs. Harrison at Dino Park. Also, eye color seemed so personal.

Niagara stopped at an intersection. "Indistinguishable from traffic lights," she said.

"In a rainy spring, one-tenth of one percent of green-eyed men disappear in state parks, camouflaged by foliage." This was the type of clowning he performed with Sheridan, who was such an easy audience she charmed George's shyness away. George was punchy with warring emotions—his mother, the Veteran, darling Niagara—which may have explained his silliness. But then he saw the Suburban Hospital sign, reminding him they were not out on a joy ride.

Niagara parked, and the Buick shook to a stop.

"Dieseling a bit," George said.

"No worse than yours," Niagara replied, and she stuck out her tongue.

The concerned-elder-engineer act was not going to work, especially because he was so amused when she called his bluff.

"You don't have to go in there," George said.

"Are you kidding? I want to see this phenomenon."

George wished his curiosity were that powerful. He bounced toward the hospital on the balls of his feet, hoping Niagara's exuberance and the Veteran's inability to speak would keep him from losing his nerve.

As soon as the glass doors opened, George smelled the mix of cleanliness and despair that permeates even the poshest of hospitals. His spirits lowered and his step grew heavy. Niagara started to ask for the Veteran's room number, but she didn't know the man's name. So George had to step forward and say, "Travis Plunkett, please."

George took Niagara by the elbow and led her down the hallway to the elevator, wishing he could shield her eyes from the gurney draped with blood and urine bags or the groggy, bandaged patient attempting a postoperative walk down the dangerously slick corridor. Taking hold of Niagara was more instinctive than premeditated; though drugged and bewildered, it was all he could do not to waltz away with her.

Ruth, the Veteran's wife, was huddled against a younger man when George and Niagara arrived. The man looked up at George as if they had met before. George released Niagara.

George had been nervous about talking to Ruth, conscious of Shackelford's early-morning phone call from her, but she hugged him with the warmth of an aunt. "You've come. This will mean so much to Travis."

"Travis," George repeated.

"George," the younger man said, and he gave George a mock salute.

"Travis," George said with recognition. Now he had it. The Veteran was Travis and this was Travis Junior. He had nearly forgotten about their son. Some grudge had erupted between the elder and younger Travises, causing the Veteran to stop mentioning his son altogether.

The younger one was around Niagara's height. He was wearing jeans, a T-shirt, and a sport coat, though it looked as if a clap on the back of his jacket would raise a cloud of dust. He seemed so weathered that George quickly calculated his age. He was sixteen when George started at Coldpoint as an eager twenty-five-year-old, which meant Travis Junior was all grown up and pushing thirty. His hair was dark and shaggy. Two long dimples creased his cheeks, rough with stubble. His eyes were barely visible, they were so slender and slightly slanted. All in all, he looked like a Husky-Lab mix, well-muscled and hyper, maybe slightly destructive. The Husky part was most clearly visible in the eyes.

Ruth bent over the man in the hospital bed. "Travis," she whispered, "Travis, honey."

The only time George had heard the Veteran called Travis was at the guy's retirement lunch. When George arrived at Coldpoint, the engineer was already "the Veteran." George couldn't recall what he was a veteran of. Was it simply forty years of refrigerator service? Had he been in the Korean War? Perhaps it was his close-cropped hair and watery eyes, his unabashed devotion to racism and nationalism and other fifties values that had reminded everyone of an old soldier.

George remembered how during his first few years at Cold-point, the Veteran would talk about his son, brag about his interest in music and electronics—then what had happened? It had something to do with college, but George couldn't quite access it.

With all his ruminating, George had neglected to introduce his new partner. Niagara pointed to herself. "I'm Niagara Spense. I work in design."

Travis Junior clasped Niagara's hand between his two palms. "Niagara Spense," he said. "Thank you for coming." He was wearing three thick silver rings on his right hand, and he had two silver loops through each ear. Was he gay? George was working hard to remember if the Veteran had given any reason for eliminating Travis Junior from their conversations or what had passed as such. The earrings rang some bell in his memory. And the motorcycle. George had last seen Junior some ten years ago, while he was still a student at Oberlin.

With his ringed hand, Travis held his hair away from his face. "Haven't seen me with hair, have you, George?"

"It was shaved," George said, relieved to finally figure out why he looked so changed. "You were a skinhead."

"Not a skinhead," he said, "a punk." Travis pushed up the sleeve of his sport coat to reveal a tattoo on the inside of his wrist; it was an A in a circle—the punk symbol for anarchy. " 'There's no government like no government,' " he said. "I still have a souvenir or two."

"Travis," Ruth said. "Please."

In the hospital bed, the Veteran was an even gray from his hair to his teeth. His eyes were open, his lungs rose and fell. Even so, there was nothing about him that suggested he was alive. He was an outlet plugged by a half-dozen tubes; his nostrils and mouth were a three-pronged receptacle. Ruth prattled away to the Veteran in a tone that suggested she was accustomed to getting no response.

How could this evenly breathing corpse have caused George a moment's annoyance? He reached out and squeezed Ruth's shoulder. "I'm sorry," he said. Then he looked to Niagara, re-splendent in her natural gaudiness—her red raincoat-liner dress, bubble-gum pink lipstick, and amber drop, orange under the fluorescent lights. Couldn't Niagara see that without cognition, without the neurons leaping back and forth across nerve endings, there was nothing? At best, George thought, it was as Mrs. Harrison had taught him. The memory of the good you do lives on as your soul. That was the best-case scenario.

"Travis, honey," Ruth said. "You have guests now. George is here to see you with his girl." To Niagara, Ruth said, "You took that Bev's job?"

"No," Niagara said. "I'm a designer."

Ruth thought about this. "You sit at Travis's desk?"

"Yes," Niagara said.

"You design refrigerators?" Ruth asked.

"Yes," Niagara said.

The joy of his father bested registered across Junior's face. "You have Dad's job?"

Niagara shrugged. "I'm one of the designers," she said diplomatically.

Ruth picked up a flowerpot of straggly mums. Something in her grip told George to take cover, and he ducked behind the back of a chair. When she did not throw the flowerpot, when she simply moved the potted plant six inches to the right, George nudged a pen from his pocket protector and elaborately retrieved it from the floor. George wished he and Niagara had flowers to hold out to Ruth rather than the news that refrigerator design required the work of two people.

"Still jumpy, George?" Travis Junior asked.

"Still?" George repeated. Niagara raised her eyebrows and cocked her head.

Junior did not elaborate. "Before you came," he said, "Dad worked in quality control. Did you know that?"

"No," George said.

"I would go in with him on Saturday, and he would show me how to hook up the oscilloscope. He taught me how to calibrate it and check out the cables."

Both men looked at the CRT displays wired to the Veteran. Two screens showed conflicting messages: a strong heartbeat and a constant line of brain inactivity.

"Isn't it weird?" Travis asked. "Now they're monitoring him."

Travis explained to Niagara, "I got into music because of these machines, and then once I chose to study music, my father stopped speaking to me."

"It wasn't the punk stuff?" George asked. "I always thought it was your band."

Travis looked at Niagara. "That was my band. The Used Condoms."

"That's awful," Niagara said. "I mean, it's awful that you stopped speaking." She began worrying the cuticle of her middle finger.

"Not really," Travis said. "Mom always said we got along best when we were sleeping."

"You can't expect a parent to cheer a band like that," Ruth said. "Not to mention a tattoo."

"That's why people get them, Mom," Travis said.

The whole dilemma was coming back to George—Junior started getting college credit for music (albeit electronic music) and Senior gave him some asinine ultimatum. Do it and I'll never speak to you again. Who knows what choice Junior had at that point? He might have egged his father on until the ultimatum was delivered. But one thing George did not doubt was the Veteran's ability to carry a grudge. He wondered how long they had not spoken—eight years? Ten?

From not remembering Junior's existence, George was now flooded with arcane details of his past; for example, he knew something about the son's early electronic promise. In high school, Junior used to compete in Morse-code contests. It was a quaint hobby, and if George had it right, Junior was the Mid-Atlantic champion in both sending and receiving.

George hoped Niagara would suggest that they had best be going, but she was staring at Travis Junior and biting her lip. George began seeing the Veteran's high forehead and short arms mapped onto the son. Even the rumpled pants were rumpled just

the way the Veteran had worn them, knees protruding, waist falling toward Travis's hips.

When George looked at Junior as Niagara might, he saw more
charming characteristics. Travis had the grin of a rock star, sly
and embarrassed. He wore heavily scuffed cowboy boots, and his
eyes carried the intrigue of a halfbreed, even though he was of
pure suburban stock.

"The oscilloscope led you to music?" she asked. Tugging at
her hair, she was in full-fidget mode. George could see she was
eager to pick Junior's brain.

Travis Junior said, "I liked the dual idea that a constant
current produced a wavy line and that a wavy line was also the
visual representation of a sound through time."

"But imperfect pitch, when measured by the scope—"

"Is fuzzy," Travis said, interrupting her. "Isn't that interesting?"

They grinned as if they had just discovered they had a friend
in common. George felt left out and slightly irritated. But that was
nothing compared to how he felt when Travis stepped forward and
slipped his fingers into Niagara's straight hair.

He made a coarse braid and showed the end of it to Niagara.
"A braid," he said, "is the same as a chord." He let go and
Niagara's hair fell out of the braid almost immediately. "But what
kind of hair holds braids best?"

"Fuzzy," Niagara said. "I get it."

"You do?" Travis said.

More modestly, Niagara said, "I think so. Wavy or frizzy hair
holds a braid better, just as imperfect pitches 'take' harmony
better."

George was still trying to figure out how an oscilloscope
would render harmony. He wondered if the two of them had read
the same article.

"God," Travis said, "you want to come to Georgetown and
be my protégée?"

"Georgetown Prep?" George asked.

"University," Ruth said. "He teaches there. He's a music
teacher."

"Yeah," Travis agreed, with his ironic smile. "I'm a music teacher." To Niagara, he said, "It's just as you said. Imperfect tones are easier to blend. So I've been experimenting with composing on slightly out-of-tune instruments. Not audibly out of tune, but measurably out of tune." He gestured to the oscilloscope.

Niagara wagged her head up and down as if he were a guru. "Cool," she said. "That never occurred to me."

She said this as if she rarely heard things she did not already know. George cleared his throat. He would rather be talking about the man with the stroke than watch Niagara slobber all over Junior.

"I'm really sorry," George said to Ruth. "I thought you had many years left together."

Ruth said, "I blame myself, really."

"Mom," Travis said, "showing him travel brochures didn't cause his stroke."

"Oh, Ruth," Niagara said. "Think of how many lives he touched."

"Travis?" Ruth asked.

"With each improvement he designed, your husband made someone's life easier."

Ruth, Travis Junior, and George were silenced; if Bev had been there, she would have shrieked. Surely, Niagara didn't believe their mission was so noble. The toughest part of making ice, which George had eliminated from most people's routine, was that long walk between the sink and the freezer, the water slopping over the sides of the divided trays.

Back in the car, George felt worse than he had anticipated. There had been no spark of malice in the Veteran's eyes, no indication there was a human presence in the bed at all. And then Travis Junior. Last time George remembered hearing about him, he was a goofy teenager who gave himself a tattoo and got picked up for urinating against the Washington Monument. Who would have thought a head of hair and a day-old beard could make him look so successful? He obviously had some ideas for music that were prized, original notions about the way we hear.

George desperately wanted to know what Niagara would do

with Junior's card, which he had presented with such a flourish. "Take a day off," the punk had said. "I'll give you the grand tour." Niagara's lips had stretched above her teeth. In what could only pass for high-tech flirting, she said, "I have a lab, too. You might be interested in my work."

Niagara did not seem to notice that George was pouting. He felt lousy, an even blend of self-pity and concern for his old colleague. After all, as bad off as George judged himself to be, the Veteran was less animated than Niagara's Buick. There was a time when the Veteran had loved to hunt a deer with a bow and arrow. There had been Monday mornings when he had described a home-repair job with pride at his own resourcefulness. Now, he'd be lucky if he lived to grouse again.

"What's the difference," Niagara asked, "between a coma and death?"

"About twenty millivolts," George said. "Maybe less." He didn't ask where she was driving; as in so many aspects of his life, he just let himself be taken for the ride.

~~~~~~~~~~~~~~~~~~~~~~~~~~~~~~~~~~~~~~~~ *Years of Icy Bliss*

When Niagara passed Coldpoint without slowing, George said, "The plant."

"I know, George." She sounded testy.

George was actually relieved they had passed work by. Bev's pills were beginning to loosen their grip, and he had no desire to spend the afternoon unmedicated at his desk. He reached into Niagara's glove compartment and picked up the Old Testament. "And now for some inspiration," he said. He flipped to a dog-eared page and began reading a highlighted passage. " 'Come, let us go down, and there confuse their language, that they may not understand one another's speech.' "

"A phase of mine," Niagara said.

"Judaism?"

"That's your religion, isn't it?" she asked.

At first George thought she had misheard him, but then he caught on to her joke. "Judyism," he said, "the story of my wife. But seriously, what are you talking about?"

She shrugged. "The writing on the wall, the tower at Babel that caused God to scramble communications—I hung out with this crowd of astral-projection-phenomenon types."

"Whatever that means," George said.

"It's silly, really. They comb the Bible looking for evidence that the Jews received radio messages from a being they took to be God. Moses going up on the mountain to get news, heaven up above as a source of the Word."

George's visit to the Veteran seemed timely, coming as it did just as he was realizing his limitations, one of which was that he would not be positing any new theories in the world of science, especially not any farfetched ones.

Niagara took the Old Testament out of his hands, and she tossed it into the backseat, nearly swerving out of her lane. "They're nuts, George."

Niagara signaled with too much notice, letting the indicator click on when lightly holding it down would have done. Today's adventure had given George a few items for the list he was trying to muster, a compendium of Niagara's unappealing traits made to convince himself that he should not want her so. Her driving and the way she had thrown herself at Travis Junior were two for the list. As Niagara looked out the back window to check her blind spot, George saw that Shackelford was right. She did resemble a sleek weasel, paws at ten and two on the wheel. With the vestiges of his imagination, George envisioned her preening her wrists with a pink weasel tongue.

Just after they passed the Circuit City Megastore, Niagara said, "Oh, yes," and executed a neat U-turn on Rockville Pike to head for the lot. She parked the Buick with a two-space cushion on each side, as if it were a precious roadster. "How about some market research?" she said.

George followed her across the blacktop, watching the way her loose dress was swayed by her hips. About thirty-nine inches, he estimated, just this side of frumpy. One hundred centimeters, he was thinking, as Niagara flattened her palm against the glass entryway and folded the door back on its hinges.

The temperature of the appliance store seemed a homage to the refrigerator. Dry, wintry air chilled George's glasses against his face, turning his elbows and forearms cold next to the slick lining of his sport coat.

Niagara and George trolled among the aisles, but as soon as

they stopped in front of an expensive refrigerator, a salesperson materialized. George actually smelled the kid before he saw him; he was wearing a dousing of aftershave best left in the bottle. A black flattop stuck out in a wedge above his forehead. He had a wide gold tooth in his straight smile, and he wore an Italian suit that must have cost at least a washer and dryer.

"The Cadillac of refrigerators," he said. "Fine machine."

Niagara pushed the external ice dispenser. The mechanism whined and then spit out a few blocks onto the floor.

"Sorry," Niagara said.

The salesman kicked the cubes under the appliance.

Niagara said, "Door ice always tastes like the inside of the refrigerator."

"I heard that," the salesman said. "What you don't know is that the '92 circulates the water once a day, like a fountain. And kids love it, they love it. Your kids will thank you. How many you have? I know they'd thank you."

George resisted the urge to set the record straight. Did he seem the type to marry a big-boned plain girl who sewed her own clothes? When people told him he and Judy looked more alike every year, he took it as a compliment. If he changed his allegiance, would he be destined to resemble Niagara?

She made no effort to explain their status to the salesman. "What do you think of the Coldpoints?" she asked.

"Oldest in the business," he said.

"Reliable?"

The salesman smiled his gold grin. "I didn't say that. No, no, I never said reliable."

Niagara picked up the card for the standard model. "Good price," she said.

"We're thinking of discontinuing them, truth be told. They're roomy, bigger than any other box, and while the warranty's good, you're golden."

"I'm getting a sinking feeling," Niagara said. George was, too, from the fake woodsy smell of the kid's cologne, but he was not disheartened by the idea that Coldpoint ranked low in customer satisfaction.

Niagara said, "Are you telling me they're worthless?"

"You want a box that will chill your chicken for five years —here's a nice, cheap solution."

"But?" George asked.

The salesman nodded to George as if he had fed him a line. "My man," he said. "Let the lady spend an extra two-fifty of your money, and you'll have a dozen years of icy bliss."

"We work together," George said, flustered by the salesman's implications and then by his need to correct them.

"What do people want in a refrigerator?" Niagara asked. "What do people pay extra for?"

The salesman said, "Truth be told, most people go for width. There's usually a cutout space they have to fit the box into."

"Or a door they have to go through," George said.

The salesman put his palm out, and George knew to slap it. "My man."

Niagara asked, "What if it's a new house?"

"Twenty questions," the salesman said, and he sucked his gold tooth. "Icemakers is number one, followed by boxes that look like pantries (we don't have those, so don't ask), and the studio audience picked as its number-three concern—this will blow you away"—he mimed a drumroll in the air near Niagara's bad ear— "energy efficiency."

"You're right," she said. "I didn't know people really paid attention to those numbers."

George was starting to get into this. His role in the icemaker was somewhat offset by the fact that he had also originated side-by-side refrigerators, which required thirty-five percent more energy than boxes with the freezer on the top. He asked the young salesman, "Do people like them side by side or stacked?"

"I don't know about you," the kid said, "but I like them with both." Then he clenched his fist and said, "Yes."

George looked to Niagara to see if he should smile or not, but she had slipped away. "Excuse me," George said, "I've lost my . . . um . . . my Niagara."

Looking for her, George wondered why he couldn't have simply said: "I have lost my friend." He glimpsed the back of her head in the foreign models, but that was actually a long-haired boy. Just when he thought she had shaken him in the chilly cave of a store, he spotted Niagara, his Niagara, a row away visiting with a couple. It took him a minute or two to navigate the appliance-store maze.

"Here's my card," she was saying when George arrived. "Call me if you have any other thoughts. George, this is Dolores and Franklin. George Mahoney."

George said, "Hello, hello." The older, doughy couple smiled as one.

In the car Niagara was spouting ideas, as if she were possessed of the recirculating feature in the competition's refrigerators. George kept making ice with the same stale water, but Niagara flushed out her system daily. Variable width refrigerators, she offered, clear ones that would expose all the brightly colored wires and circuitry (she thought this would be a designer hit), a foot pedal for the door so you could arrive at the refrigerator with your hands full. Why couldn't refrigerators be marketed like bridesmaid shoes? Bring us a paint chip from your kitchen and we'll enamel the box to match. That would give those cabinet-makers a run for their money.

With as much thought as George might give a belch, Niagara tendered a year's worth of options. The way she rattled off these innovations stunned George, who would have been happy to present any one of them, except the foot pedal. That was an example of how everything old is new again. George's childhood refrigerator had a foot pedal; not only that, but the shelves were shaped like orange slivers that swung all the way around a central pole so you could bring the food to you.

"Actually," Niagara said, "the clear one is close to what I've been working on. You want to hear my plan?"

George was nostalgic for the old family Frigidaire. Soon he would be complaining that an icebox didn't need all those fancy doo-dads and you couldn't get good birch beer floats any more. He hoped he had a few more options left in him, though even in his peak years he had never experienced the torrent gushing from Niagara.

At Coldpoint, George was famous for his false leads. Many times he had launched on a scientific study that led into ridiculous waters. Once, the Veteran told him that fish spoil more quickly because they struggle against the net. George researched the topic, and he found the Veteran was not just making it up. The harder a fish fights, the shorter it stays fresh. Flopping about depletes the lactic acid in its muscles, which decreases its shelf life. Cattle and hogs last longer because they are led to slaughter the same way they are led to breakfast. Rancor has not yet set in to spoil the meat; fear and struggle have not begun their rotting processes. George spent the better part of a month experimenting with airtight containers full of dry ice or chilled oxygen, a gas known for its regenerative properties, before Judy pointed out that people don't need to keep mounds of pickerel in their refrigerator—they either freeze it or eat it fresh.

What George had kept to himself was his empathy for those fish. Struggle spoils you for your captors—was it the philosophy of a lazy man or an adventurer? He couldn't decide, but he knew he had avoided struggle most of his life. The Veteran, he thought, had slipped into a state so devoid of struggle that he wasn't even working at his own breathing. George presumed his old office mate would stay well-preserved for many generations with that lack of exertion. But then, his mother had struggled constantly and she had come to the same end.

George said, "You're good with strangers."

"I'd say we're about par." She rotated the ignition key approximately 120 degrees to start a fire under the engine, and then she rested her hand on George's knee. "I feel horrible about Travis," she said.

Unless someone was laughing or crying, other people's emotions came as a surprise to George, who was experiencing his own agitation. Niagara's hand cupped over his kneecap was as small a demonstration as turning the key in the ignition, with some of the same consequences. "Why do you feel so bad?" George asked. The compassion and intelligence, the curiosity and ingenuity Niagara had exhibited in a single morning were enough to make

George's motor race, amplified by the cage of bone around his heart.

Niagara took hold of the steering wheel again as if no current had flowed between them. Inside the hospital, George had taken her elbow, a reflex induced by Southern manners. Could he touch her with the concern of a friend? Might he helpfully lay his fingers on the rim of her neckline and lift her dress back onto her shoulders? The question was more like a dare.

"George," she said. "They make the guy leave, as if they don't need a second designer, and then they hire me."

"He should have moved on fifteen years ago."

"Then you never would have met him," Niagara said.

George felt sympathy for the Veteran until someone else tried to express it, then he wanted to point out what a jerk the guy was. Terminally critical, capable of taking offense if George's kids phoned more than once a day or if George forgot to call out "Sharpening!" or "Erasing!" before using his desktop appliances.

"My mother died the same way he did," George said.

"I'm so sorry. Was it recently?"

"Judy and I were already married." He meant that as a way of marking time, though it sounded to him as if he were saying an important part of his life was over. "I remember seeing my mother laid out like that, mute and artificial-looking, as if she were a wax dummy."

"Or a fiberglass dinosaur, like you always wanted."

George was baffled by her remark. "What do you mean?"

"You told me the other day. Your mother was this raging ogre, and so for solace you sought out mute, extinct monsters."

"I never said that." It had not once occurred to George that he had loved Dino Park for those reasons.

"Well, that's what I heard," Niagara said apologetically. "You loved the statistics related to their destruction and that, though they were once dangerous, they were long buried and remained that way until a scientist put them back together in a lab and tried to figure them out."

"No," George dismissed her interpretation. "Boys like dinosaurs."

"OK," Niagara acquiesced.

Could he really be this unenlightened, or was she making something of nothing? The two of them sat in relative silence, surrounded by the insistent throat clearing of the Buick's V-8, until George came back to their market research. "We know nothing about our trusted buyers," he said.

Niagara swung her entire head around to look at George; strands of her hair achieved loft and, like ropes of a maypole, swung up and around. "I just read that they consume about one hundred million acres of park land each year."

"What does?" George asked.

"Forest fires."

George repeated, "I said we know nothing about our buyers."

Niagara rocked in the driver's seat as if it were a porch glider. "Oh, *trusted buyers*, right. You know, I kept asking for market surveys, and it turns out that the reason I couldn't get one is that Coldpoint doesn't survey anyone."

"We should have a phone number for people to call in suggestions."

"That's a wonderful idea, George. The Coldpoint hotline!"

How could she think up a name so swiftly? In a split second, George was alternately admiring his one original thought and sulking at her ability to improve on it. He looked out the side window, the buildings as nondescript as empty refrigerator boxes. "I'm ready to hear your plan," he said.

"What? I didn't catch that."

She never heard him when he had something difficult to say. "I'm ready," he repeated, facing her bad ear. "I'm ready to hear your plan."

Niagara coasted into her parking place at the plant. Looking in the rearview mirror, she fluffed up her bangs and reached behind her glasses to wipe off a smudge of eyeliner. "You be Shackelford," she said.

Niagara's innovation was to replace the door with an electrically coded piece of glass that could be switched from opaque to clear. With her option, the contents would be hidden until the user desired a view inside. This would cut down on Open-Door

Time, one of the most taxing concerns of refrigeration. You chill the box, control the air, then someone pries the door open and leaves it gaping while planning an entire menu. George remembered that the blue-fog demonstration of this is quite lovely: Cold air plummets toward the bottom of the door, and as it loses heat and height, updrafts turn the fog into spiral whorls that at the last minute curl up from the floor and dissipate. Room-temperature air rushes inside the fridge, and when the door is closed, the box has to chill an entire block of seventy-two-degree air.

Just introduced on the market, the glass Niagara planned to use was made with a solution of liquid crystal droplets sandwiched between clear glass layers. Judy had seen it in the windows of a special Earth Day house. It worked by running a current through the solution. With a flip of the switch, the trapped crystals line up single file, and the glass is clear; power off and the crystals free associate, turning the refrigerator door a milky white. This transformation happens at the same rate as flipping on a light. Really, it was a terrific idea. Coldpoint made pie cases and fitted restaurant franchises with glass-doored refrigerators, but in private homes, no one wanted their saucy, wilted lives exposed to view. Discounting habit, Niagara's option might eliminate Open-Door Time.

With a carnival gypsy accent, Niagara said, "Your refrigerator becomes a crystal ball, revealing its contents at the touch of a switch."

George was supposed to react as Shackelford, which was tricky because the boss was most brutal by way of his unpredictability. But this innovation, part high-tech, part common sense, had all the makings of a success. George pretended to inhale several quick puffs of a cigarette, then extinguished the imaginary butt against his palm. In a loud, gravelly voice, he finally said, "Where the fuck are people going to put their magnets? Hang their kids' art?"

"Good one," Niagara said. "I've been thinking of that, and I don't have an answer yet. Is that enough to sink it?"

"You think people buy a fridge for cold food?" he scraped,

but his heart wasn't in it. In his own voice, he said, "It's spectacular." He didn't think he had ever used that word before.

"Honestly?" Niagara said. "It's pretty simple, but it could save a lot of energy. I'm psyched that the kid at the store said people care about energy efficiency."

George studied the air vent on his side, speculating on why a car without heat or air would need a vent. He mumbled, "You already told Emilio about this."

"What?" Niagara asked. "George, you have to face me, or I can't hear you."

"I said you already told Emilio about this."

"I figured if it wouldn't work for manufacturing, I wanted to know about it."

It didn't matter if their ideas could be built or were practical. Their job was to devise new options that people would eventually pay for.

"Besides," Niagara said, "I was rehearsing for you."

George pretended to be flattered, although this day was quickly becoming too much for him. He wanted to be back at his measly little desk, poring over butter-softener refinements. Niagara did not even ask him what his bimonthly idea was, which seemed a breach of her usual good manners. At the same time, George didn't know if he could watch himself, shrunk and refracted by her prescriptive lenses, proudly announce his plans. He couldn't stand it if she were patronizing, but he wasn't sure he wanted her sincere opinion either.

Niagara must have sensed George's foul mood. She said little as they walked back indoors, remarking only on the clouds and apologizing for her ancient automobile. They ate separately: George had a sandwich and watched the pinochle game in the cafeteria. He didn't know what Niagara did for lunch.

At home that night, Judy was almost certain she had sold the mushroom-roofed house, and Harris was confident about his history exam. They rented a comedy and microwaved some caramel corn; the children lasted the evening without an argument. Despite all this, George was ornery. He tried to blame it on the caramel corn—too hot to eat and when it cooled, too hard on the teeth—but Judy had another theory.

"You are a mess," she said to him. "This stroke thing has got your boxers in a twist."

"I barely knew him," George said. Even to himself, this sounded ridiculous.

"Maybe that's what's gnawing on you," Judy said. "I'd hate to sit next to someone for fourteen years and not even know if he prefers chocolate to tutti-frutti."

"Watch the movie, guys," Harris said, and George welcomed being reprimanded by his son.

Not that George could pay attention to the comedy. He thought about how, when you flip from channel 6 to 7 on the TV, you're crossing over a plethora of radio frequencies, including the entire FM band, Secret Service communications, and a special frequency that broadcasts only in the event of prison riots. Niagara had told him all this. She had met radio buffs who regularly eavesdropped on in-flight phone calls from Air Force One and frequencies assigned to the CIA and the Drug Enforcement Agency. Niagara knew how to use a radio to detect whether there was a bug in the room, and she had heard hundreds of channels that broadcast only a monotonic voice repeating numbers in various languages.

George ate up these facts like candy. When had his quest for knowledge been satiated? He couldn't remember learning this much in years, and he both resented and craved it. Where had his curiosity gone? His need for experimentation? He used to be the one with the conspiracy theories, and now it seemed he accepted whatever he read in the *Post* without a fight. It took Niagara flexing her aptitude and sprinting without effort to make him see that he had gone flabby. He had grown from an adolescent dedicated to uncovering the truth into a placid adult who questioned only his son's reading habits. Sitting in front of the TV with his family, George endeavored to imagine the dead hosting a talk show on some undiscovered channel. He even found himself wondering, What is the frequency of souls?

After the movie, as George tucked Sheridan in, he told her

a lame story about a flock of circus bunnies who hear the moon calling them and jump high, high into Dreamland.

"Does the moon talk, Daddy?" she asked.

"Some people think so, pumpkin."

"But they're silly bunnies," Sheridan said. "Poopy puppies." She giggled at her nasty words. Then the hole opened by her missing front teeth widened into a face full of yawn, as if there were no tension in the muscles of her countenance. Soon she was humming with the quick breath of rest. George supposed that the time it took to fall asleep was proportional to the number of transgressions committed or, in his case, aspired to.

In bed, George updated Judy on the Veteran's condition. "You should have seen the guy."

"Truly bad?" she asked in her Georgia drawl. She was rubbing his back with her palm, almost petting him, which was comforting.

"Wired like a circuit board. And all one color. It was spooky." He didn't mention the appliance store.

"Oh, honey, was it like your mother?" She pressed herself against his back and hugged him from behind.

George didn't answer, though he was grateful she was making the comparison. That was the beauty of marriage to him, that he didn't have to talk about his feelings because he slept with someone who knew them all. Facing the wall, he asked Judy, "I was wondering today if maybe my dinosaur thing had something to do with her—you know, screaming, belittling mother leads boy to harmless, dead monsters. Did you ever think that?"

"Of course," Judy said gently.

George turned over to look at his wife. "Why didn't you mention it?"

"I thought you knew," she said. She blindly ran her fingers over the valleys and mountains of the right side of his face, past eye socket and cheekbone. "That's the way you talk about it. Maybelle would yell, you would get on your bike and go sharpen the teeth of some Godzilla that had been dead for a million years. I thought you had made the connection."

George didn't want to admit again that he hadn't. "What a lousy way to go," he said.

Judy tunneled her head under George's chin. "You're not like the Veteran at all," she cooed. "You've always adored your job."

"What makes you think that?" George asked.

"Well, honey, you've never said you didn't."

"I said I didn't like the Veteran."

Judy said, "I know that girl's a goon, but she must be an improvement."

George liked that everyone thought of Niagara as ugly and strange, because it allowed him to savor her, even on a day like today. When she first arrived, unmarried or loosely married men from all over the plant made excuses to visit design. In response to his colleagues' bogus requests, George ran out of mechanical pencils and tape. Within a few weeks, even the notorious and persistent stayed away. Would he have developed a crush on any woman assigned to his office? George would never have given her a thought if she hadn't landed next to him, and that was one of the things that was annoying him so. What else was he missing (in life, in his career, in women)?

Lying next to his beautiful, sympathetic wife, George found himself fantasizing again about Niagara. Judy passed her hand through the hair on his chest, scratching him pleasantly. He had enjoyed many years as her pampered pet; what made him think he could make it in the wild?

Judy said, "You just came up with that butter softener. If you're bored, you could ask for a transfer to microwaves."

"Not much of an improvement," George said. What had been his crowning innovation after fourteen years at Coldpoint? Probably the icemaker, which the salesman had said was the number-one feature. Still, if George was honest with himself, the icemaker wasn't even as good as self-defrosting.

George couldn't listen to a justification of his stupid, cautious life. If everyone believed the mind died with the body, then why weren't more people wasting less time? To divert attention from himself, he asked his wife, "Is 'poopy puppies' the kind of thing you were talking about?"

Judy's sympathetic purr changed to a hiss. "Did Sheridan call you that?"

"No, she just used it in a sentence."

"It's from that nasty Melissa. The same one who gave her chicken pox."

"Melissa?" George asked. "Do I know her?"

"You met Peter and Laney at the school auction," Judy said. "He is a used-car dealer in Bethesda."

Judy disclosed the guy's profession as if he were on a chain gang in Mississippi. No wonder she had decided Melissa was beneath Sheridan.

"Poopy puppies," George said. "It's kind of funny you think that's so horrible."

"George, don't tell me you laughed at her. The next dinner party we have, Sheridan will say, 'Pass the fucking corn, please.'"

George laughed even though he knew Judy was upset. "Lighten up," he said. "She's six fucking years old."

Judy smiled. "Am I a maniac?"

"Yes," George said. "You're a poopy puppy."

Judy wrinkled up her little nose at him. "And here I thought I'd married a passive-passive."

George patted the quilt over his chest. "As long as I sleep on this side of the bed," he said, "I'll fight for my daughter's right to say 'poopy puppy.'"

"You are a true libertarian," his wife said, resting her petite hand atop his. Her fingernails were roundly filed and they shone, though George didn't think they were polished.

George asked, "Do you know what Harris is up to with his science-fair project?"

"Well," Judy said, "I had to approve the budget."

"Is it explosive?"

"That is the extent of my knowledge. Apparently, it's so earth-shattering that Mr. Knight is afraid Harris will be accused of parental intervention."

"You think it has something specific to do with me?" George asked.

"That's what I hear on the street," Judy said. "Mr. Knight thinks he has a shot at Nationals."

George tried to read her expression to see if she would welcome this triumph. "You know Nationals conflict with Camp Smart Boy?"

"Only one kid from D.C. goes to Nationals. It's a pretty long shot."

"I'd say so, too, except last time he went with a scale model."

"We shall see," Judy said in her thickest drawl. "I picked up the SAT registration today." She held up her finger. "Don't say yes. Don't say no. Just go to sleep thinking about Niagara Falls." She kissed George wetly on the lips and then gave him a loving shove. He obligingly rolled on his side, allowing her to curl her torso around his back.

George understood Judy's need to chart a course. He saw how he drifted, how he dealt with the detritus in his path or, more accurately, how he steered around it. Judy had a theory that women's intuition was just a way women had of visualizing what they wanted and then making it happen. George tried to visualize the next year. He rubbed his bulging eyes as if to bring a vision into focus, but all he saw was pale fireworks. His childhood quest to stomp out half-truths and construct a dependable world of facts now seemed a fight to eradicate any imagination he might once have possessed.

In college, George had struggled against two other contenders to be in Judy's future. She did her comparison shopping before making a commitment, but George knew that after she chose, she stuck by her product. Sheridan's fairy tale of choice used to be Goldilocks and the Three Bears, a story that had always reminded George of Judy and her three boyfriends. Fred, also an engineering major, wanted the suitors to share a six-pack, compare notes, be a team. He was the flower-giver of the group, and several times while Judy and George were alone, Fred had called. George deduced that Fred was too hot. Hans was in the architecture school, which even at Georgia Tech meant that he stayed up all night for a week at a stretch and that he smoked. Buttoned all the way up to his Adam's apple and generally scornful of most people and all buildings, Hans was too cold. As much as George would like to think that he had won Judy because of his dark, wavy hair or his sense of humor, he was resigned to the fact that, compared with Fred and Hans, George was just right.

Judy slept soundly beside him, innocent as Sheridan, but George had fits and starts of restlessness. Preparing himself to surrender consciousness, he had fleeting thoughts of Niagara as a mad scientist who would help herself to his dozing brain. He coached himself to remain loyal to his own dogma. If anything, Niagara's conviction that she could eavesdrop on the dead should make him proud of his empirical stance. George should swell with the need to convert her, stand on his desk and yell, All that I know is that which I have proven. But later in the night, it was George in the hospital bed, gray and slack as an elephant left for dead by poachers.

The dream started out on familiar territory, a reenactment of the long drive to Pershing Academy. George had the sensation of both watching himself kick and actively kicking the back of the front seat; the challenge was to kick just hard and seldom enough to annoy his mother without her spinning around to yell. But then it was Judy in the front seat, and George knew he was being exiled to a land without Niagara Spense. In this new iteration of his dream, George lay semiconscious on the backseat of the Impala. He was not dead, or he was dead and there was only one person who would listen to him. Either way, he sent out a scream he hoped Niagara could pick up by satellite.

The girl scientist tapped her headphones, or she dozed, or her hearing aid was shy a battery. "Niagara!" George yelled. A hand came toward his face, cupping his mouth with an oxygen mask. With his last bit of strength, George screamed, "Niagara!" He struggled against the shroud of blankets, but he could not shake the mask that muzzled him. "Niagara!" he yelled again before coming to.

George's tongue tasted Judy's skin, and he awoke to find her palm completely covering his mouth. There was moonlight all over the comforter. Judy's hand was clamped down hard, the butt of her palm and the tip of her fingers pressing uncomfortably on either side of his bigamous jaw.

"You had better be screaming about vacation," she said. She let go her grip.

George stared into his wife's golden eyes until he had the sense to look away. Just before he turned his gaze, he noticed she had tiny speckles of amber in her eyes, the color of Niagara's drop.

Judy climbed out of bed and headed to the bathroom. Through the half-closed door, she said, "We'll go to Nantucket if that's what you want."

~~~~~~~~~~~~~~~~~~~~~~~~~~~~~~~~~~~~~~~~*Spirits Travel at Night*

When George arrived at work on Friday, he heard Niagara asking Bev, "What do you want in a refrigerator?" They both stopped talking to say good morning, although Niagara in particular looked as if he was not especially welcome. She was wearing the harvest version of her homemade outfit, on which garish fruits and vegetables spilled across her torso. George had expected that for her first design presentation she might actually buy something.

During breakfast, he had fought not to picture what Judy's outfit, a purple dress like a long shirt, would do for Niagara, as Judy spoke to him through the children. "Tell Daddy breakfast is almost congealed . . . Ask Daddy if he intends to leave on time."

George felt wrongly accused; he had only dreamed, for God's sake. Or maybe the problem was that he felt rightly accused. At her desk, Bev took off her glasses, fogged them with her breath, and extracted a tissue to wipe them clean. The mutual silence she and Niagara broadcast read as intimacy to George, who went into his office alone. He didn't know if he should close the door or not. He heard them walk out together, heading either for the ladies' room or to the other side of the building for coffee and gossip.

George could have used a cup of tea to soothe his stomach, but he stayed put. He always felt a little unsettled on presentation day, the fourth Friday of every other month; of course, this morning he felt worse.

Harris, for his Quote for the Day, had chosen a passage about the Chinese government shooting pornographers. "Get this," he had said excitedly. " 'The guilty party is executed by the traditional bullet to the neck, and the family receives a bill for the expense of the bullet.' "

"That's priceless," Judy had said. "Ask your daddy if he heard you."

Only Sheridan had been affectionate. Anxious for the family to avoid conflict, she had a knack for creating a distraction when someone was angry. This morning, she sat on George's lap and jabbered. When Judy made a sarcastic remark, Sheridan dropped her English muffin jam-side down on the floor. It was a dream, George wanted to explain to his little pumpkin.

Accounting for a rare vacation or sick day, George figured this would be only the third or fourth presentation he would be making without the buffer of the Veteran. He already pictured himself in Niagara's shadow, not that he had been such a star in the years of the senior engineer. By the end of his stint, the Veteran had been championing rehashed options from icebox days. When Shackelford dismissed his pie safe without even cursing, the Veteran said, "You wouldn't recognize a well-designed refrigerator if it fell on you."

Niagara came into their office around nine-thirty.

"Bev's great," she said.

"Just like that?" George asked. He had bought dozens of donuts. Using crullers for bait, he had fished out a word at a time. He wanted to tell Niagara a few of Bev's choicest remarks about her dresses, her size.

"You know what she said?" Niagara asked. "She thought I was weird because of my dresses."

"She told you that?" George was always amazed at what women admitted to. What was cattiness one second could instantly turn into candor.

"Jesus," Niagara said, "I thought these made me look normal. Listen, George, do you have lunch plans?"

"I brought some Fritos," he said.

Niagara turned her good side toward him. Her ears were weighted down with brassy bells the size of walnuts, which clanged as she righted her head. "You're free? How about noon?"

"That's fine," he said, though he doubted his judgment.

Niagara blinked her eyelids, "You've made me the happiest woman in the cellblock."

"The cinder-block cellblock," George said.

"The cinder-block cellblock of blockheads," Niagara said.

"Of blockheads using block and tackles."

"For blockbuster experiments," Niagara said.

If he had been playing with Sheridan, they would be tickling each other by now. This realization caused George to concede the game and make an immediate effort to sober up. He had to remember that Niagara was his colleague: not his girlfriend, not his child, not his toy.

Wordlessly, they both attended to their computers, keeping their heads down. This was their pattern, a blast of closeness followed by icy decorum, like the rechilling of warm air after the refrigerator door is opened. George thought about how today Niagara might change the nature of Open-Door Time, a concept that had been with man as long as the refrigerator. Though she had not mentioned the design presentation, she was unusually still, which George figured might connote nervousness on her planet. George did not hear her earrings toll once. She seemed to be consciously not looking at him, while he was completely distracted. What did she want to talk to him about that she couldn't say in the office? George took a break around ten-thirty, and Bev, bursting with news, invited herself along. The walk to the staff room, which took three minutes when he was alone, took ten escorting Bev. Women especially had news for her. They politely said hello to George, and then, that formality over, freely compared notes on a mystery Bev had lent them or chuckled at some joke about how stupid men were.

In the staff room, Bev eyed a yogurt, and George offered to spring for the snack and coffee. Lemon yogurt at a dollar twenty cents, one coffee, one tea, each seventy-five, plus tax, came to two ninety-one. When he gave the cashier a twenty, she said sourly, "Do I look like a bank?" and laboriously counted out the change into George's palm.

Bev said, "That cut looks lovely on you."

The cashier's face was made human by a smile. "Thank you, dear," she said, patting her netted head.

Was Bev talking about her hair? It was completely hidden beneath the black fishnet. Flattery, George thought, might be the simple rule for getting people to tell you things. He wished he could shake the feeling that, while Bev was approached by others to listen to their stories, he was destined to purchase his information.

After each bite of yogurt, Bev held the spoon straight up and licked it clean, probably some kind of diet trick to make the food last longer. George looked at her weird fingernails, which were alternately painted red and white. "We thought Niagara was a freak, but she has plenty of social skills."

George couldn't remember ever thinking of her as a freak. In his dream, she had been wearing the gold paisley dress, his favorite. When he summoned her face, he saw her thin, pink-painted lips in a smirk.

Bev counted off facts on her fingers: "Practically deaf in one ear, on the road most of her childhood, all those years studying engineering—it's a miracle she's not stranger."

She had learned as much in one coffee break as George had unearthed in two months. He was generous with treats and circumspect as well—why hadn't Niagara favored him with the story of her life?

Bev asked, "Has she told you what happened to her ear?"

"No," George confessed. God, he knew nothing. Like a contestant on some pitiful game show, he bought a few personal questions a day and spent the next twenty-four hours trying to guess the puzzle.

As Bev told it, Niagara vividly remembered the sound of the ambulance in one ear. She was three at the time, and her parents were away on tour in Canada. It was bath time, but when the baby-sitter dabbed inside little Niagara's left ear, big brother

Brandon screamed to be included. The baby-sitter tried to convince Brandon his help was needed at another chore, opening the shampoo bottle or soaping the washcloth. Brandon was not to be refused, and before the tender old woman could attend to Niagara's right ear, Brandon had plunged his rejected swab through his little sister's eardrum.

Bev delivered the end of the story with a thrust, and George flinched. He wished Niagara had told him the saga herself, so he could have comforted her. "I'm so sorry," he might have said, kissing her earlobe in sympathy. "You poor, poor kid."

"Hey," Bev said, waving in front of George's face, "where did you go?"

George cleared his throat. "A little tired, I guess," he said.

Fortunately for George, Bev was as preoccupied with Niagara as he was. "She told me about making the doors clear. What do you think?"

"Great," George said. Judy had once had a similar idea to curb Open-Door Time, but George could not advance beyond a dark glass door lit from within. The light had to be so bright it warmed up the interior as much as opening the door.

"I told her we thought her dresses were strange."

"Don't speak for me," George protested, offended by Bev's role as duplicitous confidante.

Bev said, "She thought that was funny."

George looked at Bev's ridiculous sailor getup. Her dress was covered by blue stars and anchors, a wide elastic belt bound her waist, and her fingernails, he saw now, were painted like flags. Niagara's outfits seemed stylish by comparison. "Why do people tell women secrets?"

"Because women ask," Bev said. She was obviously proud that Niagara had given her a personal audience, not to mention requesting her opinion of refrigerator design. "You know, I have some thoughts."

George said, "I asked you."

"Once, after your aerator flopped. Maybe I've had some new ideas in the last six years."

"Did it ever occur to you to let me in on one?"

"No," Bev said. "I don't know why."

When he came back from break, Niagara said, "Hey," and settled right back to work. George felt welcomed even though she said nothing more. He didn't speak but sat down and waited for lunch, marveling at how silence need not be oppressive.

George stared at the Christmas snapshot he kept on his desk. In the photograph, Judy and Sheridan were wearing matching holiday dresses, green velvet with white collars. Harris had on a Megadeath sweatshirt over dress pants, which were already pulling at the stress points. There was a gap between him and the girls, and George held the photograph closer to see if Sheridan's fluffy dress had caused Harris to take a step away from his little sister. In fact, Harris was standing right next to Sheridan, his thighs touching the full skirt of her dress. Was Harris so wide of butt that, even huddled against the group, he stood apart? This was George's worry, that Judy and Sheridan, prim and neatly dressed, were in the center of the family, Harris was a step away, and George was not present. George told himself that he was not in view simply because he had taken the photograph; still, he couldn't help wondering how they would get on if he were permanently out of the picture. He vowed to learn how to use the camera's automatic timer so he could slip in beside his family, draping his arm over Harris's shoulder and anchoring him more firmly than fifty extra pounds ever would.

When Niagara spoke his name, George practically jumped. "What is it?" he asked.

"It's lunch, George."

George thought he should show a little resistance, not be so eager. Of course, when she said, "Let's go," he trotted beside her as if on a lead. George reached in the pocket of his trench coat, where he harbored the receipt from an eclair he had bought Niagara her first week. The receipt was not yet a souvenir of anything, though he had inscribed the long edge with the date and, in his all-capped engineering printing, her entire name: NIAGARA HAWTHORNE SPENSE.

Niagara volunteered to drive. Evidently, she had an agenda for the two of them. They would get some take-out Chinese and drive to her lab in Gaithersburg, about a twenty-minute trek. Once they were buckled in, she said, "I didn't even ask. Do you mind?"

"Do I mind?" George repeated, as if he had a hearing problem. Did she know whom she was talking to? He couldn't remember the last time Judy had consulted him regarding the itinerary. Not to mention the fact that George had whiled away the last three days imagining the inside of Niagara's laboratory. He pictured a cozy, low-ceilinged hut with knickknacks made from pine cones and shiny objects hanging in round windows to catch the light. Come to think of it, he envisioned her lab looking like the animal dens in Sheridan's Scandinavian picture books.

It was a damp spring afternoon in suburban Maryland. Niagara drove west off route 270, and within minutes they were on a country road, lined with clever mailboxes and grassy knolls topped by vehicles with FOR SALE signs propped in windshields or against outboard motors. The maples and sweet gums, their leaves like splayed hands, were budding more tentatively here, about twenty miles north of Washington and, on the average, five degrees cooler.

George was taken back to his drives with his father through the Kentucky hillsides. Niagara had barely said a word since they had decided to split an order of spicy shredded beef and pan-fried dumplings. The grease was sweating through the bag on the seat between them. George didn't care if Niagara never spoke to him again, as long as he was riding in her Buick surrounded by the smells of old vinyl seats, oily dumpling wrappers, and sweet, sweet sweet gums. He thought of Travis Junior's musical research. This was harmony, as George understood it: a vertical slice of competing fragrances mingling over time, with fine tuning due to the season and temperature. Would someone fork over the grant money for George to pursue that?

"George," Niagara asked, interrupting his reverie. "I want to know your honest opinion about my door idea."

She was not one to beg for feedback; George deduced that her need for confidence had inspired this journey.

"I can take it," she said. Even though she was driving, she squeezed her eyes shut for a melodramatic second.

As honest as he had ever been, George said, "I'm jealous." She had once told him she was accustomed to praise, though he wondered if there was an undercurrent to the acclaim she received: You're so smart (proving that brains times beauty equals a constant), you're so clever (too clever; in fact, odd). He didn't know when she had done all the work on the magic door. She had figures for heat loss, subvention plans with Corning Glass, factory information on fitting glass doors without modifying the steel body. George had only a penciled schematic of his butter-softener compartment.

George fondled Niagara with praise. Though she was not looking at him, he knew she was listening, because she twisted her head slightly. This posture allowed Niagara to keep at least one eye on the road while she pointed her good ear toward the speedometer. It was too bad Niagara couldn't work on her satellite research full-time. While his ideas were tacked on to the refrigerator, like decorative magnets, she was questioning the given.

When he had finished his encomium, George let a long, brave pause lapse. He had this idea that people might want to tell him more if he were more inquisitive. He asked, "Are hearing aids not very reliable?"

"It's a question of balance," she said. "When I listened to my parents play, I could either wear my hearing aid and watch them both, in which case the one on the right would be louder. Or I could turn it off and put my good ear between them, which meant I could only watch one of them."

George pictured a little girl in a straight-back chair trying to choose between her mother and father.

She said, "It amplifies every little thing, as opposed to sorting the way your brain can. It always sounds like someone's whispering just behind my shoulder."

Someone usually is, George thought, guilty with the memory of him and Bev in the outer office.

The surface of the road changed from asphalt to gravel. Past a Buddhist temple, past a Ukrainian cemetery, and in the midst of horse and grape farms, Niagara switched on her blinker, giving notice that she would be turning sometime in the next quarter of a mile. George spotted a satellite dish, like an overgrown mushroom, sprouting between two plowed fields; the dish dwarfed a tiny trailer parked beneath it. Niagara drove off onto a dirt trail so rutted that she and George bounced around like atoms in the clanky Buick. When she parked, George saw that a surge protector was plugged into an electrical pole at the site.

"Speaking of hearing things," Niagara said, and led the way into her laboratory.

George was disappointed at the uncoziness therein. It had the same feel as the Veteran's hospital room though it was less tidy, with the tangled cords from scopes, amplifiers, and receivers noodled about the metallic space.

In an attempt to act comfortable, George hung his coat on a bentwood rack near the door. A sizable draft blew down the back of his collar no matter which way he pivoted.

"My home away from home," Niagara said. "You can find me here every night until twelve."

Niagara had one radio set that was his grandparents' vintage. It was labeled "DEAD." The dial was marked not only with numbers but also locations. George had forgotten this feature, which explained why Java always evoked the number 5.2 in his head; Moscow, 12.0. There were two other glass-tubed receivers with tags that read "DEADER" and "DEADEST." The cabinets were deeply carved with dozens of initials as well as crude drawings of cruder body parts. These radios had endured a hard life before Niagara, the good witch of the electronic forest, had taken them in. George ran his hand over the oval glass bulbs, like a blind man returned to familiar terrain.

"I cannibalized them," Niagara said. "Some Silicon Valley types finally gave the vo-tech schools computers to get them beyond radio repair."

"But these were out of date in the fifties."

Niagara said, "The teacher with seniority wouldn't give them up. Anyway, one man's trash is another woman's treasure."

Parked in the shade of the satellite dish, the trailer was chilly and more than a little dank. This was the odor that clung to Niagara's memos and magazines. It smelled like an old lady, clammy and stale, the appropriate accompaniment to Niagara's dresses and hearing aid.

In contrast to George's elderly notion of her, Niagara was fidgeting herself into a frenzy. She offered George a bulky man's sweater, took it back before he could accept it, and began pulling burrs of wool from the fuzzy bundle. When she offered the sweater again, George took it to make her stop picking. Her hands orbited like a satellite, until she turned her attention to her cuticles, savagely biting the skin around her thumbnail.

"Are you OK?" George asked. He wrapped the sweater around himself and was enveloped by the mustiness that he regarded as Niagara's scent.

"Sure," she said. "Should we eat? We should eat now."

Usually, she just moved around; this high-speed twitching was new and unbecoming. George halved the portions, but she was not much interested in her plate. She looked around her as if people were whispering away.

"George," she said. "You see this one?" She pointed to the machine marked "DEAD." Niagara was so jumpy she kept flinging food with her chopsticks, seemingly animating each morsel. "Last night, I picked up some static before midnight, just messing around at a hundred and fifty megahertz." As she did when she first told him about her research, she put her hand in front of her mouth, possibly hoping to trap her words on the way out. "At first it was a low drone, a whine with the inflections of voice. I thought Radio Moscow or something."

Underneath the sweater, George felt dread pimple his arms.

"Anyway, I masked some of the weaker frequencies and, clear as your voice in this room, the Veteran starts talking to me."

"From a radio set?" George asked. "He's in a coma. Besides, does he even know your name?" He hadn't known you could pick up ham operators on that kind of set.

"Not from a radio set," Niagara said. "Not ham."

"He wouldn't have any equipment in the hospital," George said, "if he was even conscious."

Niagara flung a piece of dumpling into the air. "Cut it out," she said, perhaps to herself or to George to stop him from running through the facts. Apparently what had happened had nothing to do with facts. "I heard him through that radio. He's not in a coma. He's dead."

"You talked to him?"

"No, I haven't gotten that far. I just listened." She frowned as she chewed her shredded beef. She looked as if she might cry.

George swallowed hard. He could still taste the flavor of last night's dream, the heaviness that weighed down his chest and forced out his breath in a yelp. Maybe he was starring as someone else in the hours before daylight. Maybe he was the ailing Veteran, begging Niagara to listen to his dying wish. And maybe electricity is generated by little gnomes throwing sparks at each other.

Niagara's sadness enhanced George's skepticism. "If you made contact," he asked, "why aren't you a little happy?"

"Let's just say it could have been better. I could have taped it."

"It could have been worse," George said. "It could have been my mother."

Niagara and George laughed at that possibility. They laughed until they snorted and guffawed. George said a word of thanks for his dead mother, even if it was for being the butt of a joke.

"It's incredible, isn't it?" Niagara asked. "In grad school, I worked nights in the computer lab, so I'd have my days for experiments. These last two months, listening at night over prehistoric equipment, I've come closer to the dead than I did in the last eight years. I knew there was less interference at night, but I just didn't think I was competing with radio stations for airtime."

"What did your Dr. Hanszen have to say about frequencies?" George asked, wondering if the notes she had from the dead physicist were any guide at all.

"My hero," Niagara touched her heart. "Hanszen never specified actual frequencies, but he did mention that all his contacts were after dark. He believed that dreams are our memories of the life we live in our sleep. He wrote in his journal, 'Spirits travel at night.' "

"Spoken like a physicist," George said with audible sarcasm. His face had grown tired from holding on to a smile.

"Could be faith has more to do with it than physics," she said, propelled by George's mild scorn. "I had just been thinking the dead aren't so far away—past shortwave, past cable, sure, but not in the realm of stars. And then I pick up the Veteran at a hundred and fifty megahertz. A homemade antenna could have brought him in."

What had last night's dream been about? Had he imagined himself as the Veteran, telling Niagara the end had come, or was he George, calling out for her attention? George was beginning to feel she had cast a spell on him. It was one thing to say you had a theory; it was quite another to declare you'd heard the dead speak. George asked, "How do you know it was the Veteran?"

"God, I'm so stupid," Niagara said. She beat on her chest with her fists. "I wasn't even taping."

George grabbed her wrists, intending to place them gently on either side of her plate. He didn't want any histrionics. He wanted an exacting account of her supposed breakthrough before he decided just how loony she was.

But as George held Niagara in his arms, a natural order seemed to fall into place. The impulse to make her talk sense was enveloped by a desire to hold fast to her incredibly broad wrists and draw her close to him. Perhaps his dream was as transparent as Judy had suspected, and when he'd awakened his wife with his yelling, he'd been screaming for this. He kissed each finger, marveling at how her fingernails were the size of guitar picks. Her chopsticks clattered to the floor. Her thumb tasted of soy mingled with the fire of Szechuan peppers.

Niagara didn't go limp but she didn't slap him either. "I'm telling you the Veteran is dead and you want to make out? You think this is my love nest?"

"Yes," George said, kissing her left cheek, "and yes," kissing her right. None of his dreams had covered this territory. He swaddled her lips in his and began to work them over. A lifetime spent avoiding initiative had laid him low. To touch her was to feel their age difference; the muscles in her upper arm were tauter than

Judy's, and her skin, white as an unscuffed softball, felt like one as well.

When he came up for air, she was still chattering. "Listen," she said, "just because you're handsome doesn't mean you get whatever you want. As far as I'm concerned, it is now officially two minutes ago. You let me beat myself about the chest with my fists and then give me the skeptical-scientist routine."

"What if I kiss you again?"

"You are not paying attention." Niagara took a deep breath.

Did that mean no? George wondered. Surrounded by vintage radios in the cramped tin can of a trailer, he wanted to muzzle her with kisses. Then he wouldn't have to listen to her lies about dead men on the airwaves. He could pretend, too. He could pretend she could be reformed. A little Prozac, a lot of therapy—she was obviously talented and she had called him handsome. He could show her that the world was a puzzle that had already been solved. The dead were history; their energy was dissipated among the next generation. Sure, he desired her, but he told himself he was kissing her so she would shut up.

"I want you to be my witness," Niagara said.

"I will be your witness, your manservant, your slave." After seeing Niagara right her dress no less than ninety times, George had the pleasure of pushing the damn neckline over her shoulder. For an instant, his hand rested on her flat discus of shoulder blade. Then he pushed the bra strap down, too, and he wetly kissed her neck and beyond. On the cornucopia-covered fabric of her dress, he leaned over to smooch a tomato. "Garden ripe," he said. Then he pointed to her hips. "Is that a parsnip?" he asked. "I'm partial to parsnips."

Niagara grinned. "It's some kind of tuber."

"Tubers," George repeated, "rutabagas, yams." Judy had taught him to love the sound of a list. "Don't turnip your nose at me."

Niagara groaned, and although George knew he should be worried about making a fool of himself, he was unusually self-possessed. Comfortable exploring, he fingered the amber drop that he usually saw an office-length away.

"My father bought me this," Niagara said. "You know what amber means to us?"

He wasn't sure if "us" referred to her and her father or her and him.

"*Electron*," she said, "is from the Greek word for amber. Around seven hundred B.C., some Greek observed that if he rubbed amber with a cloth, it would attract feathers and bits of paper. So he named the attraction 'electricity.' "

"Really?" George asked.

"Look it up," she said.

George hugged her chest against his. "There's amber between us," he said. He kissed her clavicle, which caused guilt to flicker in his conscience. Judy had a very kissable clavicle. Before the guilt could catch, George extinguished it with some hot breath along Niagara's neck.

A gurgle started high in her throat, a cooing that acted like a Geiger counter to gauge the pleasure Niagara got from each kiss. She cooed loudest when he smooched her just beneath her jawline, tipping her chin up to completely circumnavigate her head. George's lips were getting puffy and dry when Niagara stood up and took him by the arm, leading him to a sad corduroy sofa that someone had rightly discarded. Squatting down, she untied George's shoes, which he kicked off, and then she stood up, all six feet of her, to unbuckle George's belt and slide it through the many loops around his waist, whipping the leather strap off with flair. George unzipped his pants as Niagara slipped off her own shoes. Then she lay down on the couch and pulled George on top of her.

Niagara's dress had neither buttons nor zipper, so George couldn't get to her breasts. He settled for pressing his weight against her, delighted that after years of sleeping with a short woman, he could lie crotch to crotch against Niagara, nipple to nipple. Niagara untucked George's shirt and kneaded his softening lower back.

It was as he was holding his butt in the air and kissing the inside of her thighs that Niagara yelled, "What time is it?"

Judy had never lost herself to the extent that she had cried out during sex. This could be what the future held. Niagara had practically screamed out her question, and George was right with her. "Time for love!" he bellowed.

"Jesus," Niagara gasped. She gave George a healthy push back onto his haunches. "Design meeting, two o'clock!"

The next few minutes were pure slapstick, as George tried to shoehorn his feet into his shoes, his boner into his pants. He was mortified on about a hundred different levels, starting with kissing another woman to kissing his office mate to yelling, "Time for love!"

Niagara had a tissue for wiping the lipstick off George's face. "You're covered with me," she said. She Eskimo kissed him with her nose, a feat she could perform without rising up on her toes.

Back in the car, Niagara showed George the face of her watch—one-forty-five—before she put the accelerator to the floor. The Buick squealed around the quaint country corners, nearly eliminating some of the mailboxes they had noticed on the way in.

The last time George had made out with someone who was neither Judy nor Carol Greyson had been in junior high, and he resorted to the mature response of boys that age: he pretended nothing had happened. Cover your body with my tongue? Have a hard-on from here to Anacostia? Not me.

"Why weren't you recording last night?" George asked, hoping she would pick up from before the couch dancing. Their rush had done much to shrink his ardor, though he was still feverish with lust.

"I used to tape everything, but it seemed such a waste. How can I call myself a scientist when I am so habitually stupid?"

He tried to establish what the Veteran might say that would reveal his identity. Niagara sped up to make a yellow light. She wasn't quite fast enough, but that didn't stop her.

In his junior-high mode, George asked himself, All this time, was she fidgety because she liked me? Did she bring me out here so we could smooch? He wasn't so egotistical as to pretend that her story, along with the radios, the trailer—hell, the satellite dish—was a ruse to kiss him, though it did enter his mind. It was believe either that or her story.

"The Veteran mentioned Shackelford," Niagara said. "Said he was glad his wife bawled the guy out. He said everyone took him for comatose, but he was dead. 'Circuits off,' he said. 'Power out.' "

George had told Niagara about Ruth's call to Shackelford. He was trying to remember everything he had repeated so that he could recognize any solid evidence. He was worried that she might be playing him for a sucker. For her sake, he was equally worried that she was a talented young engineer who had spent a few too many hours listening to static.

Snagged by a red light, Niagara brought the Buick to a halt. She turned her watch to George: one-forty-eight. They were making good time.

Niagara said, "I think he was aware of me. Right before I lost him, he said, 'I knew a lady engineer once—she killed herself.' "

That was vintage Veteran. He liked to say that to the summer interns, hopeful girls from schools that, in the Veteran's era, hadn't even admitted women. But Emilio could have told Niagara that. "What did he want?"

"He left explicit instructions about his future, and they're in jeopardy. Get this, George. He wants to be frozen."

That was rich. Niagara said the Veteran had made all the arrangements—spent thousands of his pension money—but he was irate. He was enraged that he had been mowed down so soon; given that injustice, he was mad that his dead body remained on life-support.

Niagara said, "You should have heard him on anatomy. How quickly the liver's ability to metabolize proteins atrophies—oh, I don't know."

They were back on route 270. Niagara expertly weaved through the lanes; if she kept it up, they might get back by two. George had heard nothing from the Veteran to suggest that he wanted to be holed up in a deep freeze. That part of the story reeked of untruth. It hurt that the Veteran had to wait until he was dead to talk, and that even then he had to approach a stranger. Sitting five feet away from George, he couldn't speak his mind.

"I used to keep a tape going twenty-four hours," Niagara said. "The problem was, I couldn't possibly listen to it. And I didn't know what I was looking for, so I couldn't run the tapes at high speed or hire researchers to sort through them."

Did he say anything about me, George wanted to know but couldn't ask.

"Jesus, George," Niagara said suddenly. "Aren't there things you can't explain?"

Plenty. Like what did he think he was doing back in that trailer? Men were charged with harassment for stunts like that, though at least he had stopped before the possibility of a paternity suit had materialized. Keep up your end of it, George coached himself. "He just spoke to you in a normal voice?"

"I know," Niagara said. "No ooh-woos or elaborate codes."

"How do you know you don't have voices on some of your old tapes?"

Niagara waited so long to respond that George drifted back into despair. "It's a problem," she finally said. "It's like I don't have them anymore."

"Were they stolen?"

"No," she said, drawing the word out. "I burned them."

They both knew that if anyone else offered him a break-through with as many obstacles as Niagara's, he would dismiss it. At a loss, George consulted his watch: one-fifty-two. They were off the exit ramp, but midafternoon traffic was pretty thick. No one had blatantly skipped a design meeting in at least the last fourteen years. George tried to think up an excuse, a skill he supposed he might need for the future. He saw that Niagara was a little roughed up, but he doubted anyone else would notice she was abnormally rumpled.

Niagara said, "I couldn't listen to all the tapes, but I listened to hours of them. Silence, static, nothing. Do you know how hard it is to analyze tape-recorded silence with a hearing problem? And it was more than that. You know how when you get out the camera, everyone gets stiff? I got anxious that people weren't talking because I was taping."

"You got superstitious," George said.

"Yep," Niagara said. "And that's a cardinal sin in your book, isn't it, George?"

"Yes, it is," he said, a little more righteously than he had intended.

"We come to science in praise of the known. We come to shed light on ignorance and its teachings, to stamp out voodoo and acupuncture and chiropractors."

"Chiropractors?" George asked. Really, he had nothing against chiropractors.

"OK, yoga teachers."

George said, "I just think if you call yourself a scientist—"

"And, God help me, I do."

"If you call yourself a scientist," he started again, "you follow certain methodical procedures."

"Unless you are a scientist after my own heart."

George felt the test again, though he suspected she might be teasing him. He was determined to stand up in defense of science. Believe the known, don't count on a hunch, don't finesse the data. Yet even as he tried to rally on the side of facts, he remembered her tongue on his teeth. He was after her heart, her height, her breadth, her breasts.

George had heard about other men who did this without a thought for the consequences, but the details of his life were rushing in. He started the summing in his head of mortgage, plus Sheridan's tuition, life insurance, braces for Harris. He began privately negotiating: If she shows me something irrefutable, I will make a life with her. Alimony, child support, an apartment, a civil ceremony. George knew it was a testament to Judy that he could only think in terms of marriage and a family.

"May I ask you something?" Niagara said.

"Yes."

"What about accidents?"

OK, they could call it an accident. I accidentally lay down on your couch while you were already stretched out there. Such is luck.

"Like vulcanized rubber," Niagara said, and George understood she meant accidents of discovery. "Saccharine. People burn their mistake or they throw it away and find that the trash can is home to the world's next great invention."

George said, "That's the creed of flakes. They always think that sloppiness is equated with originality."

"I'll tell you, George," Niagara said, "neatness is not equated with originality."

It dawned on George that after sixteen unblemished years of marriage, he had chosen the perfect candidate for an affair. If Niagara could produce evidence that she had heard the Veteran, she would not be sticking around for the '95 refrigerators; however, if word of her unsubstantiated claims escaped, she would soon be escorted out. George felt she was destined to be notorious.

"I need more proof," George said.

"And what?" Niagara asked. "You'll drop your net and follow me?"

George pictured Niagara preaching to a crowd at the water's edge. Miracles would be attributed to her. A woman of faith and science might well walk on water, wring gold from grains of sand.

"Are you going to call Ruth?" he asked. "His doctors?"

"That would be senseless," Niagara said. " 'I was eavesdropping on the dead last night, and your husband mentioned that he would not be coming out of his coma.' "

Senseless might just describe Niagara. With her quarter-inch-thick glasses, she had no sight to speak of, and her hearing was down by half. If she could smell, George reasoned, she would have certainly done something about the basement odor of her trailer. That left touch and taste, if you didn't count anything supernatural.

George's future was flitting by as fast as the scenery. He asked, "Did he teach you any great truths of physics?"

"Nada," she said. "A half hour with that guy, and I wasn't

sure I wanted to talk to the dead. What if it turns out the only dead people with enough energy to be heard are the ones with bones to pick?"

"Bones to pick," George repeated. They had two lights to go before the parking lot. He wanted to enhance the joke, but his mind was blank.

"My mother told me physicists would be circumspect even after death."

"Your parents know about your research?" George imagined Harris telling him he was bringing corpses to life. It had not occurred to him to fear his son's science-fair project.

"I'm not ashamed," Niagara said. "Despite what you or the engineering department at Caltech thinks, it's pure, unadulterated science."

"One of the things I can't figure out," George said, "is why you thought an engineering department might go for this stuff."

"They're tight with the physicists."

"They're still engineers. Engineers basically want two things out of their research: to prove someone wrong or to take something that already works and make it tinier and faster."

"I don't see any tiny refrigerators around here," Niagara said.

George ignored the dig. "If you're not ashamed, why did you tell me not to tell Shackelford?"

"He's not interested in science, my dear."

No, George guessed he wasn't.

"You know," Niagara said accusingly, "I expected more of you."

Humiliation burned his face with the force of a slap. More what? Sympathy? Fervor? Resistance? Or was she calling him a hypocrite?

"You refute guessing as sloppy, fortune-telling as snake-oil science; meanwhile, what's your hobby?"

"Gospel music?"

Niagara laughed. "No, the weather. Don't you think it's weird that you are so drawn to the unpredictable?"

Well, yes and no. He knew the best meteorologists were accurate only about forty percent of the time and that if you just said tomorrow's weather will be the same as today's, you'd be right about sixty percent. Before he spoke a word, he tried to explain it to himself in a way that made sense. The challenge of the weather was that you can't predict the future. You can line up matrices of possible outcomes, knowing that a big wind, like a crazy uncle, may sweep in out of Canada or roar up the coast and mix everything up. But then, just as she had intimated, he couldn't figure out why he paid such lip service to a world of no surprises. Hindsight always explained the weather, but that vision was only useful for trying to predict the next upheaval.

What he wanted to articulate, but couldn't, was how could he be so opaque to himself and so transparent to her? He saw that he had much in common with the refrigerator on Niagara's drawing board. When she flipped the switch of her attention on him, his contents were clearly visible. Motivation, inspiration, impulses—all went from impenetrable to clear, as long as Niagara was nearby. Away from her, his interior clouded up again, and his logic was murky.

Niagara pulled into her assigned parking spot.

"One-fifty-six," George said.

Niagara grinned. Craning her neck toward George, she gave him a peck on the cheek. Then she whispered hot in his ear, "Time for love!"

Niagara's steamy breath resuscitated George's desire. The late-March sun beamed in on them, so concentrated that it seemed the Buick's windshield was a lens, and George had the curious sensation of his hand being warmed along the knuckles by the focused sunlight while, on the other side, his palm was cooled by the touch of Niagara's pale skin. Here was an illustration of another law of thermodynamics, the transfer of warm to cold. George kissed Niagara for a long minute, as if they had been rushing back at great peril for this.

Although it was getting on to one-fifty-eight, it was not the worry over time that finally ended their embrace but the shriek, in the large parking lot of the engineering plant, of a car alarm calling out its repetitive concern. Niagara leaped in her seat, knocking the temple of her glasses against the rearview mirror.

Rather than asking after her distress, George thought only of escape, and he clawed at the door handle until the Buick let him flee.

George tried to lope ahead, but Niagara was right there with him, like a tick on a dog as his mother used to say. Even when he lengthened his gait, she matched him stride for stride. They came in the back door, directly into the design corridor from the parking lot.

Niagara said, "I'm curious to know how the Veteran found me, if some charge from his desk or the room attracted him. Fourteen years together—couldn't you have requested a private office?"

"It never occurred to me. Believe it or not."

"Guess what?" Niagara said. "I believe you."

Approaching the bend in the corridor, George could see Shackelford's meatloaf of a back hunched over Bev's desk. Bev mumbled something in his ear, and the boss straightened himself up as best he could.

Bev gave them both the once over. "I figured you two were together."

"We were at lunch," George said, reaching in his pocket for the restaurant receipt. Instead, he felt the crumpled souvenir of the eclair. George had become obsessive about keeping the voucher casually balled up in the acute vertex of his pocket—too flat and high and it might waft out the opening, too tight and he might mistake it for trash. He vowed to sacrifice the memento to the Oldsmobile's ashtray as soon as he was back in his car; he promised himself he would burn it.

From where he stood, George saw a stack of pink message slips in his box. Shackelford had no doubt buzzed and buzzed with no answer. It made George angry to think of Bev and his boss so closely watching a clock. Bev was not his caretaker, and just because he took a few long lunches after fourteen years at Coldpoint, what was it to Shackelford?

Meanwhile, Shackelford was looking at Bev appreciatively, as if she had removed a thorn from his fleshy paw. George had never seen admiration on Shackelford's face, but he had witnessed this expression on others who gathered at Bev's desk. People from all over Coldpoint brought their troubles to Bev, who was famous for turning no one away. She listened and told them tales of worse misery suffered by other employees, so that they felt better in comparison. No secret was safe with her, and yet the way she swapped horror stories was accepted for its comfort value.

"We didn't forget the meeting," Niagara said. She held up her wristwatch for all to see. "T minus thirty seconds and counting."

"Canceled," Shackelford growled. "No," he amended. "Postponed." He massaged his gut in a clockwise circle, and he had sweat stains at his neck and under his arms. His deep black skin, which usually gleamed, was ashen.

George began to struggle in a net of panic. "Because Niagara and I were out?"

Bev shook her head. The phone began ringing. "Probably Harris," Bev said. "He's been calling every ten minutes."

I have a son, George thought.

Bev answered the phone and then said, "He's here, Harris, hold on."

Because it was Harris, Bev just held the receiver out to George, who could not refuse the call.

"I'll take it at my desk," he said, and he went into his office and closed the door.

George punched the blinking red light. "Hi," he said. "Are you home sick?"

"No, we got out early for Sojourner Truth Day. Can I have some of the cake that's on the counter?"

Surely, there was another reason Harris had called four times in the last forty minutes. "Isn't your mother around?" I have a wife, he thought.

"She's gone. There are notes all over. My note says to call you and read you your note."

"I'm listening." George could see the refrigerator awash in Judy's notes and lists. He began drumming his fingers on his desk to release some of his impatience.

"Your note starts, 'Dearest Algae Eyes.' " Harris giggled at his invented endearment. George laughed for his son's benefit. "It says, 'Tried to call. I'm dropping Sheridan off at Roxanne's. Buy salad fixings and remind Harris to edge.' It doesn't say the cake is off limits."

"One piece," George said. "Any word on the history test?"

"Her tests are stupid. It's like you're supposed to read her mind, because she only takes one answer."

"Not so good?" Now they were getting somewhere. George hoped Harris would not need a pep talk.

"I'm getting an A in Science," Harris said with mock enthusiasm.

"That's wonderful, kiddo. I was asking about history."

"She asked what Hitler called his autobiography. So I'm thinking, does she mean what did Hitler choose as the title, or what is Hitler's autobiography called, because they're different, right?"

George didn't know what Harris was getting at. It seemed like an easy question to him.

"She always tells me to answer the question she asked, so I figure she wants Hitler's idea for a title."

"You knew that?"

"Sure. *Four and a Half Years of Struggle against Lies, Stupidity, and Cowardice.* But that's not what she wanted. She got it wrong, not me."

"Did you pass?" George asked.

Harris whined, "Why is her answer the right answer? I got all the multiple-choice right, every one of them."

"You're too smart for them, kiddo."

"Tell Mom that," Harris said.

It would be a personal victory if George could persuade Judy to relax about Harris's grade point average. He used to think she kept them all on track as a family. Now her goals made them tense with fear, as if one step off the prescribed path would result in a life of aimlessness. If Harris failed history, then their vacation would be derailed by summer school. If Harris ate too many pieces of cake, his resounding chubbiness would only magnify, and he would be further ostracized, pushed into knowing freakish trivia like Hitler's proposed title for *Mein Kampf.*

Judy used to be more flexible. She could handle changes in the plan, and she was a rock in a crisis. What she had never been able to handle was no plan. And the plans she had made for Harris did not include his being chubby or requiring excess attention from his teachers. What would she do if she got wind of George's lunchtime programs?

"Listen," George said, conscious that there was a quorum outside his door, "just one piece of cake and then start edging."

"Can't I do it tomorrow?"

"What's the difference?"

"I don't know. I don't feel like it."

"An hour. That's all it will take. I'll help you rake the clippings when I get home."

"Whatever."

George hung up. As he turned the doorknob, he tried to guess Shackelford's story. The boss had said the design meeting was postponed, so George figured the plant was not closing. Sold to the Japanese? Taken over by General Electric? Either one would bring Shackelford out swinging. The president had been shot, war was erupting in the Middle East, communism had fallen. Actually, each of these things had happened in George's time at Coldpoint. A Redskins defeat affected the plant more than any global event.

Bev, Niagara, and Shackelford all stared at George with pity, a look George imagined the Veteran had received just before being asked to resign. He turned to Niagara, who was hugging herself and rocking slightly; she would not meet his gaze. George felt panic and elation rushing him from either side. The adrenaline of the unknown, the thrill and dread of suspense, was invigorating. He was becoming more familiar with the sensation. George wished he and Niagara had devised some rudimentary sign language, so she could wave her big hands in the air or arch her long back, signaling to him what was going on.

Everyone knows we've been kissing, she might have gestured.

Or, You're fired.

Or, The conference room is being repainted.

George sniffed lightly. Did he smell like Niagara? Could everyone tell they had been mixing it up? Slumped against Bev's bookshelf, Shackelford looked more heartsick than threatening. "Here's the poop," the boss finally said. George had to lean forward to hear his whisper.

Shackelford rasped quietly, "The Veteran—Travis—died last night in Suburban Hospital. His widow is planning a memorial service for Monday, which I have assured her we would all be honored to attend."

When Bev said, "Honored?" Shackelford showed a glimmer of his fire-breathing self. "Honored," he commanded.

Niagara had it right; the Veteran was dead.

"You're sure?" George asked. "I just saw him yesterday." His words, high and thin, bounced around in his sinus cavity.

Shackelford said, "Poor bastard was my age." He stubbed out his cigar in an ashtray shaped like a miniature tray of ice.

Bev said, "That's not the upsetting part. Are you ready for this?"

George plopped down on Bev's desk. The three of them were staring at him with concern, as if the Veteran's fate was somehow his as well.

"Niagara," Bev said, "you tell him."

"If you insist," the tall visionary said.

Niagara stood directly across from George and looked him full in the face. He fixed his gaze on the outside edge of her glasses, concentrating on the way the refraction distorted her face from temple to cheekbone. And so it was that George heard Niagara's voice faintly, static-filled and distant as Radio Moscow. He saw her mouth form the "o" in his name—"George"—and then he saw her bring her lower lip to her two front teeth to shape the word *frozen*. He couldn't tell if she was repeating herself or if her voice was echoing in his head. "Frozen," he heard. "Frozen, George, frozen."

# As Bad as the Worst Kid

# on the Block

George dressed carefully for the memorial service. He unwrapped the cleaner's plastic from a starched dress shirt, distinctive not only because it was pocketless but also because of its wing collar and French cuffs. The burgundy-and-white striped cotton tucked flat along his stomach into his pleated pants.

George's cufflinks, knots of twenty-four-karat gold, were a present from Judy on their tenth anniversary. George found them so attractive that he was preoccupied when he wore them, thinking of reasons to stretch out his arm under his suit coat. His gold Hamilton watch had been his father's. Though it was running when he inherited it, Judy had a jeweler take the timepiece apart, replate it, and exchange the worn-down cogs for fresh, toothy ones. "The best kind of old," Judy liked to say, "is old that works like new."

Those were exactly the kinds of houses she took on. One hundred years old with freshly laid wooden floors, bleached to look aged. The new planks remained snug up against one another and were protected by layers of polyurethane. Artisans fashioned bay windows with poured glass that would cripple incoming light rays into unparallel and distorted waves, just as the original glass had done.

Rooms for eating and bathing were always, to George, the most amusing. In the last house Judy had sold, the kitchen was designed around a re-enameled thirties range, retrofitted with a microwave where the warming oven used to be. Lining the counter, handmade tiles featured such local animals as the Chesapeake Bay blue crab and the Baltimore oriole. Upstairs, George had paced out the master-bathroom suite at around four hundred square feet. A double-wide clawfoot tub was situated at the top of flagstone steps; spots of color radiated down on the ablutionary altar through a stained-glass skylight, formerly the rose window of a downtown church.

These houses, along the same street as Judy and George's, sold for five times what they had paid eight years ago. The beauty of their own enormous home lay in how well it had been preserved combined with Judy's renovations, which were stunning in their purity. She had redone the bathroom in glass and blue tile, the kitchen in marble and white ash. In converting the spare bedroom into their closet, she'd had a carpenter line the walls with cedar drawers as in a Shaker dormitory.

Two years ago, entire office buildings in Louisville had sold for less than a fixer-upper in Cleveland Park; yet when the market plummeted, sending realtors to business school and specialty bread stores, sellers still courted Judy for the privilege of listing their homes with her. Some real-estate mogul would probably marry her just to get access to her client list. Over the years, any number of couples had broken up, leaving them with more single friends than they had known in college. George speculated that if an open competition were held today, he might not win the spot he planned to abandon. He didn't like feeling so dispensable; not only that, he was already jealous of Judy's next husband.

The pleasure of wearing fine clothes rather than his usual Monday duds was offset by anxiety. He was not sure if he had been subdued from birth or if it was from long years of practice with his mother, but he rarely dwelled on his state of mind. Infrequent crises might push uneasiness into his line of sight, and there had been occasional glimmers of contentment that he knew to be grateful for. But the turmoil he had experienced in the last week was wringing him out. What had prompted him to jump Niagara in her lab? Where had she been all weekend, that she didn't once answer her phone when he got up the nerve to call? And what would he have said if she had picked up?

There was comfort with Judy; there was desire. But fear of discovery, forbidden pleasure, newfound thrills—these evoked the Carol Greyson memories on George's hard drive. When he accessed the mental file of "girlfriend," he seemed to open the folder to a single entry. On that grassy butte overlooking Dino Park's main valley, he and Carol had been eager to taste from the tree of knowledge, that they might recognize their nakedness and be turned on by shame.

George took out his newest tie, which was emerald green with a raised pattern of roses and printed flowers in gold and sapphire. The Italian silk practically tied itself into a voluptuous knot. Gray cotton socks, black leather-soled moccasin loafers. At Coldpoint, rubber soles were required. George was surprised no one had manufactured a safety reason for requiring high-waisted, shortened pants.

Sheridan waltzed in as George lifted his jacket on over his wide shoulders. He fastened the matte gray button. "Magazine Man," she yelled. "You look beautiful!" Standing on his bed, she reached up and hugged him. George swung her in the air and listened to her squeal.

Sheridan ran to Judy to report on their fun. She often tore herself from an activity with the need to tell Judy or George about it, as if recounting was as important as experiencing. George appraised himself up one side and down the other in the three-way mirror at the back wall of the closet. Standing perpendicular to the center mirror, he turned his tanned face toward his shoulder. Then he put his hands in his pockets and stared at his reflection over the tops of his tortoiseshell frames. He looked like a mannequin that Judy had dressed for display. He had always liked colors, but he would never have been brave enough to buy such a splashy tie or to have asserted that flowers and stripes did not clash.

George tried to discern which was his truer self. Was he

Magazine Man, a suitable spokesman for single-malt scotch? Or was he Engineering Dad, comfortable with an integrated circuit and, after five, an electric fire starter? There was also, he reminded himself with equal parts contrition and conceit, Office Stud, the randy refrigerator designer. George thought of the Veteran, awakened in a hundred years by strangers. Would he be reconstituted as hunter, engineer, father, crank?

Judy came into the closet behind him and wrapped her arms around his thirty-six-inch waist. George's guilt and the multiple reflections of Judy's beauty were like rocket fuel for lust. It was as if he were already missing his life. He reminded himself that nothing had been consummated, a fact he had been lamenting before Judy showed up in the mirrors. He saw how they were the same brown hue, the same quality of person.

Judy nuzzled her cheek against the soft wool of George's jacket. In her Georgia drawl, she recited, " 'Except for the color of their hides, absolutely no imagination was used in constructing the creatures' accurate massiveness.' " She knew it was a favorite line of his, but for the first time since he had read the Dino Park phrase, George heard the joke. If a gray suit and a green tie made this much difference on George Mahoney's six-foot-two frame, how much more did the choice of blue or brown on a two-story dinosaur?

"Absolutely no imagination was used"—how could they say that? Color aside, George had always marveled at the structures Mr. Harrison had devised for his super models. An appealing combination of pirate and naturalist, Mr. Harrison had kept them bolstered against the windstorms of Louisville's early and late summer; once, a twister had levitated a woolly mammoth, setting it down intact twenty feet west of its mount. They never lost a dino during George's tenure, though several times they'd had to amputate and replace webbed foot for elephantine stub, wing for arm.

Mr. Harrison cut fangs from bleach bottles, beaks from downspouts or sheets of tin. How did he know that a blue-swirled bowling ball, when viewed from the ground, would be the steadfast gaze of a monster? What inspired Mrs. Harrison to stage her wacky game shows, which parents and kids both adored? In fact, an incredible amount of imagination was used in constructing the creatures' accurate massiveness.

Before he had known any better, when he was around the age Harris was now, George had devoted himself to weeding out all choking myths and growing in their place a neat garden of facts, six inches apart, never crossbred. From his new vantage point a quarter century later, he had come to understand that a lack of legend makes for a weak crop, one prone to drought and disease. Shouldn't he have figured out by now that the reason he never felt he was part of the world was because he was always insisting the world prove itself to him?

George had spent the last two days in a clammy state between dread and excitement. He had phoned Niagara a dozen times, always hanging up on her recorded voice rather than leave testimony that he was seeking her out. She had told him she was in her lab every night until midnight; he surmised she had spent the weekend there, too. Meanwhile, George's wife had her arms around his waist, lest he float away from his family.

Judy tipped her head around George's chest so that she was visible again in each of the mirrors, and her comeliness made his heart flutter. Every other hour of the weekend, George had vowed to leave his wife behind. Though making arrangements for Harris and Sheridan would be heartbreaking, George was convinced he could walk away. Lately, every decision Judy made on his behalf irked him, and her beauty appeared superficial and hard-won. Most of this suddenly seemed his fault, a result of his literal outlook. Why hadn't they used their inventiveness to ravage one another? That sorority nose, those slender arms and ankles, that sly bronze smile: surely there were individual positions that would take advantage of Judy's many stunning attributes. What was beauty if not superficial? Why hadn't they tried blindfolding each other, making love on a bed of coals, butt fucking? He swung round to embrace his wife and she pointed at his erection, given full sway by his pleated pants. He felt as if his penis was a weathervane bobbing with the wind toward the mother of his children, then turning wide in a gust to point to the engineering oracle.

Right this second, it was bearing due Judy, and what could he do but follow it with conviction?

"Wrinkle me," she said. "Muss me up, Magazine Man."

George tossed off his pants and jacket but kept the starched shirt and slick tie on. He shut the closet door tightly, and the two of them fell against a rack of Judy's blouses. George was reckless and excited, as he had been Friday afternoon with Niagara. Judy and George had never had sex between feeding the children breakfast and taking them to school. In over two thousand cumulative couplings (George kept a running estimate for the duration of their marriage), they had never had sex in the closet. Judy took off George's glasses, blurring just about everything. George fantasized for a moment that Niagara was his partner, but apart from routine—which he and Judy were bucking—there was little advantage to putting Niagara's head on Judy's body.

George kept his eyes open as Judy kissed him, her forceful tongue pushing against the inside of his bottom teeth. He could taste the toothpaste for sensitive gums she had recently switched to; the scent of her coconut-oil hairdressing and her grassy perfume reminded him of the beach in autumn. Age lines radiated like cat whiskers between her nose and mouth.

"We should go dancing," George whispered. "Windsurfing, parachuting. Forget Harris's weight and the price of bungalows. We should ask more questions, stop doing what we're supposed to."

"We should hush now," Judy said. She had been giving George the silent treatment since Friday morning, when he had practically woken the neighborhood screaming Niagara's name. He had felt righteously innocent at the time; he thought Judy was angry because she couldn't direct his dreams as well as every minute of his waking life. Before Friday was over, he had earned her scorn. Judy slipped out of her silky underwear; holding on to George's shoulders, she boosted herself in the air and wrapped her legs around his rump.

"Come on in," she said. "Come right on in."

She was moister than usual, practically gushing with hospitality. George pushed deep inside, thrilled that neither of them had mentioned birth control. Not that he was prepared for the consequences, but he did seem to be turning into something of a risk taker.

George stood against the cedar drawers on his side of the closet, grateful for the scarcity of knobs. He was holding Judy up and against him when Sheridan knocked at the closet door shouting, "Mommy, Daddy, open the door."

Judy and George froze. Judy's jacket was off and her blouse and camisole were up over her breasts, which were wet with George's spit.

Judy said, "Go find Harris, pumpkin. Get ready for school."

George could picture his daughter considering the request. "Get going, honey," Judy urged her on.

Sheridan dribbled on the door with her fingers, by way of getting the last word in. Then they heard her run off.

"Sheridan." Judy giggled.

"We could make another one of those," George said. Scrunching down to kiss his petite wife, he wished he were a year or two younger, so he would not have to worry about his cramping back.

When they redressed for the day, George saw he had lost a shirt button in the fracas; Judy's linen suit was a wrinkled heap. She slipped into a black sleeveless dress and hurried out to take the children to school. George pulled on his pants and gathered up needle and thread, turning on the TV to listen to the weather while he mended. The fat, goofy weatherman was wearing a ten-gallon orange felt hat and jabbering about his plans for April Fool's Week. As if they had a gun to their heads, the rest of the crew laughed along and took turns trying on the moronic hat.

As soon as he broke the thread, George thought of taking his newfound insight and laying it at Niagara's feet. Once again, Judy was out, Niagara was in. He wasn't sure if he and Niagara could continue working side by side, or if Coldpoint had interdepartmental nepotism rules. He would exercise his creativity until it was so powerful a muscle that it would lift him out of Coldpoint's frosty clutches. And do what? He had no idea. Maybe he could study paleontology, take Niagara and the children along with him to digs in Montana. He could become a weatherman, one not prone to hysterics in front of the six-o'clock audience; he pledged to reverently list meteorological information with accuracy and sincerity.

The weather news was good: a sunny March day—sixty-eight at National Airport, sixty-six at BWI—the Japanese magnolias just beginning to bloom. No clouds and no frost overnight. George turned off the TV, and he converted the high to twenty degrees Celsius—as automatic as turning eight-forty-five into quarter to nine.

Downstairs, George basked for a moment in the knowledge that the kitchen was his. At first he thought he might dig out the waffle iron and line the griddle with bacon to cook right into the batter, one of the useful things his mother had taught him. But he wanted to make a meal he knew Judy would enjoy.

He whisked one whole egg and two egg whites into a skillet, adding chopped scallions and Parmesan for flavor. As the omelet bubbled, he shook fresh ground pepper onto the back side, allowing it to set at will. He arranged the china brunch dishes into two place settings and transferred marmalade into a pot complete with its own spoon and lid. It amazed him how energized he had become. He felt wider, taller, released from some of gravity's pull. He took a vow to be less of a skeptic, an oath that sprung up like a beanstalk to outlandish heights of selfishness. Maybe he didn't have to limit himself. He could carry on as a bigamist: rent an apartment in Rockville with Niagara, keep his Cleveland Park house and life, too. He knew the notion was unreasonable, but he credited himself with having the mind of a problem solver rather than a coward.

It depressed him a little that he had been guarded for so long. He thought of the motivational tapes in Niagara's car. "Will you be present when your luck changes? Your ship comes in? When what you've been waiting for finally happens?" The lesson, Niagara had paraphrased, was that you can't depend on anyone else to bring you excitement. Lately, George had been generating enough excitement for a small army.

George had been impressed as a child that, for hundreds of years, dinosaur bones were explained away as the petrified limbs of giants, for some reason a less fantastic idea than an inhuman species. Finally, someone had stepped back and said, "Not giant." George was incapable of thinking "not giant," and even if he thought it, he would probably not announce it.

Would that change? If he left himself open, would he become more brave, more bold? What could be bolder, considering who he was, than bedding Niagara? Unless it was bolder to resist. How good was his judgment, that he would pursue such an oddball just because she was the first woman to sit next to him in fourteen years? He hadn't been aware of it before, but there were benefits to watching the world go by.

George knew enough to recognize that one of the reasons he was so receptive to a fresh start was the death of the Veteran. The elder engineer had appeared terminally unhappy, and George felt for his widow and for the man himself. He was curious to know if there was anything to his dream or to Niagara's suspicion that something about her affiliation with the Veteran's office drew his electronic waves to her. Maybe she just happened to be listening at the instant of his death. Maybe the dead are talkative only on their way out of the world, giving vent to unfinished business before they begin their slow decay.

The Oldsmobile's brakes sang out his wife's arrival as effectively as a town crier. The service wasn't until eleven, so they had plenty of time. He toyed with revealing the nature of Niagara's research and her strange success. Would Judy be angry that he hadn't told her earlier? Jealous of Niagara's mind, as he himself was? After their raucous closet episode, would it be stupid to even mention Niagara?

Judy was rigid about many things, but she wasn't as stapled to the facts as George was. She was receptive to friends who had ventured into reflexology, ashrams, red hair at forty. It might be enough to fold Niagara into their family, let her be a science role model for Harris, a spontaneity prototype for Judy. Here was a compromise George hadn't yet deliberated; it could be that having Niagara around would perk them all up.

George opened his arms to the slender curves of his wife, but Judy dodged his embrace. Sitting down without a word, she crossed and uncrossed her legs. She was either about to cry or recovering from tears.

"Honey," she said. "Baby, we have to talk."

George split the omelet in two and flipped half onto each of the plates. "Harris?" he guessed quickly, taking the offensive. He tried to remember if he had heard this morning's Quote for the Day, often an indicator of trouble to come.

"Harris," she said, "and then some."

"What's wrong?" he asked.

"I am afraid that you're turning my child against me."

She had it exactly backwards. He should have told her of his lobbying effort on her behalf before she began suspecting he and Harris were in cahoots. "I'm trying to turn Harris toward you," George said, relieved that their son was the topic of concern.

"And why is that, George?"

"You're mad at him as soon as he's in the house. He eats too much before he comes home or he eats too much or too little at the dinner table. It's clear he knows more than the teachers, but everyone except me thinks that makes him a discipline problem.

"Judith," George said, and he stroked her velvety nose, "he's grown terrified of you."

Judy shooed George away. "Why did you dislike your mother so?"

George wished Judy had majored in art history rather than psychology. He wanted to talk more about Harris. "I've told you most of the stories."

"What's the worst thing she did to you?"

George thought about his mother's cruelty. Her long silences were torture. Her ability to belittle all his interests, most of his talents, that was bad. "The worst thing," he said, "was punishing me for what other kids did."

Judy said, "Like when something is broken and no one fesses up?"

"No," George said, impatient that he had to tell this story again. "She would come into the house and announce, 'Kevin wrecked his brand-new bicycle. What are we going to do about that?' and I had to stay home from basketball to clean out the garage."

"I don't get it," Judy said.

"Well, it was something like preventive punishment. She would say, 'You've probably been just as careless, except you were lucky.' "

"Some luck."

"To her, I was as bad as the worst kid on the block. What's the good of bringing home all A's if you're going to be punished for someone else's F?"

"She would do that?" Judy asked with genuine sympathy.

George said, "Once a kid in junior high got caught for plagiarism—he put his name on a story out of another school's newspaper. Anyway, the principal sent out a letter explaining why the kid was suspended. I was afraid to go home."

"Grounded?"

"That time she hit me," George said. " 'If I ever catch you copying'—whack—'I'll hit you so hard'—whack—"

"It's sick," Judy said, "I know it is, but it helps to hear that there are worse mothers in the world. I'm sorry it was yours."

"You're a good mother. You just have different ambitions for him. Maybe Harris will become the first person large enough to create his own weather."

"That's what I'm afraid of," Judy said. She dabbed at the corners of her bronze mouth with the linen napkin George had put on the table. She was substantially narrower than the dining room chair. "You would spoil them," she said. "They need some limits set."

*Spoil* was a word George heard often in his line of work. It had different meanings at home and at the plant. Overindulge, but it really meant make rotten. Love too much, give in too often, and the children would go bad, like chicken left to thaw too long on the kitchen counter. For a second, George suspected Judy of putting herself forward as the better choice for single parent.

"I get them to bed on time," George said. "I enforce kitchen cleanup. You act like I come home with my pockets full of candy and encourage them to swing from the curtains." George appreciated this was not a time to be enumerating his talents as a father, when he was thinking of jumping ship.

"OK," Judy said. "So my son is a wreck, and it may be my doing. Let's see if everything else is my fault."

George enveloped her fist in his hand. When he pried open her fingers, to his complete surprise, she was harboring the eclair receipt, the souvenir of the first cream puff he had bought for Niagara. Though just a pale wad, the crumple was immediately recognizable to George, who had been carrying it in his trench-coat pocket for weeks. George felt his eyebrows shoot above his glasses; with no effort from him, he sensed them traveling up his forehead, pushing the skin like a window shade.

Judy's little hand was cold and clammy, and George lacked the desire to warm it up. She had tricked him, pretending she was upset about their son, her parenting, George's own childhood, when she had this on him all along. It was appropriate that they'd been discussing George's mother, for here he was, back in the soup again. It was a broth with a recipe he was destined to re-member: leave yourself open, get yourself in trouble, prepare for exile.

But a balled-up receipt was not a baby in the stomach of a sixteen-year-old. Besides, he and Niagara had not shared the car-nal pleasures George and Carol Greyson had enjoyed. This ra-tionalization, he knew, glossed over the existence of his wife and two children. Technically, an adulterous kiss by a father and hus-band might be tallied as worse than teen sex; certainly, the wife would count it as such. For a man of limited imagination, George had a profound idea just then, one that might keep him from being scalded. He saw how letting go his grip on the facts left him open to grab the lip of the cauldron, and thereby swing himself out of the soup. Get yourself in trouble, lie for all you're worth.

Judy said, "You wake me up screaming the name of the ugliest woman to come to town in years. Your work clothes smell like a root cellar, and then I open the ashtray to this." She un-folded the receipt and George saw his unmistakable printing down the side: NIAGARA HAWTHORNE SPENSE.

Despite the hot water he was in, George was intrigued that

Niagara's scent was seeping into him. He took the paper from Judy so it would be back in his possession. "It's nothing," George said. He knew he could not sustain a filibuster, so he chose to perjure himself as simply as possible. "It's her name written on paper. We had some silly discussion about whose name was more pretentious: George Bledsoe Mahoney or Niagara Hawthorne Spense. Honey," he said, "you know dreams better than me. Doesn't everything represent something else?" He was glad he didn't have to look into her eyes as he made excuses for himself. What he was really thinking was, It's not so hard to lie.

In the closet, George had held out the hope that they could step out of their routine. It was Judy who had loosed the bolt of lightning that had illuminated his morning: "Except for the color of their hides, absolutely no imagination was used . . ." He regretted that Niagara had come between them, especially on the day they had expanded their experience. He had wanted to ask Judy what proof she required for her personal canon. He had wanted to teach her about faith in their children, just as he wanted to be taught about faith in unexplained powers.

Judy pushed herself away from George. "Mama used to say, 'When a man asks you to try a new position, it's time to ask a few dozen questions.' "

So, in the end, it was good sex that had made Judy leery, a situation that riled George. With each year spent together, their mutual attentions had lapsed and their inhibitions increased, until now, any departure from habit was viewed with mild scorn or, worse, misgiving.

"Take your mama's advice," George said, belligerent. "Ask me a few dozen questions."

"Have you porked that girl scientist?"

"Nope." Once that was under his belt, he wasn't sure how he felt about gambling with his marriage this way. Thus far, George was only guilty of lip mashing, thigh stroking, and adulterous intentions. Ironically, he was under interrogation because he wanted to make love to his wife with boundless ardor.

Judy asked, "Are you doing it with someone else?"

"Nope," George said. Judy's hand was cold and limp as jam.

Sometimes when he wanted to have sex and she did not, he would give her a good rubdown, but it was like trying to warm up marmalade in your hands. If her pilot light went out, no amount of blowing or coaxing would kindle a flame.

George stared at the delicate jam pot, antique white china with tiny hand-painted poppies on the side and lid. Judy touched his chin with her other hand, frosty and damp.

"Well then," she asked, "what the hell is wrong with you?"

~~~~~~~~~~~*Enough Donuts to Feed the Dead*

While George slumped in the passenger seat of his wife's convertible, sullen as a dog being taken to the vet, Judy reached across him to disengage the latch for folding the top down. From the driveway, George noticed the spate of broad, heart-shaped leaves engulfing his lawn. No matter how many violets he pulled, their rhizome roots the size of small potatoes, he could not cultivate an island of Kentucky bluegrass to surround his homestead, which, this March morning, was deteriorating both inside and out.

These are the worries that come when real danger is past, George thought. He wished he could forget the funeral, change into his gardening jeans, and dig his way out of his funk. He would conquer the violet problem once and for all, earn a place in this household by sweat equity.

If George ever left, he expected Judy would hire landscapers to fill the yard with hostas, liriope, and daylilies—plants that thrive on neglect—then mulch the weeds out of existence. George felt that subscribing to a lawn service would be like paying someone to come over and start his barbecue.

"What are you scowling at?" Judy asked. She seemed more curious than piqued.

He studied Judy in her purple scarf, its pale ends fluttering over her plywood-colored shoulders. "The lawn," he said. He put his palm on the stick shift, covering her veiny hand with his own. Judy's interrogation about Niagara had done much to constrict his earlier leap of faith. George had a good job with a steady future, and he looked nice in a well-made suit. Maybe he should live with that.

George was usually apprehensive riding in Judy's posh car, which seemed an obvious target for car-jacking or worse. A silver BMW with vanity plates was the car of choice not only for successful real-estate agents but also for drug dealers. The dealers' cars had darkened windows, spiked wheel covers, and license plates exclaiming "XS=SUXS" or "IN YR EAR" bordered by a thick chain; whereas Judy's car looked as if she had just driven it off the lot, except for her "PI PHI" sorority vanity plates. If George suggested it might not be wise to flaunt her affluence so, Judy would say, "Why be a Pi Phi if no one knows it?"

On this particular morning, George welcomed being in the convertible on the way to Maryland. As they picked up speed, the noise of the wind made conversation unnecessary, and he was left to his own thoughts. A scant eight weeks ago, he had attended a luncheon wishing Travis Plunkett a fruitful retirement. The poor brute. Going from Coldpoint into a frozen time capsule was like jumping out of the frying pan into the fire. Having lived only in the steamy climes of Louisville, Atlanta, and Washington, George shuddered at the thought of shelving his joints in a deep freeze for eternity.

It was comforting to remember that the Veteran enjoyed ice fishing and late-autumn deer hunting, crouching in the snowbanks with a highly strung bow and arrow. The old man had tried to make the outings sound peaceful. He would describe covering himself with powdery snow near fresh hoofprints and hearing the feathers of the shaft fly past his ear when he released the arrow. Throughout the Veteran's monologues, George was plagued by the needly stab of cold toes in damp boots. Maybe the Veteran was trying to ensure a blanket of quiet for himself, the cold keeping even his flesh from falling off the bone. A clean, well-insulated space might have been the draw.

George pondered different resting places for his body. While he had never believed that the person survived the corpse, he didn't know if he could stand the ridicule of medical trainees toying with his intestinal tract. In light of Niagara's most recent discoveries, and because it was the most common approach, he wanted to be buried with everything intact. There seemed a chance of regret in donating yourself for parts; likewise for cremation.

At the Smithsonian, George and Harris had once seen an Indonesian corpse measure that had been buried with someone's ashes. Hammered gold rectangles were strung together with wire into a life-size stick figure. The intention was to inform the gods of the deceased's stature so the person could be re-created when the time came. George had pointed out that height was hardly the measure of the man, but Harris replied that human scale might be the only concept gods had trouble with.

It might be helpful to leave clues, if not for the gods, for the scientists. In George's case, a refrigerator could serve as his corpse measure. He'd pack a stack of bologna sandwiches and enough donuts to feed the dead in the vicinity of his mound. George speculated that he might want a picture of Judy tacked on to his refrigerator. He looked his tony wife up and down, from the muscle at the back of her calf that flexed and softened as she worked the gas pedal, to the black dress that hugged her shallow bowl of a stomach, to her face, masked by the wraparound sunglasses tucked behind her dainty ears. She looked grand, on the gaunt side of slender, with the stature that comes from fighting both age and gravity gracefully. Would she be flattered if he asked her for a nude photograph?

While George was plotting what to pack on his final trip, they came upon the Veteran's little chapel. Situated a hundred years ago on the main wagon road through Rockville, the Methodist church was a quaint clapboard building. Now the wagon road was a six-lane highway, and the little church, with its wooden roof and white plank siding, had taken on the appearance of a fruit stand. Judy pulled into the gravel parking lot next to Niagara's gray Buick, its trunk garnished with stickers proclaiming "Subvert the Dominant Paradigm" and "Visualize Whirled Peas," apparently a California joke. No matter what kind of car Judy might be forced to drive, she would never allow bumper stickers, and if she did, they would certainly be consigned to the bumper and not the trunk. "Mean People Suck," another declaration, sent George into a pleasant logic spin.

"Don't tell me," Judy said in an uppity tone. "I'm sure I can guess."

George knew from his Southern upbringing how a Georgia belle could make nice all over you—dab honey behind your ears and along your eyebrows—before opening her purse to release the red ants.

As soon as George and his wife approached the crowd, Shackelford gave Judy a bear hug, then Bev took her aside for some quick briefing. They hadn't seen each other since Harris quit going to soccer. Bev leaned into Judy, who kept herself ramrod straight even as she whispered. George wished he could hear what they were talking about, but Massoud wanted him for something. He was wearing a robe and matching fez, their deep burgundy and loamy green more evocative of sorrow than black.

"Is this a custom of the Methodists," Massoud asked George, "to freeze the body?"

George confirmed it was as weird as it seemed.

"At what temperature might you guess that freezerproof containers crack?" Massoud wanted to know.

Although he wasn't sure why Massoud cared, George assumed someone in the Coldpoint crowd should know the answer. "Why do you ask?"

"Maybe his family will use plastic bags for his next-life food. Will he have grains or some beeves?"

"Beeves?" George asked.

"Cattle," Massoud clarified.

Bev was always making jokes about the Jewish tendency toward an oversupply of food, but George didn't think Massoud was talking about the burial customs of their synagogue. "I thought you were Jewish," George said.

"Yes," Massoud said, "but also not Jewish. My countrymen have their own ways."

Just minutes ago George had been mentally packing his eternal lunch bucket. Now Massoud was talking about the same thing. George asked him, "What do you think happens after you die?"

"We assert it is not for us to know. So many of your people are troubled by this uncertainty. We say, have a glorious time in this life, and, upon death, it will be revealed what is next expected. Death provides the invitation to some other feast."

"Nice," George said. "And are you having a glorious time?"

Massoud laughed. "You pull on my legs, right? You, who know my Bev so well and see the source of my joy."

George nodded. "Of course," he said. Although he personally got a kick out of Bev, sometimes he laughed at her jokes because he didn't want to be the target of her humor. She could do withering impressions of Emilio in manufacturing and Bob, the patent lawyer.

Massoud wandered off, and George looked around at the crowd. Frank, head of quality control, was there, as was Shackelford's secretary. Was her name Peggy? Penny? George should have learned her name; in the five years that Shackelford had been his boss, she was one of the few who had remained for three design meetings. George hadn't seen Sandi, the effusive marketing director, yet, but there was Bob standing apart from his coworkers. He looked the same as he did at work. Because of the nature of his tasks, he was allowed to wear real clothes to the plant, though George felt he overdid his ensemble. Sometimes during design meetings, George had tried to imagine what magic an automatic lathe might work on a double-breasted suit and a silk club tie. Bob gave people all sorts of reasons not to like him; what chafed George were the lawyer's suggestions of modifications to new patents that would allow Coldpoint to walk away with another plant's ideas. George could not see Niagara, but his heart was beating as if they were embracing on her pitiful divan.

"You think you know someone," Frank said to George, "and then this." He gestured toward nothing in particular. Except for his light blue sport coat, Frank also looked the same as he did at work: white walking shoes, pastel pants, and a golf shirt.

Bob and Peggy/Penny each took a step toward them, forming a small circle. Bob stopped grooming himself for a split second. "I have to say, his desire to be frozen is rather ironic."

"Oh my God!" Penny/Peggy gasped. "Refrigerators and frozen, I just got it."

The three men stared at her. George was astonished that she had only now made the connection. He was relieved to know he was quicker than some.

"Poor bastard was Shackelford's age," Bob said.

Shackelford stepped up behind Bob. "Speaking of poor bastards," he said. The circle widened to include the boss. Shackelford reached toward George's stomach, and George instinctively protected himself. "Nice tie, Mahoney." Shackelford grabbed the end in his thick fingers. "Why don't you show this much taste at the plant?"

"Let me tie my own and I'll show some flair."

"What are you talking about?" Shackelford growled.

"Shop rules," George said. "You think I'm drawn to clip-ons?"

Shackelford shook with his smoker's cough, halfway between a laugh and a spasm. "Don't tell me you missed the memo, Mahoney. I'm here to tell you, read your fucking in box."

Bob said, "The dress code was abolished in ninety."

Shackelford elaborated, "We finally noticed that you guys never go to the factory floor."

George looked at Frank, who shrugged. "I thought it was because we send out all the machine work," Frank said. "We only wire our own circuit boards on the floor."

"That could be dangerous," Shackelford said. "Most of you would go up in flames if a soldering iron touched you."

George didn't know if he was referring to the fibers in their clothes or the fact that most of them hadn't held a soldering iron in a decade.

George looked to Frank again. "You knew this?" He didn't

want to insult Frank, but he couldn't fathom that anyone would wear elastic waist pants except under duress.

"Sure," Frank said. "But what are you going to do? It's like I tell my kids—it's a look." He rubbed his hand over his flattop, the same haircut he had been wearing since George first met him.

George excused himself from the group and walked toward the church. Recognizing almost everyone else as being from Coldpoint made him sad for the Veteran. Ruth was standing with one or two unfamiliar guests, who George surmised were family members. He could identify Travis Junior from the back. The rumpled son was cradling a woman against his hip, someone a little taller than Niagara, more like a motorcycle babe than a long-term love. Though Travis might be married, George couldn't shake the image of the kid at sixteen, his shaven head and slanted eyes making him look like a Buddhist mendicant.

Travis's escort looked over her shoulder at George. It took him several moments of tallying similarities (pointy nose, wire-framed glasses) before he realized it was Niagara in heels and a hairdo. She must have sprung for a store-bought dress, because if she had sewn it, she could have made sure the sleeves came down as far as her wrist bones, which were especially prominent above her white lace gloves.

Niagara detached herself from the Veteran's family and walked toward George, who saw something like antennae poking out of her head. As she came closer, he recognized the chopsticks that had sounded a drumroll on the trailer floor the moment he had begun kissing her. Bobby pins also stuck out from her head —she seemed to need a separate clip to keep back each strand of thin hair.

"Hi, George," Niagara said.

"Hello, hello," George answered. Niagara's bun showed off her hearing aid to distraction; the unappealing mock-flesh color filled her right ear like wood putty patching a wide hole. He hoped Judy would find Niagara too easy a target to take aim.

Niagara swatted at his pockets. "Have any treats hidden in that attractive suit?"

"No," George said. He sucked in his lip so he wouldn't be caught beaming at her. "You talked to Ruth?"

"And his son," Niagara said. "Don't forget he has a son."

"Did you tell them?"

"I told her the Veteran wanted it this way," Niagara said. "She didn't ask me how I knew."

"And the son?" George asked. "Don't forget he has a son."

"I was reminded all weekend," she said, and she exaggerated a wink.

Which of the times that George had phoned had she been in Junior's arms? Was it possible George's earth-shattering desire had made no impression?

"He's sharp, George," she said. "Makes me wish I had met the old man before all this."

"You were brought here because the old man was not sharp." George was feeling rather unsharp himself. He pictured her riding Travis Junior like a well-oiled Harley, lashing his chest with her limp hair.

Niagara was attending to the end of her velvet sash, which apparently needed shredding. She looked up at George. "On his nightstand, Travis has a telegraph key, which is hooked up to his computer. You would be amazed by some of the stuff he's tapped out in the middle of the night."

"He was a telegraph champion," George remembered. "He won contests in high school." So she had seen his nightstand. She had met the guy less than a week ago, at the deathbed of his father.

"Some of them are dreams," Niagara continued, "but there are inventions, too, and entire melodies, spelled out note by note. Isn't that incredible?"

"Good inventions?" George asked.

Niagara thought about this. "I'm not sure what his intentions are."

"*Inventions,*" George said.

"Oh, beats me," Niagara said. "The point is, he's doing the same thing I am, except he's both transmitter and receiver."

With the chopsticks behind her head like rabbit ears, Niagara resembled a six-foot-tall receiver. Her appearance both broke and warmed George's heart. He looked toward the frisky professor, stifling any he-man thoughts about taking him out with one punch. After weeks of begging for personal information, George didn't want to be privy to Niagara's adventures with another man.

He led her back to their secrets, hoping to make himself indispensable. In a low voice, he asked, "What do you hear from the dead?"

Niagara looked puzzled. "I don't fear anything from them. It never occurred to me to fear them."

"*Hear* from them," George said, disappointed that a whisper was inaudible. He moved around to her left side, and he pointed to his ear. He could see Judy striding toward them, her heels sinking slightly into the damp grass. Another one of his colleagues sidetracked her, and George repeated, "What do you hear from them?"

Niagara pretended to pout. "No one talks to me anymore," she said. "Not a soul." Her deep brown eyes caught the sun as if they were enameled.

"I called you this weekend," George laid himself bare. "You weren't home."

"Did I give you my number?"

"No," George said. "I'm more resourceful than you imagine."

"George," she sighed, "you don't want me. You just want a change."

"If you knew what I really wanted, you'd probably slap me." His pulse was in his throat now. "Niagara," he said, to keep her eye contact, "why are you at Coldpoint?"

"My people sent me," she answered, gesturing skyward with her eyes. A moment passed as George gauged the plausibility of her reply. With practiced timing, Niagara waited for George to close his mouth before waving her hands in front of his face. "No, no, no," she said. "Jesus," she dismissed her own answer, politely passing on the opportunity to tease him further.

"I have to work." She was back to worrying her sash. "I make my own clothes, drive a rattletrap, live in a dump—all so I can squander my salary on satellite dishes. I just wanted something mindless—oh, God, I'm sorry."

"It's all right," he said, and he meant it. Travis's arm around her was a blow, but this news didn't hurt, because he had already assumed that for Niagara, designing refrigerators was the equivalent of an actor waiting tables.

"I'm almost there, George," Niagara said. "You can't conceive what it's like to be this close."

He dared not tell her he had felt that way all weekend.

Niagara pushed and prodded various clips back into her hair. "My mother expects I'll hear early Renaissance music—she's sure that's the sound track in heaven."

"And your father?"

"My father doesn't understand why I have to work nine to five at engineering. No offense, George, it embarrasses him." Niagara started to say something else, but Judy appeared in the midst of their secret-agent talk.

George said, "You remember my wife?" Judy draped her arm around George's hip, a little proprietarily, George thought.

The two of them had met just after Niagara had arrived, at the christening of Emilio's newest baby. That party had been a lavish blowout at a Catholic church not far from here.

"Niagara Spense," the gangly girl scientist said. "It's a pleasure to see you again."

Judy shook Niagara's hand and smiled. "What a pity it's not under happier circumstances." George wished his wife would stop staring at Niagara's great white gloves.

"Actually," Niagara said, "I see you each morning in our office. George has a lovely picture of you and your children on his desk."

"They're his children as well," Judy said.

George stiffened a bit. At the moment, neither woman appealed to him: Judy, groomed to her pointy teeth, mentally compiling a list of Niagara's shortcomings. Niagara, overgrown waif with a boyfriend, interested in George only because he was her sole witness that she had made contact with the Veteran.

The service was short and bland except for a brief talk from the cryogenics expert, a blond statue of a man with a radio voice who professed to having grown fond of the Veteran. He called the deceased "this farsighted scientist." George smiled at that description, which was inaccurate in more ways than one. George liked the idea of the Veteran in a silver bullet-shaped coffin, frost covering the glasses he had needed because, for him, anything farther than three feet away was the blurry future.

The minister was next at bat. It was possible the meek reverend had not met the Veteran; he read from notes on an index card that the deceased worked at Coldpoint and that he had a wife named Ruth and a son named Travis Junior, who was now an esteemed professor of musicology at Georgetown University. George saw Niagara squeeze up against Junior. For all practical purposes, the minister could have been reciting a direct mail solicitation for the dead. You, Travis Arnold Plunkett, of North Bethesda, have been selected . . .

The reverend talked about Travis's love of the outdoors, especially fishing, and read the scripture about Jesus making his apostles fishers of men. George knew how close that passage was to Jesus commanding them to drop their nets and follow him. Then Shackelford gave a thin eulogy, which George recognized as an abbreviated version of the guy's retirement send-off. Shackelford covered the Veteran's years of service and described the advances he had made in self-defrosting technology. George dreaded the part about the door.

"I'm here to tell you," his broad, panting boss began, "the power of a simple design. You may not believe me when I say that one magnet on a refrigerator could save a child's life. Well, good people," he said and he slammed his fist down on the pulpit, "believe it."

This preamble to the Veteran's humanitarian innovation did not inspire Judy to squeeze up against George. She pinched his thigh through his pants and he winced. George hoped they could take his terrible mistake of not having given Judy's idea enough credit and lay it in the Veteran's grave.

"This man," Shackelford said, aiming a finger toward the audience. But his gesture pointed nowhere, for the coffin, or whatever cryogenic box held the Veteran's body, was not on display. Harris would be disappointed—he was eager to hear every detail about the shape and design of the capsule.

"This man designed a door that closed magnetically rather than with the mechanical claw that meant suffocation and death to untold numbers of children." Shackelford looked at the crowd. "He did that," he said, as if anyone who knew the Veteran would dispute it. "And I'm the one to tell you, we are grateful."

Where is the old man? George thought. Is he watching this pitiful ceremony, hovering above as an astral projection of his former self? Is he otherwise occupied with Aristotle and Edison, nattering on about the joys of self-defrosting? Or is he just part of a puddle of energy—an electrical purgatory of souls with a charge weaker than that of a chlorine ion? George didn't suppose there was a chance in hell that the Veteran's body and soul would ever be reunited. But then he hadn't thought there was a chance in hell that Niagara could have tapped into his energy pocket.

A stab of pain hit George behind his right eye. As the Veteran's office mate, George had been chronically uncomfortable, but he did not remember having had the anxiety, self-doubt, and headaches that he had experienced in the last few weeks. Worry, curiosity, fear—all converged into a beam of intense pain that burned a hole in his vision. At the first stab, he had squeezed Judy's hand, and she squeezed back, pumping comfort his way. He tried to concentrate on ignoring the pain.

He postulated how the cryogenics industry would get by in the absence of chlorofluorocarbons. The irony of the concept occurred to him as soon as he had registered it. The Veteran was dead, and if his silver bullet thawed, he would be room-temperature dead. However, if the refrigeration industry didn't find some fitting substitutes—not just less ozone-depleting hydro-chlorofluorocarbons and hydro-fluorocarbons but entirely new alternatives—George's own livelihood was in jeopardy.

For decades, industry and the consumers it fed had been sending refrigerants and propellants into the air, from the coolant in air conditioners to the pressurized gas that pushed fluffy ribbons of whipped cream from a can. These effluvia were cumulatively eroding the atmosphere's mantle of ozone such that there was an actual rip in the sky over Antarctica. A no-ozone zone meant that radiation from the sun beat down unabated on water and vegetation and skin below.

The president had already signed legislation outlawing American chlorofluorocarbon production after the last day of 1995. Shackelford thought they had more than three years; the National Refrigeration Association and the chemical companies were busting a gut lobbying congressmen over lobster lunches. Optimism surged with the administration turning its back on the spotted owl. Although the president had initially banned all logging in the owl's habitat, he rescinded his decision shortly thereafter, announcing that the timber industry had suffered enough. Most likely there would be an extension to the CFC ban, or the refrigerator lawyers would open some loophole for Coldpoint to jump through at least until the millennium.

If only chlorofluorocarbons weren't so damned handy, George thought, focusing on the evolution of coolants in hopes of curbing a migraine. Beginning with the advent of heat-exchange technology, ether had been the first coolant, followed by ammonia and sulfur dioxide. The early choices were all toxic, corrosive, or explosive. CFCs didn't eat away at rubber seals, so refrigerators lasted twenty years or more; if they did leak or lose their coolant in a puncture wound, the vapor would neither blow up nor rot anyone's lungs. George recognized the limitations of his thinking. He had to go further than concocting a substitute; chances were, no new coolant would work with the existing box. Someone would have to redesign the way the gas was housed, circulated, and stored to keep it away from food as well as customers, manufacturers, and repairmen.

George remembered reading about scientists in Los Alamos returning to the Malone refrigerator, a 1920s invention that used incredibly high pressure to compress carbon dioxide for use in cooling. What a hero he would be if he made any progress on this front. Even Niagara's keen door innovation couldn't compare to saving the planet from extinction. Just having these Big Picture thoughts ennobled George; lately, his fantasies had been limited to seeing Niagara's underwear.

As people filed out of the service, George fixed on each one that he knew. His migraine had progressed to the point of morbid thoughts, and he saw with the acumen of a prophet. The dark circle in his line of sight occasionally occluded someone's head, like the privacy spot that protects a rape victim in a televised hearing. While Niagara had insisted that the soul remained fresh long after the body's expiration date, the vision George experienced through the pain and the spots was not as comforting.

The foreman and his wife marching down the aisle: they would die. George's wide, explosive boss, followed by Bev in her long plaid shorts and Massoud in his hat and robe: they would all perish. In this brooding context, lucky was falling asleep in your spouse's arms—your children already established as adults—and never waking up.

The idea of his coworkers and especially his boss turning to dust clogged George's head with images of bones, which in turn filled his thoughts with his dear dinosaurs. He could still get obsessed about whether they knew what hit them. That seemed more important to George Mahoney than what had actually killed them. How much warning, if any, might they have had of their own doom? A million years? A generation? Did they foresee their extinction in the streak of a comet's tail blazing orange across a starry, prehistoric sky?

George liked Massoud's version of death as the portal to a banquet of heavenly delights. Lately, he had begun to wonder why most people's avowal that it's over when it's over did nothing to help them walk away from demeaning jobs, wasteful habits, unloving marriages. He had been struggling anew against his net of passivity. Why hadn't he demanded his own office? He had known for years that the dress code was unnecessary—why hadn't he challenged it? Why hadn't he taken the twelve weeks of vacation he had accumulated, if only to reseed his lawn or drink beers on the wraparound porch? Why couldn't he hold Judy at bay and give his children a little breathing room?

George assumed every thirty-nine-year-old man decides life is too short to waste, or Porsches would have long ago gone begging. Still, civilization must be founded on a powerful need to conform; otherwise people would devote themselves to exhausting their seven or eight decades on this earth, selflessness be damned.

When Ruth came down the aisle, Travis Junior and Niagara were still with her. Niagara was weeping noisily.

Coldpoint, George understood, was not going to be the death of him. Just because the Veteran had been phased out didn't mean George was next. He was now the senior engineer on a stable, familiar project. He had just learned the value of outside help: market research, talks with the folks on the line or in quality control, brainstorming sessions among staff, maybe even a suggestion box. With the steady progress of a tortoise, George had enriched year after year of refrigerator models, from separate temperature controls for refrigerator and freezer (so ice would be ice but milk would be milk) to eliminating those pesky egg cups that used to fill the inside of the doors and gather goo. He was encouraged by his earlier thoughts about new technology.

So George was not the Veteran. But he was not Niagara either. Muse of his dreams, namesake of his potential vacation spot, eater of his donuts, great big woman who wore electricity round her neck like a charm, Niagara could perform any number of mental gymnastics at no risk of headaches or whiplash. She would prosper with or without him, with or without Coldpoint. George truly wished her success, though knowing her haphazard approach, he doubted whether she would ever convince another person she had achieved a breakthrough.

The pain came again into George's eyes, the dark shadow eclipsing his vision. He squeezed Judy's palm once, twice, in tempo with the throbbing of his temples. Judy lifted his hand to her face and brushed his knuckles with her lips. They had love and history and a future between them. Why had he doubted their connection? He wondered if her parents would consent to come up for a week so the two of them could get away without Sheridan and Harris. Sheridan was old enough now, provided that someone like her grandparents was around to give her unlimited attention.

He and Judy could regress to the time before children, when Judy was known to read a book for enjoyment rather than a leg up.

George's conjugal devotion lasted the remainder of the processional and into the reception. Since the Veteran's body was being stored, there was no graveside service. The Veteran had not even made an appearance at his own funeral—he was already tucked into his airtight resting place.

Ruth had arranged a small buffet at the church, a light spread that seemed more festive than dour. George prepared two small plates, one for himself and one for Judy, and he was circumspect in his choices for his wife. Though she loved sesame noodles, he knew she would not eat them standing up. Nothing with spinach, broccoli, poppy seeds, or parsley, and no whole strawberries, any of which would cause her to worry about carrying seeds or leaf tips in her teeth. He doted on the puffs, the individual bites.

George liked knowing what would please her and what she would eschew. He realized that he had felt the same way earlier, during their closeted sex, even as he had praised the unfamiliar. This was intimacy, George reconsidered, knowing not only where to touch but also what to feed. He skewered a melon ball to see if it was fresh or frozen, because the unthawed ones hurt Judy's back fillings. He was aware that certain foods repulsed her, a trait he found amusing rather than significant. (She didn't like the way cherry tomatoes exploded in her mouth and she would not eat sprouts, simply because they looked too much like sperm.) It seemed he knew her tastes better than his own; for some reason, watching his wife clean her plate when he had cooked or selected the food satisfied him no end.

Filling his own plate was easy and without method. His vision was starting to return, though the pain was not altogether gone. He spread pasty cheeses on salty crackers, scooped a sample of each salad—it did not matter if he finished everything. Also, he nabbed a few unknown things, hoping for a foreign taste or two. Judy, he knew, was not fond of the strange.

George could smell Judy's lawn-inspired fragrance in the

breeze as he walked up to an animated cluster that included her, Emilio, and Inez. It wasn't until he had presented Judy with her plate that he realized she was arguing with Emilio.

"Even after you die," she was saying, "there are too many choices. Cremate? Donate? Bury? Freeze?"

Judy's dogma regarding the secret to free time, money, and contentment espoused the limiting of options. He wished she did not feel a need to convert the masses.

"People in a dictatorship are in some ways freer," she said. She typically advanced that capitalism paralyzed people with possibilities. "Toilet paper is like mosquitoes," she said. "Are a hundred different kinds really necessary?"

Emilio's wide face ballooned out and his broad chest expanded; the effect was something like a rooster preparing for battle. Emilio was known for being unflappable in the face of plant disasters, such as drill presses crushing expensive components or suppliers continually shipping the wrong parts when each delay cost a point in Coldpoint stock. He had come to America in the *Mariel* boat lift, and George had only ever seen him argue defending Jimmy Carter on the rare occasions the ex-president's name came up. The Cuban scooted up until his belly was practically touching Judy's. Inez grabbed his arm, bulging with muscles visible through his coat.

"You can't tell me I am fortunate," Emilio said to Judy, practically spitting out each word, "because I sit on a boat with criminals and crazy people. If they weren't afraid for sharks, they would have cut me just to take the buckle from my belt."

"She doesn't mean you," Inez cooed in her mourning-dove voice. To Judy, she said, "As far as Emilio knows, he had only one choice—freedom—and he do what he needs to get it."

"Of course," Judy said. She quickly changed her tone to one of flattery. "You did what you had to do. George and I, we would never survive a journey like that."

Emilio was placated by her retreat. Shackelford lumbered up to the Coldpoint gathering, embracing Judy for the second time that morning.

"Lovely eulogy," she said.

"Thank you," Shackelford accepted. "Sound familiar?" he asked George.

Travis Junior appeared just then, escorting Niagara on one arm and carrying a bowl of ice in the other. Ruth was following them to the group. George would have expected Ruth to stay with her own people, though he remembered how she had been oddly calmed by Niagara's presence in the hospital. Perhaps she sensed that Niagara had knowledge of her husband and his eternal needs.

Because the ice was melting into a glob, Junior knocked the cubes about with one of his chunky silver rings. The mass broke into lumps the size of golf balls, and Niagara fished them out. She plopped a piece into each person's glass, periodically shaking her hand until it came unstuck from her glove.

George didn't trust the biker professor. In a show of ill manners, he glowered at Junior and then surveyed the group. What he saw was a circle of enmity. Only Plunkett the Younger and Niagara were smiling. Ruth's nostrils flared as she stared at Shackelford, who, for no known reason, was looking daggers at Inez. Inez was gripping Emilio in a pincer-tight hold. Emilio was scowling at Judy, whose eyes and nose were wrinkled toward Niagara.

"A toast," Junior proclaimed. He had that bad-boy grin that reeked of tomfoolery. "To my father," he said. "For whatever cosmic reason, he brought us all together."

George realized that only the Veteran could make this a more uncomfortable gathering. Perhaps the dead engineer would continue to chat with Niagara and make himself known as a spokesman for life beyond the grave; otherwise, he had infused this group with nothing more than his bitterness and spite.

Travis Junior raised the ice bowl, like a loving cup, above his head. "To my father," he repeated. "May he chill in peace."

Shackelford decided he had seen enough of them at the funeral, and, rescheduling the design meeting for nine o'clock the next morning, he granted his department the rest of the day off. Judy dropped George at home and set out for an afternoon of impromptu appointments she arranged over her car phone, beginning with tea in Georgetown and ending with a bonus visit to the health club.

In the middle of the afternoon, the unpopulated house felt vast and stuffy. George opened a few windows and a bottle of beer, then left a message at the school for Harris's science teacher to call. He wanted to make sure Harris wasn't pestering the patient instructor, though he wasn't above snooping for clues regarding the mysterious science-fair project. What would Harris make with George in mind? A gas-powered weed puller? A combination beer cooler/footstool? Actually, George recalled, the science fair wasn't for inventions; the projects were supposed to explain concepts like thunder or static electricity. George remembered Harris's interest when he told his son how a simple model of a telegraph had started him on electrical experiments. Perhaps Harris had put together a telegraph—George hadn't done that until high school.

Each spring, returning to the varnished school auditorium, George had to suppress his amusement at the Washingtonian nature of the children's projects. "Seven Days in the Life of the National Debt" had been a particularly memorable display in which one little girl had used kidney beans to depict the interest compounded on the debt in a single week. Honorable mention went to a poster-board explanation of how C-SPAN beams legislative proceedings from the floor of the House to your home. George wondered how much more technical sixth-grade offerings would be than those of fourth or fifth graders. Maybe Harris had made George a barometer using human hair, a project George himself had once tried unsuccessfully.

Shortly after George got home, a neighbor came to inquire if Judy had any couscous in the pantry. She had not expected to be greeted by George, dressed in a suit and holding fast to the neck of a Rolling Rock. George wished he had left the beer in the kitchen.

"Beer?" he asked Beatrice, a well-bred woman in jodhpurs and riding boots. George didn't know if her costume was one of fashion or sport.

"It's only two," she said by way of refusal.

"My watch must be fast," George said and smiled.

Judy had two boxes of couscous, so he gave Beatrice the unopened one, though he didn't understand why his neighbor couldn't go to the grocery store just up the street.

"Tell her I have pilaf if she needs it," Beatrice said. "With Moroccan you must have couscous, don't you think?"

"Absolutely," George agreed. "Pilaf would never do." He shut the door and, for his own amusement, imitated her mincing steps as he hustled back to the kitchen for chips and salsa. He filled a bowl with each and carried both bowls and his beer to the bedroom.

Beatrice's request was not uncommon. Neighbors often knocked on their door to borrow maple syrup when they discovered they had a batch of pancakes and nothing to pour on top. Or they came for saffron, cardamom, dried vanilla beans—rare and expensive spices they knew Judy stocked. If she wasn't able to meet the request, she could usually offer a viable substitution.

George felt lucky to be in such high spirits and thinking well of his wife. His headache had peaked then miraculously ebbed, and he was no longer compelled to mull over thoughts of mortality, his own or the Veteran's. George called the weather line, and today the abbreviated report satisfied rather than annoyed him. He turned on the bluegrass radio station and carefully hung up his good suit. He was still vexed about discovering that for the last two years he had dressed like a Georgia Tech nerd even though it wasn't required. Once his incarnation as Magazine Man was known throughout the plant, they would recant their scorn.

A pair of khaki shorts and a peach polo shirt transformed him into Magazine Man at the Beach. All he needed, he thought as he looked in the mirror, was to trade in his stockbroker glasses for some Secret Service shades. George scooped up hot sauce with a corn chip, careful not to dribble chunks of tomato down his shirt front.

On the radio, he heard the twangy banjo introduction to "Get Ready for Tomorrow," one of his favorites. It was an old cowboy gospel tune, complete with yodeling and hokey lyrics. George had it on tape, but he never thought to play it. His delight at hearing it now was such that he actually yodeled along. As the chorus wound down, it occurred to him that being married was like owning all your favorite songs. They were so familiar that you often forgot to play, let alone enjoy, them.

The phone rang, and at first George expected someone else to answer it and buzz him if he was needed. He caught it on the seventh or eighth ring.

"Mr. Knight," he repeated the teacher's name. "Thank you for returning my call."

"What can I do you for?" the teacher asked in a Midwestern accent.

"Well, I didn't want you to think we were putting Harris up for adoption or anything," George said. "I hope he hasn't overstayed his welcome in the lab."

"I welcome him overstaying," Mr. Knight said. "The place is crawling with other kids, not like Harris, who got themselves a late start. Besides, Harris is about the brightest boy I've met in all my days in the sixth grade."

George looked down at his long deck shoes. "I'm proud to hear that," he said. He was mighty proud. Not only was it a joy to have a good teacher compliment his kid, it was a relief to be talking about Harris's brain and not his girth.

"Wait till you get an eyeful of his project, Mr. Mahoney," Mr. Knight said with the glee of a grade-schooler. "Your life may never be the same."

George laughed. "That's a lot to ask from a science fair," he said.

"Well, I'm only one judge, but if this kid doesn't go to Nationals, I'll eat my grade book."

"So he's working on something electrical," George took a stab in the dark.

"Oh no you don't," Mr. Knight scolded. "I'm authorized to tell you, 'None of your beeswax, mister.' "

George wondered if Mr. Knight naturally gravitated to sixth-grade language. "I have to admit, I'm curious," George said.

"Well, then, haul your fanny down to the gym at one p.m. on Wednesday."

"Will do," George said.

"You're good to call," Mr. Knight said and hung up before he could give out another morsel of information.

George was gratified by the teacher's assessment. Without prompting, he had deemed Harris the brightest boy he had met in all his days. That was unanticipated enough. If he hadn't been so preoccupied with his own curiosity, George would have asked Mr. Knight about the smart camp, how Harris was doing socially, and whether he had overheard any of Harris's other teachers refer to him as a discipline problem. He considered phoning the teacher again, but he thought it would sound as if he were begging for more praise.

Was it so important that Harris belong to a clique? When George was in sixth grade, he had been down to two friends, and they actually liked each other more than they liked him. George was neither fat nor eager to volunteer answers in class; instead, he'd been abnormally skinny and so frightened of making a mistake that he became silent as a stone if the teacher dared to call upon him.

Although he hadn't heard it from his mother, adults who yell apparently perceive themselves as commanding respect. They contend that raising their voice is a necessary means for keeping their subjects in line. But George was proof of the fact that being screamed at serves to make a person jumpy. Rather than grooming him to respect her, May-belle Mahoney had prepared George to expect failure and ridicule at every turn. George's father did not join in the derision his wife practiced, but neither did he protect George from it. He never offered an explanation of why he had married May-belle Potter, and he did not apologize for her touchiness or her suspicion. His father's personal style alternated between healthy teasing and an easy silence that father and son enjoyed when they were throwing pitches or washing the cars. George remembered him gently suggesting solutions to the toughest math problems; he wished he could ask his father some of the tough questions now that he was firming up his nerve.

The Harrisons had done the most to inspire George's independence. Just riding his bike along the small stretch of highway to Dino Park showed more daring than he had previously possessed. When Mr. Harrison began asking for George's help in physically demanding tasks, George found he could scramble up a ladder carrying a two-handed load. He discovered a knack for simple machines, too, and using pulleys, levers, and inclined planes, he helped Mr. Harrison maintain their personal equivalent of the pyramids.

George hoped his children would be braver than he was. He tried to bolster their self-esteem and inspire courage in them. So far, Sheridan was socially fearless; if anything, she could be too bold talking to strangers or running up the high-dive ladder. Harris always seemed to have one eye on the task and the other on Judy or George or his teacher. George was encouraged that Harris had undertaken to surprise him. Also, what parent wouldn't be heartened to hear what Mr. Knight had to say? Science might just save Harris, George thought, science and a little more exercise.

Peering into the darkness of his son's room, George could make out the posters for Megadeath and Metallica, bands that celebrated tumult and destruction. Except for Sunday mornings, George was hardly ever alone in his house. Staring objectively at Harris's lair, with the *Mad* magazines stacked next to *Electricity Explained, Columbia History of the World,* and *The Big Bang: Fact or Fiction?,* he marveled at what a funny kid his son was. Eccentric, immature, plump, hilarious: so many traits that made Judy uncomfortable.

George supposed that was part of the attraction to Niagara as well: in looks and style and humor, she was an amalgamation of Judy's pet peeves. The sorority knowledge that he had admired in college (not only grooming and dressing tricks but also the wisdom that being too smart or too funny, especially absurd, put people off) George now recognized as Judy's need for conformity. She was frankly unsympathetic to glandular conditions, not to mention obsessions or slapstick.

George finished a second beer and his snack out on the front porch. The street was quiet except for the occasional toddlers strolling with their Ghanaian or Filipino nannies. The beer gave him a pleasant buzz, and his thoughts left his home and cascaded toward Niagara. He smiled at the memory of her funeral getup—what did she see when she looked in the mirror? He didn't know if it was witnessing that or Niagara vined around Travis Junior that had lessened his appetite for the girl with the kaleidoscope mind. In this relaxed state, he relished the sensation of reaching under her harvest print dress to stroke her oversized butt. Her tongue had tasted like the fake fruit of movie candy, and the long strings of her hair had rested between the ribbings of the corduroy divan.

George stood up and brushed the dirt off his backside. His self-praise for not thinking about her had turned into a hard-on, and he surveyed his ailing lawn in lieu of a cold shower. Lazily, George dug up a few violets in the island of plants between the lawn and the house. Then he broke open the two bags of mulch that had been sweating in the sun for at least a week. Although the shredded bark smelled like rotting melons, the dark mounds at the base of the shrubs and the dogwood instantly made the lawn look more tended.

Before George could tackle a second project, Sheridan was dropped off by her car pool. She threw down her Baby Agatha backpack. "Daddy, Daddy!" she yelled, out of breath with excitement. Judy was always home to receive her; George loved how a small change in the schedule could make a six-year-old's whole day. He took off his garden gloves and scooped her up; they both waved to Sarah, the Monday car-pool mother.

"What do you want to do until dinner?" George asked his little girl.

"Play with Baby Agatha!" she squealed.

Holding her around the waist, George let her fall backwards toward the ground. She swooped up her precious backpack as George righted her. The pinkness of every Baby Agatha accessory was like camouflage among Sheridan's wardrobe. Today she was wearing her favorite outfit, a pink-and-white-polka-dot dress over matching bicycle shorts. She was paler than either George or Judy, with a beauty recently marred by a few missing front teeth.

"Can we go to the store, Daddy?" Sheridan asked. "Dominique has this coat that Baby Agatha wears in the rain, and, see, I know where she got it."

"I don't think so." It was a sticking point with George that Judy bought the children whatever their hearts desired. If anything, she was the one who could be accused of spoiling them, though it might just be a difference of upbringing. Harris didn't seem affected, but Sheridan was apt to throw quite a fit if denied. George laid his hand on her head. "Seems to me Baby Agatha has more clothes than you do."

"No, Daddy, I have more." Sheridan zipped and unzipped her backpack, obviously concocting another strategy. "What if it rains, Daddy? All her clothes will get ruined."

"Pumpkin, you're her mommy," George said. "If it rains, you have to bring her inside."

Sheridan plopped herself on the porch swing with a petulance that George expected might give way to a rant. She lay face down on the flowery cushions, and he couldn't tell if she was crying. George was newly sympathetic to her flutters of mood; after all, he had vacillated between despair and elation, Niagara and Judy, for days. He pushed the swing gently, so she would not be startled by the movement. The breeze from the swing animated tendrils of the ivy in standing wrought-iron planters, which flanked the front door of the house.

Sheridan lifted her head, and George saw that her face was dry. Although he had basically denied her toy-store request, she looked hopeful that he would change his mind. He knew their afternoon could go either way, one of the aspects of parenting he did not enjoy.

At the base of one of the ivy stands was a shoebox, probably on its way to the recycling bin. "Here, honey," George said, "here's something for Baby Agatha."

Sheridan shook the empty box. "What's in the box?"

"Pretend it's a toy."

She removed the lid, rustled the tissue paper inside. "What came in the box, Daddy?"

Was she materialistic, unimaginative, or just asking? "Invisible shoes," George said.

"They were invisible or they make you invisible?"

"Both," George answered.

"How do you know they're not in here now?"

"I don't. Better look carefully."

Sheridan took to pretending. She lifted a pair of imaginary shoes out of the box. "So heavy," she said. She put them on the porch and stepped into them, bringing a strap around the side to buckle it. She stood up on her toes. "High heels," she said.

"Just the right size," George said. "They're beautiful."

"Beautiful, fountain blue, good and true." It was her highest form of praise. On tiptoe, she ran to George and poked him hard in the ribs. "I'm invisible, you can't see me."

George pretended not to know where she was as she not so gently pinched his waist and the back of his knees. He tackled a few small lawn jobs, steadily calling out, "Where is that minx, that magpie, that mushroom?" while his little girl found ways to touch him from a distance with a whip of ivy or a rake handle, and eventually the rim around the shoebox lid, which she had ripped off in a long peel.

Although dinner was scheduled to be leftovers from Friday, George felt at liberty today to do what he wished. Around four-thirty he took Sheridan inside and parked her in front of a video, then washed up and reviewed his many dinner options. He thought steak would be good, and he knew Harris would agree. He settled on kabobs because the kids liked them and Sheridan would get a thrill out of helping in their assembly, though he would have to watch her carefully around the skewers.

In the freezer was a nice cut of sirloin that could be thawed in the microwave. Sirloin was a little extravagant for kabobs. What the hell? They could afford it. Opening the freezer and watching the clouds of cold air puff out brought George back to thoughts of the New Refrigerator, improving itself in front of his eyes. George imagined a freezer filled with gel that could be contained in malleable plastic. This mass would be frozen but also soft and compactable, so that the gel would take up any available space not filled with food. (Keeping a full freezer cold requires about one-third the energy of chilling an empty one.) When you removed a steak or a package of waffles, you would pull it from this oozy cushion (George vocalized the science-fiction sucking sound that extracting something would make), which would immediately re-form to plug the gap where the package had been. The gelled pillow would act both to insulate food and to ensure that gasps of air did not escape whenever the door was opened.

Where had this idea come from? George was sure the beers had worn off, and yet all afternoon he had enjoyed an absence of tension and self-awareness. Maybe Shackelford would get him a modem, let him design away in the privacy of his home. It was a worthwhile suggestion, though George knew it was about as likely as turning on his radio and hearing the Veteran make a speech.

Sheridan was no help in preparing dinner, but she thought she was an equal partner, which was all that counted. George had diced up red and green peppers and onions, and there were cherry tomatoes for the kids and George, as well as chunks of pineapple.

Estimating Judy's arrival time, George started the charcoal and tossed four potatoes in the microwave, anticipating a joyous family meal. He hoped Harris was staying in the science lab until dinner and not stopping over at some grease pit for snacks.

When Judy came home from the gym, she was a little confused by George's dinner choice, as if someone had switched calendars on her.

"I'll take the ravioli to work tomorrow," George said.

"Fine," Judy said, adjusting herself to the surprise. "I'd rather have kabobs."

George looked for signs of irritation but she seemed sincere. She was always calmest after a workout. While George prodded the coals, Judy sat out on the deck with their little girl, and she brushed Sheridan's tangled hair until it was all of a piece again. Then the two of them went inside to squeeze some lemonade and set the table.

Harris came home right on time, and George was relieved to see he was hungry.

"Kabobs," he said, gawking at the grill. "Man, I can't believe it. Kabobs!"

You would have thought George was grilling an entire chocolate cake for him. Throughout the meal, Harris kept up a constant chatter that entertained them all. With Judy and George so dramatically relaxed, Harris had the table nearly to himself. Sheridan loved it when anyone got a laugh, making her a joy to play to.

"You should see Carly's project." Harris had started a new science-fair story. "She's doing this thing with beans, right, but —get this—she planted whole beans instead of just the seeds."

They all laughed at the silly girl.

" 'Mr. Knight,' " Harris said in a girl voice, " 'I think Justin poisoned my soil. I put a string bean in each of these cups, and not one has sprouted.' " Harris was laughing now, too. Judy didn't even remind him to keep his mouth closed, that's how much fun they were having.

In the middle of dinner, George had a strange longing to set a place for the child he had fathered with Carol Greyson more than twenty years ago. Combinations of his and Carol's traits suggested themselves to him. Was she a voluptuous girl with a dimple in her cheek and a mysterious mechanical aptitude? Or might he be a dark-complected high diver with admirable nerve and bad eyesight? Would that child—now an adult—appreciate George's humor, enjoy the meal he had lovingly prepared for this, his second family? It dawned on George that Judy would somehow link his philandering to this unfinished business.

"George," Judy said, "Harris is giving out clues."

"Clues?" he snapped to. "You're going to let me guess your project?"

"If you can," Harris said. He was smirking like crazy. "Ready? Your clue is 'You're getting colder.' "

"Hmm," George said. He tried to remember the guesses he had made before. He had been heading for something electrical, so now he said, "Is it car-related?"

"You're getting colder," Harris said.

Judy tried her luck. She had ventured earlier that the topic was food. "Are you brewing beer?"

Harris grinned so widely that George could see braces were inevitable. "You're getting colder," he said.

George remembered his weather idea. "A barometer?" he asked.

Harris bounced in his chair. "Colder," he said. "You're getting colder."

"Ice!" Sheridan yelled excitedly. "You're making ice!"

By the expression on Harris's face, which changed as drastically as if he had dropped a hot fudge sundae in the dirt, George knew Sheridan was onto something. Harris recovered quickly, pretending to be thrown by the simplemindedness of his little sister's suggestion. "Right," he said with mock sincerity, "I'm making ice." Then he revved his belly laugh again, and he mussed up her hair with his oily kabob fingers.

That night, as George threw his dirty shirt and shorts into the hamper, he told Judy his hunch. "I think Sheridan guessed the project," he said. " 'You're getting colder, You're getting colder,' and she nailed it. I think he is making ice." He climbed into the steaming shower and tried to predict Harris's method.

Judy was standing there with a clean towel when he was done. She lovingly dried his back. "It's too complicated," she said, picking up their conversation. "I think he was flustered that Sheridan guessed something beyond him. Who knows how to build a freezer?"

"Besides me?" George asked.

Judy kissed a vertebra midway down. "Who in the sixth grade?"

"What a day," George said. He raised one of the windows a crack, careful not to show his naked self to Beatrice and Seth across the street.

"We should go to a funeral every Monday," Judy said.

George turned his side of the antique quilt back and climbed into the sleigh bed, leaving his glasses on the nightstand. Even a few feet away, Judy was blurry, and the clock on her side of the bed was unreadable.

Judy worked cream into the balls of her feet. "I thought you were getting a migraine this morning."

"The throbbing was there," George said, "even the spot in my vision, and then, when we were driving home, it disappeared. I think that's why I felt so grateful all afternoon."

"You could use a day off now and then," Judy suggested. "Don't you have about two months stored up?"

"At least. I was thinking of trying to do some of my work from home."

"Here?" Judy asked. She rubbed her fingertips together. George could smell the camphor radiating from her.

"All I'd need is a modem," George said. "You could use it, too, for house listings."

"I'm not sure that's a good idea," Judy said.

For the first time in his married life, George wondered if Judy was having an affair. The day had started with him in the hot seat, but her response was mighty suspicious. Why wouldn't she want him around the house more? He could be here when Sheridan came back from school, and he could take Judy's turn at the car pool, a duty she disdained because of the possibilities for damage brought on by a BMW full of six-year-olds.

Judy didn't offer any explanation for her reticence. She went through her evening regimen, seemingly unaware that George was staring at her. Watching her routine, George decided that it wasn't that she was entertaining anyone else in his home, it was just that she liked having the house to herself. One night off the dinner schedule was acceptable, welcome even. Too much of that, he could see, might be threatening. When she finished the scarecrow exercise, both arms straight out to the side, she gave her hair a wicked brushing. Lovely, tightly laced Judy, destined to stay at her proper weight, wedded to a budget and a goal. Wouldn't he be miserable without her?

"I love you," George said. It wasn't something he told her every night.

"Sweetheart," she said, "I love you too." Judy let her head drop all the way back, her chin pointed at the ceiling. Then she slowly brought it forward in an exaggerated nod, until her chin rested in the hollow between her collar bones. She repeated this motion back and forth and then sideways, stretching her ear to her shoulder on each side. When she lay down next to George, she fell asleep almost immediately.

George didn't toss much himself. He felt pure and parental, as if he had renewed his devotion to Judy and the kids. Though he was home plenty, today he had been part of his home. He realized, too, that he was getting excited about the unveiling of Harris's hard work. He prayed the kid wasn't setting himself up for disaster, like his overstudying of history facts.

Before Wednesday, there was presentation day at work, Niagara's first. Maybe for the hell of it George would try out the freezer-full-of-gel idea, without drawing up any plans. Shackelford would choke on that. Also, it would make Niagara's idea seem less radical, thereby helping her cause. George wondered if he was hiding behind his family because he didn't know how to face her. He had thought he wanted to train her, then he had thought he wanted to (as Judy would say) pork her, and right this second he thought he wanted to avoid her.

Travis Junior seemed to know what to make of her. Maybe George could just take in her teasing and feed her an occasional donut, enjoying her wackiness as a change of pace. There would be some kind of cosmic symmetry in Niagara coupling with the Veteran's estranged son. George tried to talk himself into this arrangement, even as he remembered that this afternoon the simple fantasy of lifting her skirt had given him a hard-on.

In sleep, he was driving south on the I-75 of his childhood. The route had become littered with outlet malls and fake country shoppes, but his dream preserved the barns painted with advertisements for chewing tobacco. There were horses galore. This was just after I-40 and I-64 were transversed by 60 and 75, when people could afford the dime that a gallon of gas cost.

Familiarity flew by the window of George's dream car. He passed the red-and-white-checkerboard water tower, the car wash in the shape of a whale. He smelled the metallic scent of water from the car wash's jets and the stench of the long, crowded chicken barn a good ways from the road. Kudzu was already fashioning the fallen trees into a horrific topiary garden; high clouds wicked the moisture from the airy highway. In general, a magnificent Kentucky spring was working the landscape over. George sang the chorus of "Ready or Not, He's Coming," yodeling like Gene Autry, and someone in the passenger seat snickered.

It was Niagara who was sitting next to him, laughing at his singing. She was wearing one of her office uniforms, but it was the lavender silk of Judy's nightgown. Her nipples poked out like pencil points; the silk also revealed the definition of her thighs. Her stringy hair blew away from her face, which was a nice effect, and she wasn't wearing any glasses.

"To Dino Park," she yelled over the wind. "And step on it."

George raised his fist in the air. "To Dino Park!" he yelled, too. His tie whipped up and over his shoulder, something a clip-on could never do. George remembered that he was free to choose his own clothes now, and he looked down at his shirt with its thin, elegant pinstripes of black and green. His tie was black paisley on white silk, a nice match he had made himself.

Out of the corner of his eye, George could see Niagara twirling a strand of her hair around her finger. She tugged at her safety belt, and she changed the radio station three, maybe four times. He always loved it when she squirmed.

George was conscious of regretting that the Harrisons had been reduced to Christmas-card acquaintances. He should have taken his family on a road trip through Kentucky and the Carolinas. Judy was an adventurer, a good wife. It wasn't her fault that George had not been in for adventure in marriage. He had been through with feats of daring since Carol Greyson had sucked him dry the week before she left for the Little Flower Home.

Now he was interested in risk once again. Mrs. Harrison was at the opening gate, and rather than shrinking his desire, her presence only strengthened it. Parked at the entrance booth, George lifted his arm and studied a scab flapping on his elbow. Slowly and unwisely he pulled it from his wound, which was rimmed in white and cratered with scraped flesh.

"Baby, you're hurt," a voice said. It came from outside, but when he looked up, Niagara was in the tiny booth. She took his arm through the open car window and kissed the area around the scab.

Somehow George was out of the car. It seemed Niagara had pulled him through the window with the intensity of her kiss. Even though the paved lot looked like the parking area at the plant, George registered it as Dino Park. Likewise, Niagara seemed to have something of a Southern accent, and the breasts caressed by the purple silk were round and large, ripe as Carol Greyson's.

"Where shall we start?" Niagara asked. "Prosauropod? Sauropod?" She licked the inside of George's ear. "Theropod?"

Taking Niagara's arm, George led her to the back of the preserve, where the brachiosaur was parked. She stepped lightly along the path, her dress smooching her hips with every step.

The dirt-brown brachiosaur was shabbier than when he and Carol had cuddled up inside. Standing in front of the thick-legged brute, George observed that it was not much taller than he.

"Seems smaller," he said.

Niagara looked him up and down. "Big enough," she said. Her laughter was sexy and promiscuous.

She stood near one of the dinosaur's hind legs, then held on and slid up and down. "Oh, brachiosaur, baby," she said.

George took her to the cave of the dinosaur's stomach. No one was in the park today. Probably no one came at all anymore. He was afraid he might scare her off with his desire.

"Reptiles are ectotherms," Niagara said breathily. "They derive body heat from external sources. Birds are endotherms; they generate their own body heat."

"Yes," George agreed. "Yes."

"So were they reptiles or birds?" she asked. She palmed the zipper flap of his pants. "Did they get hot from external sources?" She took her hand away. "Or did they generate their own body heat?"

Reptile or bird? This was an age-old discussion in scholarly circles (almost settled now on bird). He had to be true to the facts as he knew them; however, he couldn't bear for her to pull away.

"Reptile?" she said, cupping his penis and squeezing gently. "Or bird?" she asked, her hand on her head. Like an optometrist testing lenses, she repeated the drill. "Reptile?" hand on penis. "Bird?" hand on head.

George would face the facts later. "Reptile!" he declared. He kissed her on her graduate-school bangs, her hearing aid, the clasp of her amber drop. He loved to kiss. Niagara massaged his shoulder blades, spanning his pectorals as easily as a pianist covers an octave. Her kisses, which had started out as strictly lips, were now wetter and more fragmented.

George felt he could kiss her all night, even as he hoped things were going further than that. "One question, Mr. Dino Park," Niagara said. "Just how did dinosaurs have sex?"

"Perhaps we can accurately construct their massiveness," George paraphrased from the Dino Park pamphlet. He unzipped his pants, relieving some of the ache he had felt since they'd arrived.

Niagara said, "My left pocket."

Suddenly, her dress was covered with pockets. There were pockets over each breast, in front and back, in the side. George experienced some confusion as to her left, his left, and each pouch he reached in, she would laugh and say, "You're getting colder."

He couldn't remember which he had tried, so he began again in a methodical way. "You're getting colder," she said in response to his efforts at her breast pockets. She tittered and repeated the phrase for the front patch pockets. When he reached into her left inside pocket, he pulled out an accordioned column of condoms.

Now it was George who was delighted. "Good for you," he said. He ripped off the last pouch and put the rest back into her pocket.

Niagara was not wearing a garter belt or string panties with a triangle of red lace. She was plain through and through. Lifting her skirt above her shin, George saw the tourniquet elastic of knee-high hose, which her calf spilled out slightly over the top of. Her underwear was cotton, full cut, with bands of fabric around the legs, like men's underwear. George thought this was a guarantee that his experience was genuine. If this were a dream, he reasoned, he would have seen a black garter belt cutting across her flank. He would have smelled that musty nylon crotch scent as he frisked her pockets.

Niagara wriggled out of her clothes and worked George's heavy jeans down his legs. His underwear was the army green color his miniature plastic dinosaurs and soldiers had been. When Niagara pulled the elastic away from his waist, George felt the Kentucky spring wind cool his balls, and his erection was stiff as a perch. Like a bird come home to roost, Niagara grabbed his penis and rolled a blue condom expertly around it.

In a fake Southern accent, she said, "Time for love!"

George pushed her against the brachiosaur's wrinkly hind leg, the both of them grunting like cave people. Before he moved inside her, George registered that someone was calling his name.

"Georgio," he heard, in a nasal Kentucky voice. "Georgio." And then as the woman came closer, the greeting took on a scolding tone. "For heaven's sake," the woman said. "George Bledsoe Mahoney!"

Looking over his shoulder, he recognized his mother's walk and voice before he saw her face. The blue gingham housecoat was coming toward him, one bony arm on her hip and the other extended with finger pointing. She looked so young, about the age she'd been during the Carol crisis. Even in his dream, George calculated that she was thirty-four then, younger than George was now.

George wasn't with Carol, and although the woman he was with wasn't Judy either, they hadn't actually done more than kiss. He prepared to defend his innocence. Except that his pants were around his ankles and his penis was swathed in a light blue condom.

"Where did you learn this behavior?" his mother screeched. "Who is this slut?"

George hadn't remembered how pretty her hair was. It had the flat waves of old movie stars, and it was a shiny auburn. She had nice legs, too. But her face was contorted in anger and shame. Her mouth had long lines on either side like a wooden puppet; her cheeks were sunken and sallow. "George Bledsoe Mahoney," she said again. "I am waiting for an answer."

"You're dead," George said. He pushed away from Niagara and reached for his pants. "She's dead," he said to Niagara.

Niagara had withdrawn a tape recorder from her purse, which George had not even seen she was carrying. Was this part of her experiment? Is this how she conjured up the spirits she sought?

"What are you doing?" he yelled.

"Taping," Niagara said with a grin. "You said she was dead, didn't you?"

Mercifully, George woke up, his breathing intense as a piston. He was hot and sweaty, but he was also cold. The sheets were damp around his tingling legs. George stumbled into the bathroom, hoping to throw up. He wanted to be physically sick, to be assured that he had food poisoning or the flu, and that anything occurring in his subconscious was the result of an outside virus. More than anything else right now, he wanted to demonstrate that a sick little germ had taken hold of him, a viral invasion that would be gone by morning.

Clad in nothing but his boxer shorts, George slouched in a corner of the study like a washed-up fighter, supporting his weighty head with his hands and torturing himself with replays of his action in the ring. No matter what angle he viewed the dream from, it turned his stomach. He was sickened not only by guilt but also by Niagara's teasing, which activated his fantasies and glands to no release.

The pounding of his heart and ears was shaking his viscera the way Harris's heavy-metal music did when George opened the door of his son's room. George rubbed his temples and took deep breaths, a relaxation technique he had previously scorned. Over the next hour, he mapped a variety of flowcharts in his head. Alternate futures branched out like tributaries; however, each hypothetical rivulet sprang from the same source. Logic even more than desire dictated that he had but one choice. All things were possible if he was willing to jump into a barrel and throw himself down Niagara's falls.

Energized by decisiveness, George picked up the phone. Niagara had told him she stayed at her lab until midnight; surely, George rationalized, she would not be too deeply asleep within an hour of that. He pulled the lap throw around him. The last time he had seen Niagara, she had been draped like a stole around Plunkett the Younger. With a clarity that manifests itself only at ungodly hours and in dire straits, George imagined an easy victory over the cynical, smooth-talking Travis Junior.

He was so far down the river that when the answering machine clicked on, George was nothing short of enraged. It struck him as another testament to Niagara's indifference that he would be manufacturing a lover's oration and battling convulsions of nausea while she greeted him with a recording.

George was thinking about visitation rights and an equitable split of his and Judy's retirement money, and he couldn't even get Niagara's attention. Didn't she see what he was prepared to sacrifice? That ought to be aphrodisiac enough. Because they had consummated nothing, George continued to react on a junior-high level. She kissed me. Doesn't that mean she's my girl?

George sneaked back into the bedroom to retrieve his sweat suit from where it hung on the door. Lifting the weighty second skin, he seemed to be bringing himself back down to earth, setting himself free from the rigid finger that hooked under the back of his neck and kept him an inch above the ground. Like a cat burglar, he palmed Judy's keys from the dresser, aware that the Oldsmobile would wake everyone in the house. He waited until he was in the garage to step into the spongy pants and pull the sweat shirt on over his bare chest. Because the laces on his sneakers were rotten, George had to leave the shoes flapping. These were the sneakers he wore to change the oil or spade manure into the garden, and they looked particularly suspect behind the driver's seat of the BMW.

George was amazed at how many cars were out at one in the morning. Although his family had been sleeping for hours, other people were still eating or looking for a place to have a cup of coffee after the night's last movies. No gospel music was on this late, so George listened to an AM weather channel, repeating the current temperatures of the Mid-Atlantic region like a mantra: Philadelphia, 55; Wilmington, 53; Dover, 50; Salisbury, 61.

Traffic thinned as soon as he passed the Maryland line. After he was on the beltway, George realized Niagara was probably home and tucked into bed, her answering machine netting any calls that might come scampering, like rambunctious squirrels, over the wires. He could use the car phone to call information for her address, but even George in his mad dash understood that going to her house would be overkill. The fact that she had once escorted him to her trailer lab, where sparks had flown between them, allowed George to pretend he was more visitor than stalker.

To drive was soothing. George's route took him from the beltway to 270 and then west. The BMW's center of gravity was in or near his lap, so when he turned the wheel he took the car with him; in the Oldsmobile, it always felt as if the car took him and in its own time. Housing developments sprouted in clumps off the interstate, interspersed with industrial parks and unlit expanses, which he guessed to be fields. When he found the narrow road that burrowed into farmland, the dashboard clock glowed one-twenty-five. The occasional spotlights in the country dark distorted landmarks or else they disappeared altogether, and George had to double back to the Ukrainian cemetery for a second attempt at Niagara's blessed trailer of the fields.

George had been unaware he was even paying attention to the route on Friday, so engrossed was he in the smell of their lunch and the anticipation of seeing Niagara's lair. But when his lights lit up the red reflector she had pasted on the nose of a deer-crossing sign, he knew the trailer was on his right.

George coasted off the road about twenty yards past the sign and cut his lights. He was snug up against someone's farm; freshly plowed dirt gave a loamy scent to the air, which was notable for its lack of exhaust. George was unprepared for how much cooler it was here than at home. He wasn't wearing a T-shirt or socks, just boxer shorts under the sweat suit. His dilapidated sneakers felt clammy on his feet, and a lone lace trolled the roadside for burrs.

Niagara's weathered Buick was moored in front of the trailer, which was brightly lit in the inky field. Here and there, night herons called out in hopes of finding mates, their shriek-HONK seemingly amplified by the still air. Crickets fiddled around with their back legs, and spring peepers chirped as well. George felt like one more randy creature out on a spring night with a hopeful agenda.

As he tiptoed past Niagara's car, George saw what he assumed was Travis's Harley-Davidson nestled in close to the trailer. The motorcycle shone purple with the escaping light, and when George put his fingers on the chrome exhaust pipes, they were hot to the touch. He returned to Niagara's Buick and laid his palm on the hood as a healer might, but the combustion within had long subsided. So Travis had been summoned or given license to drop by. The anger that had dissipated in the drive out flared anew in George, who was conscious that his was definitely stalker behavior.

George crouched on the step leading to the front door. Would his weight rock the tin-can laboratory? Slowly unfolding himself like a human extension ladder, he peeked in at the bottom of the small window to see Niagara and Travis Junior drinking from champagne flutes. Neither the noise of George's approach nor his eyeballs in the window disturbed their gala.

Niagara was wearing tight black jeans and a long-sleeved ribbed shirt that would have been right for the weather except that it stopped several inches short of her relatively small waist, heretofore unseen. George had not pictured her as being so trim. Circling her right arm, a mass of bracelets was coiled like a spring. George glimpsed her long, jangling earrings, and he fantasized that if she were outside with him, the air would play her like a giant wind chime.

Niagara and Travis each took a sip of champagne and clinked their glasses, then they cocked their heads, as if they were savoring the sound. Travis had his right arm stretched out in the gesture of a conductor, pontificating, no doubt, on some musical-genius notion. Travis's voice carried but Niagara's was just a tuneful buzz. They tipped their glasses once more toward each other in a salute. After swallowing, Travis took the champagne from Niagara and gave her a big wet kiss. George could see the man's tongue, which repulsed him.

"Bye-bye, physics," Travis heralded. "Hello, metaphysics." His grin flattened his eyes into narrow slits.

Niagara hummed something.

"You bet they'll bite," Travis said. "They might also give you money." He stood up and swiveled her chair around. Then he pulled her hair back behind her head and kissed a spot on her neck just behind her right ear. George wondered if she heard a loud, gross "smooch" through her hearing aid.

What were his options here? He could jump up and down on the step, make the pitiful trailer rock with the wrath of a shunned suitor. He could knock on the window; he could knock the window out. George tried to figure out why this man had been granted access. Given, he conceded, Travis was younger, funkier, electronically more innovative, and unmarried; still, George had to consider himself the better man, or (kept awake by a burning need to commit adultery) he would have taken an antihistamine and gone back to bed.

Until this moment, George had not thought to wonder what Carol Greyson had seen in him. When she had come on so strong, all George had to do was receive her, which he gratefully did. They fell together—friendless egghead and friendly hedonist—to share sympathetic stories about his mother and her father, to touch and be touched, to explore territory new for each generation. Some effort had been required to garner Judy's affection, but it was more as if he fit the picture she had already sketched.

Niagara and Travis were toasting again, but to what George couldn't discern. Travis had pulled Niagara onto his lap and brought down his volume accordingly. The wall near George's porthole was struck by a projectile, signaling the uncorking of another bottle of champagne. A few peals of the flutes were followed by Travis's voice. "And let's not forget George," he cried. "To George."

This time Niagara joined in audibly. "Hear, hear!" she said. "To George."

To George, who brought us together! That was the kindest spin he could put on Travis's salute, which might have been a tribute of sheer mockery. George felt shriveled by the night air, and his back ached from standing on his toes. Still, he watched the action within change from celebration to leave-taking. Niagara pointed at her huge watch and began clearing away their trash. Very tidy she was, George thought, as he watched her wipe out the champagne flutes with a reluctant Kleenex. Coat and purse on, Niagara tugged at Travis's sleeve. He was languishing on the sofa George himself had warmed to.

George climbed off the stoop to hide on the dark side of the trailer, but many more minutes passed, the early-morning dampness stiffening his neck, before he heard Travis's voice.

"Who's driving?" Junior asked. He sounded as if he were wearing a muzzle.

"Are you kidding?" Niagara asked. She jingled her keys. "I just toasted. You're the one who finished off two bottles of champagne."

"That's what you do at a wake," Travis said. "I'd planned to share with the rest of the mourners."

"Honey, get off the bike. We'll come get it tomorrow."

What was George to do—leap out of the darkness and declare his love? Niagara had called Travis "honey," inflecting the word with the condescending affection reserved for drunks and toddlers; George didn't suppose she would leave Travis in the gravel for him.

"You're beautiful when I'm drunk," Travis slurred.

"Some compliment," Niagara said. Their steps merged into a shuffle.

Teeth chattering in his drafty head, George held his pose until the Buick spit out gravel from under its big wheels. He reached for the trailer door, thinking: Get warm, piss, and unlocked, unlocked, unlocked. When the doorknob gave in his hand, he credited Niagara's carelessness over his mental powers. It was just like her to leave a trailer full of electronic equipment, parked next to an extra-large satellite dish, unlocked.

Distinct from the mustiness of the trailer was a pungent fried-chicken odor and the pharmacy smell of alcohol. George had been brought here too, also with food; he had been invited as well to lay his head on that dirty brown couch. As his extremities warmed, his blood began to boil. Just as he expected, there were no tape recorders hooked into the radio sets. She evidently appreciated neither his kisses nor his sage advice.

It was Niagara's indifference that ultimately wounded him so. He turned on all three big consoles and blasted the room with static. On the key chain George had filched, Judy had the foresight to carry a small Swiss Army knife; George unfolded the narrow blade and held it like a pen. Choosing words that would injure and demoralize, he scratched "DEAD IS DEAD" into an ancient radio's wooden chest. So many had gone before him, the cabinet was a virtual bulletin board, though his message stood out as the newest and least carnal. He thought the carving might be his first act of vandalism, and it seemed long overdue.

But then the smallness of the gesture emboldened him. He was tired of making no mark. He was sick of his puny refrigerator plans. His great leap of marital infidelity, what had it amounted to but a bunch of kisses and some bad dreams? He seemed not to do anything more than halfway. It takes two to pull taffy, his mother used to say when she implicated him in crimes he hadn't committed, but now that he was interested, he couldn't get his hands on the sugar.

George was determined to stop holding himself back. He swept Niagara's papers onto the floor, keeping an eye out for implements of destruction. He vowed to burn the place down if a match showed up. In the bare-bulb light, a champagne bottle in a wire trash basket cast a long shadow, and when he retrieved it, the dense glass felt lethal as a lead pipe in his hands. George swung the magnum down on the radio, smashing first the cabinet, then the glass tubes within. Why old radios anyway—did she think resurrected equipment would attract its own kind? He perversely imagined he was doing Niagara a favor: she probably kept the vacuum-tube models more out of superstition than sensitivity.

Such exertion was new to George, who was amazed at how thrilling rage could be. Niagara would regret leading him this way and that. He remembered with derision Travis's self-inflicted tattoo in praise of anarchy. The punk. Split open and inside out, the shattered radio emitted a smell of ozone and dust, like an electrical storm in an antique store. It was easy to be destructive, he thought, working off his passion.

That was the first wave. The second one, equally compelling, was born of curiosity. He was too much the engineer not to see dismantling as the step before putting back together. Brushing slivers of glass aside, George sat down between the eviscerated console and the other sputtering radios. Within seconds, he was as absorbed by manipulating Niagara's gadgets as he had been by wrecking them. Only a few trips up and down the dial were necessary to give him a vague notion of her setup. She had coupled antennae to amplifier to filter, basically constructing a giant megaphone for the faintest whispers. George fiddled with the settings, manufacturing feedback to gauge the sensitivity of the radio marked "DEADEST." He wondered if the feedback could act as a net to snag vagrant, albeit nearby, waves and carry them back to the speaker. He was timing the delay between sending a signal and picking up feedback when someone spoke up.

"Sure as I'm talking to you," an older woman announced, "those teeth were false as Nixon."

George spun around and was blindsided by a stab in the hand. He yelled out, even as he saw his wound was self-inflicted; he had sliced himself against a broken radio tube. Blood ran freely, and with it George's nerve. He was woozy with fear and pain. The sentence had come not from behind him but from the very radio he had been toying with. Weirder still, he knew that voice.

George's flailing had caused him to spray the couch with red. He needed something to stanch his bleeding before he could discern how seriously he had been cut. There was no toilet paper in the tiny bathroom, some three steps away. What he found instead was an open box of sanitary napkins that seemed capable of absorbing all the blood in his body. With all his might, George hugged a giant pad against the side of his palm.

George stumbled back to the couch to lie down, thinking his sweat suit might blot up some of the mess. He elevated his hand, propping both arms against the back of the sofa. Of what he had heard, was it the speaker or the line he recognized? "False as Nixon" was almost familiar, and so he tried to concentrate on the distinctive tremolo. It was the voice of big hats and silk lampshades, an accent that could only have resulted from a lifetime in Kentucky. George had a rare twinge of homesickness, and his nostalgia was enhanced when the voice spoke again.

"Then she says to me, 'Let the man have his dessert, why don't you? He looks as if he's been rode hard and put away wet.' "

George closed his eyes to pastureland kissing a cornflower sky. Dozens of picnic tables laden with food, one devoted just to pies. Freshly dug horseshoe pits, a maypole fluttering with wide ribbons, plodding ponies carrying elated children who clutched at their manes.

"Well, when he bit into that praline, I knew we were going to be there all night long."

"Aunt Fanny," George said, astonished by his recall. Fanny, his mother's great-aunt, was long dead. The gathering her voice so vividly elicited was a family reunion, held on Derby Day circa 1959, when Nixon was a relatively young liar. George treasured the notion that this might be Fanny's heaven, a field full of food and kin.

No explanation came to him as to why Aunt Fanny would be on the radio. Given that someone had written her remarks down, a stranger reading Fannyisms would not evoke the Technicolor vision George beheld; had some folklorist captured her on tape, a recording of that vintage would at the least have a hiss or a hum. Loath as he was to admit it, dead might not be dead.

A shiver of apprehension accompanied George's potential conversion. Niagara's first success was to listen in on the final exhalations of the Veteran's sour breath, as the old man begged to be unplugged. Perhaps the afterlife was no picnic for Aunt Fanny, and that was why she was contacting him.

George's imagination switched from the joyous family reunion to zombie relatives dragging their grudges onto the airwaves. Torture and mayhem; chaos like the primordial ooze with an ax to grind. Were the dead restless and angry, hot and crowded? Reduced to strange and charmed particles, did they cramp up?

In the throes of this dark vision, George heard another woman, clear and whiny, from the radio set.

"Who's there?" the second voice said. "Is someone on the line? Is someone listening?"

"May-belle," Fanny scolded, "you are out of your ever-loving mind."

Whatever blood was left in George's body was pounding. He would surrender to the authorities, testify that Niagara's claims were true, have his teeth extracted one by one—anything not to hear what his mother might say from beyond the grave. He had been willing to concede he had been visited by Aunt Fanny, but he hoped this was shock. If he could just hallucinate a chest pain, he thought, he could die and get this over with.

"Must we endure another complete confession?" Fanny asked.

"You don't have to listen," George's mother snapped. "Lord, Jesus, Saint Peter, whoever is out there, hear my sins."

"For the love of Adam," Aunt Fanny sighed.

"I guess you know everything," his mother said, "so I'll just ask your everlasting grace. I coveted my whole life away. I coveted my friends' houses, their appliances, their vacations. You tried to show me the vanity of my ways. That time I scrimped like a miser for an avocado dishwasher—soon as we plunked down the money for it, avocado was out and I was coveting Norma's white appliances, so bright they could have been in a hospital."

That's where it came from, George thought, the feeling that he was one step behind, that all the excitement ended just before he walked into a room. Her shame assuaged George's mortification. George's mother went on and on about the outside-looking-in phenomenon. Though George's phobia centered around events, his mother's was fixated on possessions.

". . . and when Cadillacs were all the rage, I begged Will for a Cadillac. Then George needed braces, and do you hear me, Lord? I held those braces against my son. I did. Every time I looked into that mouth full of chrome, I saw the grill of a '68 Caddy. I couldn't speak to him I was so embarrassed by my longing."

George was fascinated by how much of his childhood his mother was clarifying minute by minute. He clearly remembered her silence lasting a month after the bands had been cemented to his teeth. He hadn't wanted braces, and he had guessed that his mother was angry at him for not being a willing patient. Even if he was inventing her speech in his delirium, it was riveting. George had never heard his mother talk so long without raising her voice. She was still condemning her own covetous nature when she said, "I was so busy worrying about material goods, I never even knew George was in trouble."

Here we go, George thought, steeling himself to be cuffed by the past. Then a worse possibility occurred to him. What if she meant impending trouble? A warning from the grave would be more than he could stand. What if Harris were in danger, or Sheridan? He tried to assure himself she didn't know the future, only the past and her own death. She couldn't see ahead, he didn't think.

His mother's reproach crackled through the speakers. "Two years he consorted with that slut. Years of fine behavior wrecked by one persistent fleshpot. Oh, he'd ride to work on his bicycle, and then she'd drive him home in that rattletrap of her daddy's —and he was white trash, believe you me—"

"A ride home," Aunt Fanny said. "God, ask her what Maybelle gave George in return."

"Shush, Fanny, I'm confessing, aren't I? Oh, Lord Jesus, I couldn't even look my boy in the eye my shame was so vast. I was his mother and it was my duty to protect my Georgio. If I sinned by keeping my boy out of her clutches, then I'll pay with interest."

"Get out your checkbook," Aunt Fanny quipped.

"Fanny," George's mother said, "do you mind ever so slightly? I will tell you true. I marched over to Chuckie Greyson's shack with five hundred dollars that I had been saving toward a summer cabin. My boy was going away to school, I told him, and it would do him good to think he had gotten Carol in a family way. I explained how it may have happened already—we didn't know if she was or wasn't—and I wanted George to know we had chosen him a good path, the only path. Chuckie's mouth like to hit his filthy kitchen floor. He took my money. He said, 'This will work better than a fire hose on dogs.' Turned out his girl was dry as a bone; some fever had shriveled up her eggs when she was eight or nine. Course, I had to learn that from Reverend Kelly's wife; Carol's daddy didn't have the decency to tell me. But the point is, it could have happened, and I like to think George was lucky that we took care of it before he was in trouble for true."

If George had garnered anything from his experiences with Niagara, it should have been how to take a surprise. He was trying to keep his emotional knees bent, his joints loose, to absorb the shock of his mother's tale.

George could never have suspected that Carol was pregnant, because Carol had not been pregnant. He was saddened to think that his mother knew something as personal about Carol as her infertility, when George hadn't known that himself. Even confessing, his mother hid her deceit behind George's rehabilitation, rationalizing that he might have been guilty.

May-belle Mahoney was winding down. "I suppose he was what you would call a good boy," she said. "I hadn't hoped for him to be an engineer, but he could have done worse. Will and me, we had to face people counting off the months between the wedding and George's birthday. Sure, we told George it was April of fifty-one we got married, but he's a bright boy. Sometimes I'd lecture him and he'd give me a gaze that let me know he was onto us. He's no dummy, my boy. Will, with a baby and me to support, he couldn't go to college. His parents said he was smart enough to knock me up, he was smart enough to be on his own. I figured I wrecked his chances . . ."

George leaned close to the speaker as his mother's voice dwindled to a faint sibilant or two and then died out, the feedback chaser squealing through the set after her. George turned off the two working radios and began to survey the damage. The memory of Niagara drying a champagne flute with a tissue struck him as absurd, surrounded as he was by shards of glass and splintered wood. Her colorless couch was now an expressionist tarp slashed with red.

Forget cleaning up. For an instant, he entertained the thought of masking his work to look like a kid prank. It wouldn't take much: a message in blood ought to suffice. But he would have to come clean to Niagara anyway; if his mother could bare her soul, so could he. Weary and elated, wounded and healed, George closed the trailer door behind him and made sure it latched securely.

Flexing his hand caused the blood to flow again, a stain that even proof of life after death would not excuse in Judy's car. One-handed, George shimmied his sweat shirt off over his head and wrapped it like a boxing glove around his fist. Driving a BMW in the middle of the night, no wallet, no identification—most incriminating of all, no shirt and a bloody pillow for a hand—George understood that the slightest infraction would get him locked up.

George's dream, where his mother had arrived to point and accuse, had galvanized his desire to finish what he had started with Niagara. Now, her revelations had taken the defiance out of his sails and allowed him to appreciate the safe harbor of his family. Why would he step out of their loving embrace for the sake of Niagara's touch? Eager as he was for home, George paid close attention to the speed limit, not to mention the rearview mirror.

First the suburbs and then the city came back to him. The return seemed much shorter than the drive out, but wasn't it always easier going home? Soon enough, once the leaves that were currently budding had bloomed and turned, George would be forty. Old enough to know better, he thought, now that he did know better. The pity he felt for his mother was about equal to his anger toward her, which signified a profound increase in pity. She had lied and then punished him for misbehaving. A round robin of punishment, the reverse of Niagara touching a lamp to connect to her parents' loving touch.

Mostly George regretted the concern and guilt he had wasted on a problem that had never existed. All that energy, gone to nothing. He tried to reserve judgment against Carol, whose silence and disappearance may or may not have constituted betrayal. Who knows what the adults had told her about him? Close to home, nearly all lights had dimmed, and there was no traffic. George wished Niagara were in the car with him now, so he could tell her the news. He had the sensation of being inside Niagara's head, having looked through the door she had opened. To see with her eyes was more intimacy than he had planned for.

"You think I'm such a skeptic," he said out loud, "but I never suspected my mother was expecting me when she married. My father told me he wasn't interested in college, and I did not doubt him. I'm a bright boy, all right," he said. "I am a man who is not easily fooled."

George returned home safely. Figuring a missing sweat suit was less suspicious than a bloody one, he disposed of his entire ensemble in the supercan outside, then streaked to the guest bathroom, where he parboiled his sinful, redeemed self in a scalding shower. The cut on his hand was deep but small; George covered it with a generous wrapping of gauze. Swaddled in his plush robe, George visited each of his children to plant a kiss on their cheeks, silently rededicating himself to them.

The clock on the nightstand read three-thirty when he cupped himself against Judy, who surfaced for a second or two. "Did you hear a noise?" she asked. "I did too."

"It was my mother," George said, certain Judy was actually unconscious.

There was something to be said for exorcism; George drifted off quickly. In the hours before dawn, he entertained no relatives, staged no orgies. Slumber alone carried him on its healing currents, rafting him down a dreamless river. For the first time in many nights, he never left his body and he never read his mind.

## 12

~~~~~~~~~~~~~~~~~~~~~~~~~~~~~~~~~~ *The Lines of Resistance*

George sprinted through his morning routine as soon as the alarm sounded. Pleading work as an excuse, he begged off breakfast and being assigned to Harris, then ran out the door like some cartoon father, with his shirt untucked and his briefcase an arm's length behind him. He avoided Sheridan, who would panic over his wrapped hand; neither did he want to be there when Judy realized the BMW had been driven in the night. He knew any explanation he gave would be suspect. As for Harris—it would be just my luck, George thought, if he took the kitchen trash out on his own initiative for once and came across a bloodied sweat suit in the supercan.

Having gained an hour, George stopped at the diner on Rockville Pike where Niagara had explained her electro-spiritual stirrings. George sat at the counter studying the current in his coffee cup and taking stock of his position in the altered cosmos. Niagara's research had seemed especially hokey to him considering her scientific pedigree, an elite group of intellectuals who knew how to make electrons sit up and beg. What would the Caltech cronies think when she began to amass evidence supporting her theory?

At that memorable lunch, the first fortune earring Niagara

unfolded had read, "You will do foolish things, but you will do them with enthusiasm." George barked a laugh, drawing stares from down the counter. Niagara had appropriated that fate as her own, though it could now be seen to have predicted George's week with alarming accuracy. More evidence that as much as you choose your fortune, your fortune chooses you.

Departing from his usual high-fiber, low-fat morning meal, George ate eggs and sausage, then pancakes and bacon. It was like a feast from his childhood, an era when fat warmed your heart and eggs were touted as brain food. Stingy as she'd been with affection, George's mother had fed him generously, coaxing a rise from the toughest biscuit.

George tried to outline what he would tell Niagara. He didn't suppose his respect and admiration for her would be clear in his act of destruction. From innumerable excursions with his kids to the National Zoo, he vaguely remembered there being some animal that defecated and then rolled in its own stink before courtship. Maybe he could start explaining himself on that note.

After he finished both breakfasts, George thought to remove his flag of a bandage. The skin was white and puckered, as if gasping for air; however, what looked four or five hours ago as if it might need a stitch was already on its way to healing. He had cut himself in an opportune spot, one that barely pulled or stretched, and he decided to leave it uncovered. Anyone bent on mystery, George mused, would do well to study the restorative powers of the flesh.

"You look like day-old doo-doo" was the way Bev greeted George at work.

"Rough night," George yielded, willing to fold with the slightest inquiry. The prospect of facing both Niagara and a presentation meeting was making him regret his second breakfast as well as his first.

Bev shook her head in sympathy. "You and me both," she said. "Last night, Mike nearly lost a finger working on that science-fair project."

It was no wonder. George had expected Bev to put a stop to Mike's flammable experiments even before this year. Maybe refusing a pyromaniac brought on more trouble than it was worth. Feeling a little unsteady, George perched on the corner of Bev's desk. "Don't they have to get them approved? Mr. Knight seems pretty conscientious."

"Well, this one slipped through his crack. The project should be called 'How Firecrackers Put Your Eye Out.' I just pray he doesn't win an award."

"Are you and Massoud going tomorrow?"

Bev rolled her eyes. "Of course."

"We could all drive together," George suggested. He took off his glasses and swabbed his forehead with the back of his wrist. He smelled vaguely unfresh, like a stand of boxwood.

"You are a mess," Bev said. "Presentation day?"

"Yes," George said, "and my mother."

"I thought your mother was dead."

"Me, too," George said. "But that doesn't keep her from torturing me."

Bev, for once, wasn't interested in more information. "Nice pants," she said. "Not your usual attire."

Dressing against the clock, George had already robed his top half when he remembered he could wear real clothes. Because he didn't want to start over, he pulled on a pair of pleated khakis and found his favorite belt—dark brown, crocodile leather with a silver buckle at one end and a silver tip at the other. Though he felt like a modern Minotaur, half nerd, half man, he had doubted anyone would notice the transformation.

Niagara was wadded up in her chair when George entered their office. It may have been because her glasses magnified her eyes in makeshift wonderment, but it seemed to George that Niagara stared at the computer screen with as much love and attention as Sheridan viewed the puppet monsters on TV. Whereas Sheridan could tuck herself into the crook of the sofa's elbow, Niagara's long, bony body rose from the office chair like mountain peaks. She had her shoes off, and her feet were tucked under her, though they stuck out quite a bit from under the chair. She was back in uniform; today's plain dress was the color of a paper sack and just as flattering.

George wanted to hold up her hair and kiss her neck, the way he had seen Travis do through the window. "Hello, hello," he said nearly in a mumble.

Niagara leaped forward, whacking one of her prominent knees against the desk.

"Sorry," George apologized.

Niagara held on to her knee. George could see that she had trimmed her bangs yet again—that was twice in one week—and overdone it on the eyeliner. This was George's favorite look, a style right out of his high-school yearbook.

George understood why Niagara would be made nervous by his entrance; he was mighty jumpy himself. Three hours of sleep and three cups of coffee were enough to make him break a sweat along his upper lip. He had navigated the Oldsmobile to work by force of habit, coming to at distinct points in the trip—Chevy Chase Circle, the entrance ramp of the beltway, the neon clock of the diner. He marveled that he had arrived at the plant without plowing over the back of another car.

"Your first presentation day," he said to Niagara. "There's no need to be nervous." He sounded patronizing where he meant to be attentive.

"I guess," she said. She fluttered her hands in front of her face. They had been chewed on, peeled at.

It took all the self-control George could muster not to tell his story. For the sake of her presentation, he had promised himself he would wait.

Niagara left the office with her body bag of a purse and returned subtly transformed. She had cleaned her glasses of stray clipped bangs and fingerprints. She had also tried to comb her hair over her hearing aid, but the strands couldn't manage it. Bright peacock feather earrings stuck out between stringy pieces of hair. George helped her round up her poster-board graphs and the transparencies with pie charts.

George had one sheet of paper with the butter-softener schematic drawn on it. Feeling grossly underprepared, he had made copies for the eight people who would be at the meeting. Fourteen years ago, when he had unveiled the side-by-side plan, he had carried in a box full of data. Judy had coached him over breakfast: how much refrigerator space would be lost (surprisingly, a few cubic inches were gained); what were the advantages of such a spacious freezer (more households were buying auxiliary freezers to hold summer vegetables or half a cow). The Veteran had openly yawned when George fished out the sixth or seventh comparison chart of the meeting.

"Break a leg," Bev said to the two of them as they left their office. When neither of them replied, she called out, "Niagara, good luck."

George kept up his inane cheerleading all the way to the conference room. Three people were already there, each with an empty seat on either side. Emilio pulled out a chair for Niagara between him and Frank, head of quality control. Emilio winked at George, who was relieved to see that the Cuban wasn't holding Judy's funeral argument against him.

Bob, the patent lawyer, was also there, sitting with his feet arrogantly perched on the conference table. There was no visible wear on the heels or soles of his Italian shoes.

"George," Bob said, "what's the good word?"

"Hi, Bob," George said. No one wanted people thinking they were buddies with Bob, even though Bob pretended that he was blessing specific individuals with his greeting.

Sandi, director of marketing, popped in, followed by Shack-elford's secretary, and finally Shackelford, who was dogged by the smell of soot and sage, his specially mixed brand of tobacco.

The boss sat at the head of the conference table and immediately lit up another cigarette. George could see he had regressed to rolling his own.

"People," Shackelford called them to attention. "Let's get down to it."

No one mentioned the absence of the Veteran or even the funeral. They were not a crowd for small talk; still, George thought they might have acknowledged that time passes, things change, the Veteran had died.

These meetings had always been awkward, what with Shack-elford's desire to leave the refrigerator alone and the many ideas tottering between practical and useless, even comical. On the fourth Friday of every other month, George always felt like a help-less villager at the base of Mount Shackelford. Discussion and questions ensued in the anxious minutes before Shackelford erupted. Depending on the extent of the boss's rumbling and the personalities around the conference table, they would either run terrified from the lava flow or else step up to the caldera and throw in sacrifices.

George was hopeful that the dynamics might change. It was Tuesday, the Veteran was gone, and Niagara's debut was prom-ising. Shackelford, however, stared at the two of them with the smoldering intensity George had seen at fourteen years of design presentations, nine with Shackelford in Emilio's chair as foreman and the last five with Shackelford at the head of the table. The boss looked from Niagara to George. "You want to flip a fucking coin or what?"

George regretted his lapse of manners. He should have asked Niagara if she would rather go first or second.

Niagara said, "George, you want to start?"

"If you prefer," George accepted her invitation. He handed out the copies of his schematic, gray from the dark setting needed to duplicate the meager pencil drawing. Sandi rotated hers every which way; unable to make sense of the schematic, she began doodling away at the lines of resistance. Altogether, his butter softener was unveiled, explained, and accepted in under five minutes. It had the sound of an extra feature with-out changing much. The additional software and thermostat would be inexpensive and compact—there was plenty of unused space in that part of the door. The speed with which George's trial was over underscored to him what a small idea it was. Or maybe it was a credit to his talent. He lifted an eyebrow in Niagara's direction, as if to say, See how easy this is? Go get 'em.

"And now, ladies and gentlemen," George said, "our newest talent, just in from the coast. May I present Niagara Spense."

Mostly they just stared at George, Niagara included. Finally, Emilio clapped, prompting Frank and Sandi to follow suit.

Niagara stood. "Thank you, thank you," she said. "You're too kind." Three-fourths of the group smiled at her. George recognized in her fake curtsy the grace of a comedienne.

Niagara laid out her bar graphs and detailed drawings. The refrigerator is milky white; a switch is flipped; the refrigerator is clear. The box gives up its contents without the loss of a single degree. Emilio beamed as she furnished the manufacturing numbers they must have crunched together. George could tell that the group was pulling for her.

Shackelford began his rumble of displeasure the second Niagara stopped speaking. "Forget it, sister," he said. "You know what that pissy idea would cost us?"

He probably thought he was asking a rhetorical question, but Niagara had estimates and subvention proposals for splitting costs with both Corning Glass and the federal government.

Bob was evidently torn between kissing Shackelford's ample ass and sinking his teeth into some potentially interesting patent law. George knew where his face would end up.

The lawyer said, "We'd have to pay royalties on that kind of glass. Whoever invented it would require a cut."

Emilio said, "We save so much, we can afford to make inventor rich, too." It was unlike Emilio to argue a point in favor of more work for himself; none of them thought that altruistically of refrigerators.

Sandi, too, had something to say. "It's so different," she started, which made George think she was going to underscore Shackelford's rejection. But then she burst forth with marketing ideas. "What choice is there in boxes? You either get a ready-made or a custom cabinet. This could be both status- and energy-conscious. Energy efficiency is very important to buyers these days."

"There are some quality statistics available on the glass," Frank said. "We're talking a two-percent fail rate with a ninety-nine-percent confidence factor."

"I'm no engineer," Sandi admitted, "but I don't see any reason why it wouldn't work."

Shackelford jeered at the lot of them, from whom he had

come to expect either offerings or a quick retreat. "You want reasons?" he asked and pounded his fist on the conference table. By now, he had exhausted the room with his custom-blended smoke. "Where do you put junior's artwork and the grocery list? Magnets won't stick to glass, and if you want to see through the fucking door, you have to keep it clean."

Niagara took the offensive. "There are vinyl adhesives that stick to glass," she said. "They might be less dangerous than refrigerator magnets, which kids are always swallowing. You can't put magnets on pantry refrigerators, and those are already out-selling Coldpoints." She was frenetic but sensible. "Maybe another part of the kitchen will become the bulletin board. Are we responsible to the magnet industry?"

Sandi was right on her heels. "We could do a cute promo where we give away a magnetic bulletin board with every refrigerator. 'Put your pictures here, but put your food in the new Coldpoint.' "

George spoke up. "No magnets hardly seems a reason to dismiss it."

"You people," Shackelford snarled. He counted on his thick index fingers. "One," he said, "glass is heavy as cement; and two"—he held up the V of two fingers—"glass fucking breaks. The shithead who has to move that son of a bitch wants a lighter, stronger box—not a block of glass."

Niagara shrugged her shoulders, surrendering to his objections despite the fact that she had matching rebuttals. "So much for vision," she said. "Open-Door Time just seemed a good place to start. I looked at the energy surge there and figured I'd give it a stab."

Half the people in the room sighed in sympathy with the junior engineer, but George was annoyed by her acquiescence. What had happened to the champion of unpopular ideas, the patron saint of basement science projects? He was tempted to tell Shackelford, the pragmatic dullard, what Niagara was capable of.

Niagara took a deep breath and started in again. In fact, she was not folding to the opposition, she was folding into another shape. "I also thought of mounting a miniature closed-circuit screen on the existing door," she said. "And I'm working on the possibility of some kind of object reader that could be taught name association for liverwurst, Parmesan, etc., and answer a user's question of, 'Do I have a pound of liverwurst in there?' with 'No, there is only a half pound.' "

"And don't forget," Sandi prompted, "different colors."

"Oh yes," Niagara said. "Sandi and I were thinking people might pay a premium for a refrigerator that matched their kitchen paint sample."

Frank and Emilio were shaking their heads in disbelief at this spray of ideas, which extinguished Shackelford's fire. The boss squinted at Niagara, apparently trying to figure out if she was mocking him. "Maybe," he said. He pointed a fat finger at George. "That's the stuff I want—butter softened by a computer chip, that's design."

George thought he had never received such undeserved praise. "I had another option, too," he said, "but it's just in the planning stages."

"Two in one meeting?" Frank joked. "You'll pull a muscle, George."

"Listen to this," George contributed. Though he would not have suspected it last week, he now felt he possessed the strength of character to sublimate desire into teamwork. "What if the interior of the freezer contained a semisolid gel mass kept in some kind of flexible pouch? The gel would conform to the shape of whatever food you put in, and it would insulate the freezer. You'd push your food into the gel, which would contract, and when you needed it"—George made the sucking sound that would accompany his futuristic freezer—"you would pull the food out. In the meantime, the freezer would be easier to chill, because it would always be full."

Emilio imitated the suction sound. "I like this noise," he said.

"One proposal per person," Shackelford decreed. He blew some smoke Niagara's way. "That gel idea; that's another one of yours, isn't it?"

Shackelford had managed to insult both George and Niagara

with a single question. The first innovative device George had come up with in years, and Niagara was punished for it. It was a cruel reversal of all those years at home, when George had his mouth washed out with soap because some other kid swore at the principal.

Niagara did not answer the boss's accusation. As if repulsed by their very presence, Shackelford ended the meeting. The last person he addressed was George. "Give her a hand," he said. "Help her out, for God's sake."

George remembered how helpful he had been in her laboratory on Friday, sliding Niagara's cornucopia dress past her shoulder blades, sharp as wings, and then returning last night to wreck the place.

Niagara walked down the hall just ahead of him. She shoved her drawings into a recycling basket in the hallway. As they neared their office, she muttered, "Give her a hand."

Mistaking Niagara's murmur as a victory announcement, Bev applauded. She sensed her blunder after three loud claps. "Not good?" she guessed. "Was there yelling? I think Shackelford's getting an ulcer."

Niagara scurried into the office like a mouse down a hole. George was right behind her, and he slammed the door before Bev could insinuate herself. His chastened coworker was paler than usual, and they were both shaky. George opened his arms to the girl genius, who folded like a marionette. In the solution that surrounded his heart, he sensed the mixture of passion and compassion had changed to favor the latter.

"It serves me right," Niagara whimpered. "Whenever you think a job is beneath you, this always happens."

"He's not known for his foresight," George said. He was the model comforter, resisting all temptation to stroke or even pat. Once she had heard him out, she might want to keep her distance. He took a deep inhalation, aware that Niagara's scent was no longer the single note of mildewy dampness but a chord. Her muggy aroma—like the underside of leaves after a solid week of rain—had picked up road dust and the whiff of tanned leather, which George recognized as the state smell of Kentucky but which he assumed had more to do with Travis's motorcycle jacket than his own home ground. It was as if the musicologist tomcat had sprayed Niagara as his territory, and as repugnant as that image was, George found himself willing to respect Travis's rights.

Niagara pulled herself together, that is to say, away from George. "I'm not so good at taking criticism from idiots," she said. Her makeup was smudged all over her eye sockets. "I can't believe he got to me like that."

Simulating nonchalance, George sipped from his coffee cup, which had not been refilled that morning. The day-old office brew was like a dirty thumbprint on his tongue.

"I have a confession to make," George said. "Or it's more like an apology. I drove out to your lab last night, and Travis's Harley was parked next to the trailer. You guys were in the lab." He had forgotten to open with the good news, and he could tell he was making her uncomfortable.

"Travis was depressed about the funeral," she said.

"What were you and the professor drinking to?" he asked.

Niagara spread her hands over her eyes. "Jesus, George, you were spying on me?" Embarrassment blotted her skin in altocumulus formations.

He had started all wrong. "Just for the record," he said, "your glass door *is* spectacular."

"You'd say anything to stay out of prison," Niagara said.

George said, "I thought Shackelford was buying your object-reader idea. When did you come up with that?"

"Dr. Hanszen says you have to have an alternate story for people who don't think the way you do."

"What did your Dr. Hanszen tell the masses?"

"He peaked before satellite communication, so he would say radio-wave research. He taught me that if it sounds boring, no one will ask a second question."

George saw in that instant that, except for the shock of disapproval, Shackelford's poisonous fuming was nothing to her but hot gas. Neither was she impressed that the plebes had stood up for her, which was more than they had ever done for George.

Niagara steered him back to the topic. "I had already told

Travis about what his father said over the radio. Last night, I showed him how I had done it. He thinks the university might take me in."

George remembered Junior waving his glass about. "Bye-bye, physics," he had chanted. "Hello, metaphysics."

"I waited for you to leave, then I broke one of the radios."

"You blew a tube?" Niagara asked, puzzled. "Oh, you mean the tuner; that knob falls off all the time."

"I clubbed it with a champagne bottle."

Niagara gasped. "Were you drunk?"

"Jealous," George conceded. "I had come to throw myself at your feet." He held up a hand. "Don't say it, I'm back on track again."

Niagara pointed to his shriveled hand. "Radio bite?"

George nodded. "Which would explain the blood all over your couch."

"George, you're creeping me out."

There was a rap on the door, and Bev poked her nose in. "Everyone all right in here?" she asked.

"Not now," George snapped.

"Please," Bev said. "I thought you might need a medic or something." Bev was accustomed to people unburdening themselves to her—George knew she enjoyed hearing gossip as much as imparting relief.

When she left, George said, "I'll pay for everything; I swear we'll find you a replacement." He wasn't sure that was possible. "We haven't even gotten to my confession."

"I don't know that I can stand any more," Niagara said.

"I turned on the other radios, and I familiarized myself with your equipment." He winced. That sounded like he had had his way with her amplifier. "I scanned the frequencies, and then I had this idea that manufactured feedback might usher some other signals in with it."

"Feedback," Niagara said, shedding some of her disgust. "That's how I got the Veteran."

The sensation returned of his being of one mind with Niagara. He hoped her imminent discoveries would extend beyond his family and acquaintances. George said, "I'm afraid I heard my mother. She was the one on the radio last night."

He expected Niagara to be radiant, levitated perhaps, her hair a static electric halo about her face, but when he brought his eyes up from the floor, she had that devastated look that had made him grab her in the trailer. He wondered why all her advances made her so sad.

"You must be some kind of carrier," she said. "First the Veteran, then your mother. Just as you prophesied."

"What do you mean?"

A twitch ran through Niagara like a muscle spasm in a horse's shoulder, and she rapped her knuckles on the wooden desktop in a spooky fast knock that sounded like hooves. She licked her teeth, she chewed on her lips. George was reminded of revivalists back in Kentucky. Niagara was perpetually adjusting herself, but this was more like a fit.

"Remember," she said, "when I admitted the Veteran contact would have been better if I'd had him on tape, and you said it could have been worse . . ."

George moved his head in a catatonic nod. "I said it could have been my mother."

"Right. George, she was practically in the room with you."

"Who knows?" George said. "Last night she was just to the left of public radio."

They were mutually flustered for a complete minute, and it was as they quietly appraised the same square of linoleum that Travis Junior swung open the door.

"George!" the rock-star professor boyfriend bellowed. He clapped George on the back, his silver rings striking George's scapula like brass knuckles. Under his left arm, Travis carried a glossy black helmet shaped like a slanted cone. George wondered if he had several bikes or if he had been out to the trailer.

Travis put his futuristic dunce cap on Niagara's desk and took hold of her face in his two hands. "Have I got schemes," he said. Then he let go of Niagara and sat on her desk, bringing one heavy motorcycle boot up next to his butt.

George could see by Junior's expression that, like the frisky retriever he resembled, he was eager to offer his mistress some prize he had wrestled or stolen for her. Travis enumerated the courtesies he had offered several department heads earlier in the semester. "Tours of the music lab, computer-synthesizer demonstrations, impromptu recitals—I was banking for future redemption," he said, playing up the Catholic-school angle. Then he told them that this morning he had happened into a squash game with two of the heads and a dean.

Having seen him drunk and disorderly within the last ten hours, George was impressed that Junior had been able to hit a ball.

"After I made nice all over the slobs, I mentioned a certain lovely scientist and her groundbreaking research."

"You told them?" Niagara swung her head with glee, sending her feather earrings fluttering.

"Baby," he said, "they were hungry for it." He slid his rings back and forth on his fingers, like beads on an abacus. "Wait until I find Pontchartrain; he'll drool all over his hair shirt."

Apparently there was research money available in at least the religion department, if not every department Travis had baited. "It seems that the Jesuits are dying to find some high-tech proof of life after death." He was selling Niagara as if she knew exactly how to conjure up and even converse with the voices. "There's a bidding war going on," he said. "Religious studies against the Kennedy Institute of Ethics."

"What?" Niagara asked. She turned her good ear round, like a directional antenna, to the source. "A building war?"

"*Bidding*," Travis said. "The medical ethicists would sell their mothers to get you."

George tried to imagine what they might want with Niagara.

"Are they thinking about posthumous malpractice suits?" she asked. "Do they want me to talk about death as a privacy issue?"

With his bright pink tongue resting on his lower lip, Travis was practically panting. "No," he said. "It's better than that. They think you might lead them to some dead Kennedys."

Niagara sat still, both hands in her lap, and a sly grin rested comfortably on her unlined face. So lightly did her years rest upon her that George was ashamed of the lecherous plans he had entertained. It was the first time he had seen Niagara at peace, and her beatific countenance was the look of a woman deeply in love. While George's news had made her twitch, Travis had soothed and pleased her.

Niagara stirred from her reverie. "I suppose they'll want proof."

"Not if religious studies is the winner," Travis said. The leathery musicologist came close enough for George to smell a whiff of tequila on his breath. "Living expenses and a lab of one's own," Junior said. "Isn't that every woman's dream?"

## 13

# What If You Have Powers

# You Don't Believe In?

For the first two months following Sheridan's birth, Judy had been transformed by depression. George remembered what a surprise it had been to everyone who knew her that she was truly unable to get out of bed or dress herself; she was barely able to eat. Mostly she wept and apologized to the passel of friends, relatives, and baby-sitters who pitched in during the crisis. George volunteered for the night watch, a post he maintained after Judy came back to her self. He had helped plenty with Harris, but to be completely responsible for his newborn daughter—even when she was mostly sleeping—was a heady experience.

The world took no notice of their plight. Clipper ships sailed into New York Harbor to celebrate the one-hundredth anniversary of the Statue of Liberty, an earthquake leveled San Salvador and its surrounding villages, *Voyager 2* discovered another ten moons orbiting Uranus. Meanwhile, George was becoming adept at a new set of tasks; for example, to avoid startling Sheridan, he learned how to change her in complete darkness. It so happened that a white plastic diaper was luminous enough on its own that he could distinguish the plain white back from the patterned front, and when the cold months came, George witnessed a phenomenal occurrence. In the winter dark of the nursery, its air dry enough to require the constant steam of a humidifier, the act of ripping open the tape tabs on his daughter's diaper caused sparks to fly on either side of her tiny hips. Thus far, it was the closest George had come to a mystical experience. Seeing his family as a microcosm for all that existed, George beheld the laws of the universe dancing round the rump of his baby girl.

Here was a story he would like to be telling Niagara, rather than the sordid tale he had begun back at the plant. He always felt small-minded compared with her. He wished all along he had been volunteering more examples of himself as receptive and loving. George was piloting the trusty Oldsmobile; despite his truancy of the last week, he had suggested they leave the cubicle before he continued the mother saga.

"Would I go for a drive?" Niagara had repeated, making sure she had heard correctly. "Listen, I'm ready to clean out my desk."

If only he could drive, he had thought, he would be able to order his thoughts. There were rules out there to be obeyed—red lights, merge lanes, speed limits—man-made rules he could contend with. Niagara had watched him sweep his desktop for his keys, root through his top desk drawer.

She lifted her dress back onto her shoulder. "Left pocket," she had said.

"Beg your pardon?"

"They're in your left pocket. You were jingling them earlier."

George had hesitated. He wondered if he was still in last night's dream, if the entire trailer episode and presentation meeting—not to mention Junior's sniffing around—had been part of his sleep, and he was scared to see what might be hidden in his pocket. Should he hope to wake up or not? But when he reached inside, his pocket held no surprises, just keys and a half roll of antacids.

Now he was turning left off Rockville Pike to take them up the hill behind the Mormon Temple. The stiffness in George's shoulders dissipated into a slack exhaustion; the ups and downs of this last week were giving him an emotional case of the bends. Inspired in equal parts by heaven and Hollywood, the gleaming temple was pure white, with thin golden spires like divine lightning rods rising from each corner. From the tallest spire, an angel trumpeted the word to twelve lanes of cars and trucks, acting as God's traffic-control reporter.

"What if you have powers you don't believe in?" George asked. "Sort of like a hidden talent, but worse. A hidden talent would be that you had the potential to become a prominent pianist but you never took a lesson. Powers like psychic powers, but you didn't believe in psychic powers."

"If there's proof of your powers . . ." Niagara trailed off.

Just driving helped ground George. He was more a transmitter than a medium, more a medium than a psychic, he reasoned to himself. If Niagara hadn't been out there, her one good ear listening to every snap, crackle, and pop, George would not have even known he was attracting the dead. He hadn't foreseen the Veteran's death; he had merely dreamed he was the ailing engineer calling out for help. Judy could interpret that scenario with little effort—might George be afraid of becoming obsolete, of being regarded as a comatose designer? She would have some creative explanations for what he'd heard last night as well.

George followed the roads into the visitors' parking lot, enjoying the prospect of finishing his story of the afterlife here. It was a bright March noon, and George guessed the predicted seventy-degree high had already been reached. He parked the Oldsmobile under a budding oak.

Once the car settled, George removed his shoulder harness. "You want to walk?" he asked.

"If you need to," Niagara replied. She gave him his lead, but he still felt the cold bit in his mouth. It was in the interest of science, he told himself, though a condensed version would suffice.

They set out for the fountain near the entrance. Fresh-mown grass, the same fragrance as cut watermelon, scented the air, which seemed clearer up on this mount. The cars filling the lot bore license plates from all over the world.

"I've had these dreams," George said. A blue jay on a fence post caught his eye.

"Sleeping dreams?" Niagara asked.

"Yes," George said. "What did you think I meant?"

"Well, you've got me spooked here. For a second, I had this notion that you were going to start talking about us running away together or something. Dreams of a new life, I don't know."

She was ripping a leaf along its veins, and George couldn't detect if she was mocking him or not. Looking past her, he was surprised to see a couple in a sedan passing a paper bag between them.

"Last week," George started, "Thursday night, I dreamed I was the Veteran in his hospital bed and I was dying. The gist of the dream was that I had to call out to you. I kept yelling your name as I was going under."

"Thursday?" Niagara asked. "The day we went to the hospital?"

"The night he died."

Niagara had been chewing on the leaf stem she had just denuded. She took the frayed stem from her mouth and flung it away. "Around what time?" she asked. "Do you remember when you had the dream?"

It was a couple of hours after he had gone to bed. He knew that much because once he had woken up (Judy's hand clamped hard over his mouth), he had left their bed for the couch in the TV room. The midnight talk shows were winding down with marginally famous guests. He remembered flipping between the channels and seeing a child genius, an unfamiliar music group, a bird-call specialist. "Coming up on twelve-thirty."

"That's when he died," Niagara said. She folded her arms across her chest, but not before he noticed that her nipples were making a tent of her dress. She said, "I heard him after eleven, when he was dead but the hospital didn't know it. And then Travis told me they discontinued life-support at twelve-fifteen." Neither of them was walking anymore. "George," Niagara said, "he called out to both of us when he died. He contacted you."

"Would you believe me," George asked, "if I said it gets weirder than that?"

"Maybe. Don't forget, I'm the gullible one." The fountain spewed behind them, and the smell of chlorinated water coming through a pipe reminded George of washing the car with his dad. The sun glanced off the tower angel to brighten Niagara's murky brown hair. Her peacock earrings were iridescent blue, then green as the breeze blew them around. When she raised herself onto her toes and kissed George tenderly on the cheek, he must have flinched, because she said, "Don't be so frightened. Aren't there some things you abide without proof?"

Maybe it was the setting, but she sounded to him like the angel comforting the shepherds who watched their flocks by night.

"Why did you kiss me?" he asked.

"Because you're adorable," Niagara said. "Especially when you're nervous. Relax and tell me everything."

"Kissing is not going to relax me."

Niagara laughed. "I'm done kissing, George. It's all out of my system. It will never happen again."

"God damn it," George said with tremendous sincerity.

It was easier than George thought it would be to relate last night's dream. He felt himself redden when he got to the condom part, but she didn't heckle him in any way. When he said he'd heard a voice behind him scolding him and calling his name, Niagara gasped and covered her mouth.

"Not your mother," she said.

"In her gingham housedress," George concurred. "Coming at me with that pointed finger."

George wished he had a brown bag to chug from. "So I drove out to your lab, did some damage, started fiddling, and the next thing I know, May-belle's broadcasting her sins and mine." He felt a surge of anger toward Travis. If Junior hadn't been there last night, Niagara could have heard this from May-belle firsthand. It would have been nice for her to know without him having to tell her. Though if Junior hadn't been there, George might have familiarized himself with different equipment, and he supposed he would be in for more than a hefty repair bill.

"Come on, Psychic One," Niagara prompted him.

"Can I tell you my side first?" He felt a need to divulge every little detail, an urge he had resisted even among the bragging boys at Pershing. "Carol had breasts a full year before she started calling me. I was completely ignorant—no sisters, a mother who would say 'My friend is visiting' once a month—but these were not breasts to be ignored."

George was remembering sixteen-year-old obsessions, but he was eager to unload. "It seems absurd now, but I honestly had no idea what exactly caused pregnancy—not that ignorance absolves me."

A crowd of a dozen or so people trotted past them toward the door to receive a young, fresh-faced couple who were stepping into the sunlight. She wore a white dress so simple it appeared to be made from a bedsheet; with his short hair and blue, slightly shiny suit, he looked as much Moonie as Mormon. George knew the temple was the site where the devout wed for time and eternity. The sincerity of that gesture shooed him back to the Olds.

Partial shade rendered the car dark as a cave to eyes accustomed to the afternoon sun. Niagara belted herself in. "You know," she whispered, "these people perform baptisms for the dead."

"I could use one of those about now," George said.

Niagara laughed, but he hadn't really been joking. The notion of floating robed and weightless in a tank of water was incredibly appealing.

In honor of the setting, George left out some of the lurid details. "Our two years together, I kissed every inch of her. I committed her to memory before she could reject me. As it turned out, we were separated before that could happen."

Niagara was facing the windshield. George knew that meant she was listening intently, offering him the full use of her left ear. He said, "Carol encouraged me to be spontaneous without worrying about being laughed at, which was as new a sensation as sex to me. We danced naked in the belly of the brachiosaur; we wrote letters to each other about our parents, our favorite music, our fantasies."

Before he started his litany, George had imagined it would be moving and exceptional. Even to himself, he now heard it as a simple first-timer story. If he could, he would have explained to Niagara how loose and trusting Carol made him. It may have sounded entirely hormonal, but George remembered coaching himself to surprise Carol, whether it was with a poem or a silly treasure hunt to lead her to a Goo Goo Cluster. As in a philosophy seminar, they had taken turns presenting discussion topics: What would you give to the family of a man wrongly put to death? Would you tell your mother off if you knew it meant an eternity in hell? Meeting George as a high-school sophomore, Niagara would have been impressed at his capacity to embrace both things proved and those only dreamed of.

"George." Niagara pretended to slap his face, as if he had passed out at the wheel. "The suspense is killing me. What did your mother say?"

He remembered the monologue nearly word for word. He told her about Aunt Fanny leading off, and how her voice had unleashed a vision. Then his mother, talking first about her envy before moving on to George. "Years of fine behavior wrecked by one persistent fleshpot." Deceit upon deceit: hush money, sending George away thinking he was responsible for a child he would never see, Carol's infertility, his mother's indignation that Chuckie Greyson had misled her, and the crowning touch, his own parents' shotgun wedding. Niagara seemed relatively unmoved by his eavesdropping; he had expected to bring the house down.

When he was finished, she scratched at a stain on her dress for quite some time. "I don't mean to be rude," she finally said, "but her soliloquy has all the makings of a dream."

"You don't believe me?"

"I want to, I do. I'm just saying she went down the list and answered the dream questions: 'Was I really guilty? Why was she so hard on me?' "

"You expected me to believe the Veteran came to you," George was getting the Harris whine in his voice.

"No, I never expected it. I only told you." She unbuckled her seat belt so she could face him with her whole body. "I want this to be true more than you do. But we're scientists here. Think what you would say to me—look up their marriage license; find Carol Greyson, for heaven's sake."

"What happened to our kissing?" George asked, almost academically. "You may not be flattered to know this, but in all my married years, I have never done that before."

"It's like lightning discharge," Niagara said. "Electricity builds up and if it can't travel, beware the ball of fire."

George thought she had misconstrued his question. "What happened to our kissing?" he repeated, enunciating each syllable.

"I heard you," Niagara said. "The electricity was building up between us—you were positively crackling—and it was getting pretty hot in here. I thought we had dissipated it."

"I'm not intelligent enough for you?" George asked. "You aren't attracted to me?"

"Let's just say I came to my senses, like you," Niagara answered. "Anymore, I try not to be attracted to men who aren't available. No matter how phenomenally they kiss."

"Anymore?" Had she been in love with married men before? "Anymore."

"Tell me," George begged. "If you think I can stand it."

"This is not for public consumption," Niagara said. She cleared her throat, obviously struggling for the right words, and her voice broke when she said, "I shouldn't even go into this."

"You know the worst about me," George said by way of comfort.

"That's true," Niagara said. "Fair's fair." She seemed to be silently arguing with herself. "Here we go." She was mustering her courage on the one hand and talking herself out of it on the other. "George."

"Niagara."

"I am doing all of this—throwing away a Ph.D., going into debt, giving up on a normal life—in hopes of finding Algernon Hanszen."

"The sound-wave man? I thought he was dead." Niagara had pointed the physicist out in the circle of photographs that crowned her desk. The ghost of tuberculosis sucked at Hanszen's cheeks;

with fifty pounds on his frame, he might once have been hand-some. George must have had his physicists switched. Might that portrait have been a waning Michelson? A young de Broglie? "I assumed he was dead before you were born."

"That's right," Niagara said. "He died in 1918, after Planck won the Nobel that should have been his. He doted on Planck, though of the two of them, I'm sure Algernon was the visionary. Their colleagues in Berlin called him 'Planck's Constant.' "

"How do you know all this? I've never heard of him."

"I have all his notes. It's pretty unscientific of them, but Caltech's engineering library was cleaning house. They thought he was a crank, not that they know a blessed thing."

"And you love his notes?" George didn't get it. What had he been calling love if not reveling in someone's physical presence, muscling up when they spoke your name?

"Everyone knew I had these ideas about electricity, so the librarians passed his archives on to me. They said I'd get a kick out of them, but I think they also hoped I'd preserve them."

George sided with Niagara in her scorn of such unlibrarylike behavior. Of all schools, Caltech ought to know that the distinction between genius and crackpot is slight. On the other hand, George thought, of all schools, Caltech probably suffered from an over-abundance of each, with the crackpots no doubt keeping more copious records.

Niagara said, "I read through everything four or five times. I would get to the final page of his last journal and pick up the first shabby notebook to start over again."

"You love him?" George asked.

When Niagara looked up, her eyes were misty and red. "I love him more than nuns love Jesus."

"My dear Niagara," George said, laying his hands on hers. While it remained to be seen how accurate George's predictions were, he foresaw a lonely future for his sweet conjurer. Even if she were successful—finding the dead and then finding one among the billions—she would have at most a voice crooning to her from the other side.

"All those photographs," George said, "over your desk."

"Mad scientists, mistresses or sisters who were the real brains, a few mathematicians. People whose reputations I would love to restore."

"What about Travis Junior?"

Niagara tried a wan smile. "Well now, you can't kiss a dead man, can you?"

## 14

*Sweet Forgiveness*

Getting ready for work Wednesday morning, George was undone by the possible permutations of shirts and ties, and he found himself sympathizing with Judy's arguments against freedom of choice. Ordinarily, he showered and dressed in eight to ten minutes; stymied in the closet, he had already heard the high and low temperatures broadcast twice. He was keenly aware that today was the unveiling of Harris's science-fair project, for which he wanted to look like a proud, casually handsome Washington father. And his relationship with Niagara having entered a different plane, George still hoped to impress her without obviously trying.

Lately, when Judy mentioned their potential summer vacation, she would dwell on the Adirondacks or the merits of Quebec, presumably so she did not have to speak the words "Niagara Falls." If she was avoiding it, George couldn't mention the tourist spot either, which saddened him. He wished his wife would say Niagara over and over again, the way she had before, because George ventured he would soon be lonesome to hear her name.

Provided George's experience with his mother was genuine, Niagara posited that others must be transmitting the spirits of ancestors and ex-coworkers. She planned to track down Algernon Hanszen's relatives, no matter how remote, and stand next to them, hoping something of him had rubbed off on his progeny.

"At most," Niagara had told him, "you have served as my missing link to the dead. At the least, you invited me into your dreams. Pretty impressive, if you think about it."

"I think about it," George had said.

"And you led me to Travis Junior, for which—who knows—I may be eternally grateful."

That hurt, even though George pitied the suitor who had to compete with a dead man. He'd felt compelled to ask, "Did you ever consider I might have led you to me?"

"More than once," Niagara fluttered her clumpy eyelashes. Then she pushed her wire-rimmed glasses up the bridge of her nose, transforming herself from coquette to scientist. "Compared to you, I'm just a technician. You're the one with vision."

His vision detected a shyness heretofore unexhibited. Niagara randomly pushed buttons on her calculator rather than meet his eye. "You know," she said, "I've spent thousands on equipment, where you're picking it all up intuitively. At the risk of sounding like your mother, I'm covetous."

That convinced George that whatever he was, he was not psychic, because he never would have divined her saying something like that to him. In fact, he hadn't actually predicted the future—the most he had done was scare the complacency out of himself.

The third time the traffic report came round, George forced himself to decide, choosing an Egyptian cotton, long-sleeved shirt with a tab collar and regular cuffs. For a tie, he picked out a dark-blue silk number, redolent of the forties, which had an asymmetrical red swirl and an elongated green olive at the widest point. George donned pleated blue pants and leather-soled wing tips.

As he buttoned and belted and tied, George reviewed his mother's deposition, which had been both enlightening and demoralizing. His resentment had begun to soften when he recognized that her resolve to discipline him had been prompted by regret for her own sloppiness. It was something like Christians atoning for original sin. Furthermore, he now understood what it meant to have a son cause you worry. While George was not quite ready to release his mother from blame, he was starting to grieve over losing her.

Judy had this theory that if people were only brave enough, they could get whatever it was they desired. Maybe, George had often concurred, but who knew what that was? Judy knew, and it impressed George that Niagara knew as well. That's probably why he clung to these women, hoping one of them would either teach him how to find his bearings or drag him along as she raced toward the sky.

George consulted the closet's full-length mirror, satisfied with his wardrobe choices, and he pledged to his image a commitment to take part in his own life. He had never intended to remain passive-passive in perpetuity. What had started as a coping mechanism for living in his mother's house had become a habit and then a way of life. In marriage, he had stumbled on a woman with an eye for beauty who gladly arranged a pleasant home in exchange for his appreciation. George had lately begun to exert his own ideas about dinner and the children, much to Judy's surprise but not necessarily chagrin. It was quite possible that Judy was tired of making all the decisions. After sixteen years, she could use a break.

With the optimism of a child dressed up and slicked down for the first day of school, George walked into the kitchen to greet his family. Oatmeal sputtered on the stove under Judy's watchful eye. Morning light refracted by blinds striped the marble counters, and the outdoor thermometer read fifty degrees. George automatically converted it to ten degrees Celsius.

"Today's the day," he said to Harris, who was slouched over an empty cereal bowl.

"You're getting colder," Sheridan giggled. She loved the idea that a surprise was brewing.

Harris's plump face sagged with a scowl. He looked as if he might throw a tantrum. "Where's the funeral?" he asked.

"What do you mean?"

Harris tugged on George's tie, which stayed firmly knotted around George's neck. "This. What's the occasion?"

George counted on the guys at work to be less observant than his twelve-year-old. "The ban on good taste has been lifted," he said to his son.

"I told everyone you were an engineer," Harris whined.

George didn't understand the problem. "I can wear regular clothes to work now."

"Mom," Harris practically cried. "Look what Dad has on."

Judy stopped stirring the oatmeal to inspect her husband. "Pretty snazzy, though you'll probably need your ID to get into the building."

"They'll think I lied," Harris said. "They'll think he's a lawyer like everyone else's dad."

"Oh, I get it," Judy said. "Honey, you do look a little jurisprudent. Maybe something with a front pocket."

Thus was George sent to his room. Just his luck that Harris valued his father's nerdiness the day George realized it was optional. George returned his tie to its maple rack and slipped the brass collar tabs out of his starched shirt, regressing from Magazine Man to Engineering Dad.

He changed into a short-sleeved shirt and took a red-and-blue-striped clip-on from the snaky bundle in his closet drawer. He practiced hiding his disappointment in his reflection. Like yesterday, his top and bottom halves did not match, more so today because he had spent so much time on his ensemble.

Back in the kitchen, he squeezed Harris's shoulder. "You're right. That's much better."

"When are you coming to school?" Harris asked in his anxious wail.

"Whenever you want," George said. "I, for one, can't wait."

Harris sighed. He turned a spoonful of porridge over and over. George thought he understood what his son was going through. It would be difficult for the experiment to be as impressive as Harris had implied. He might not win the fair, in which case, he would brand himself a failure in science and a disappointment to both Mr. Knight and George. Harris was biting his lower lip, and George thought if he addressed any of the boy's insecurities, Harris might spray the table with tears.

George threw out a false guess. "Does it have to do with plants?"

Harris let his left dimple show a bit. "Plant stuff is for girls, Dad. Fourth-grade girls."

"You're getting colder," Sheridan said, and then she became nearly hysterical with giggles, prompting Harris to tickle her under her chin and inside her elbows.

George luxuriated in their silliness. It seemed as if a cloud had passed over them, bringing a relief none could have predicted. Taking stock of his own condition, George felt sadder but wiser than he had a week ago. Judy used to say that was the goal of analysis, to make you sadder but wiser about yourself; heaven knows, the most extensive therapy could not have exceeded the revelations of his mother's confession, which George was convinced had originated outside his head. Not all the pieces fit; for example, reviewing his father's behavior, he was unable to isolate examples of longing or regret, though, admittedly, George had wanted to trust him when he said being a machinist was a fine way to make a living.

George couldn't decide if he should update Judy on the possible truth about his high-school girlfriend. Disclosing the Carol Greyson bulletin would mean telling her about Niagara's hobby as well.

"Daddy, Daddy, Daddy, Daddy," Sheridan chanted at the breakfast table.

"Are you with us, sweetheart?" Judy asked.

"Absolutely," George tried to sound enthusiastic. "Harris, I'm driving Bev and Massoud to school, too. How early do you want us?"

"Mike's going to blow up an apple," Harris said with more awe than George wanted to hear.

"What a surprise," Judy said. "Let's see. He burned a phone book last year, he ignited something the year before . . ."

"It's different, Mom. This time he's doing a real explosion."

"I'd better wear my asbestos dress," Judy said, which got a smile out of him.

"Is one o'clock OK?" George asked.

"It starts at one," Harris whined.

George was getting a little exasperated. He just wanted to know what time to show up.

"How about twelve-thirty, honey?" Judy said. "That way you'll be done with lunch, and if your fourth-period teacher lets you out early, Daddy will already be waiting."

George was impressed that Judy knew Harris's schedule.

"OK," Harris said, "but if Mrs. Troy doesn't let us out, you can't look on your own."

George drew an X across his heart, and he winked at his little girl. "I promise Sheridan's allowance that I won't peek."

"You better not," Sheridan said.

Judy tapped at her watch. "Get going. I'll take both of them to school."

"Don't make any plans tonight," George commanded the group. "I think we should go to the Zebra Room for science-fair festivities."

"We're having pizza?" Judy asked. "I already took the lamb out of the freezer."

"Put it back," George said. "We're going out." Then he kissed each and every member of his sweet little family and headed spryly out the door.

Driving up Connecticut Avenue, George admired the effects of last week's rain. Past Chevy Chase Circle, forsythia and daffodils yellowed the showy yards bordering the street. The trees had branches full of lime-green buds, and corn-colored cars, dusted with golden pollen, abounded. Traffic was slow but amiable, and George turned to the bluegrass station for fellowship. When he knew the song, he would take a stab at the low part, a pastime no one on earth knew he enjoyed. He drove up the entrance ramp to the beltway singing "He's Coming Tomorrow and I'll Be There."

Both Massoud and Niagara were hiked up on Bev's desk outside George and Niagara's office. Niagara was wearing an alarming dress, black with a lemon-yellow stripe on either side of the center zipper. The outfit hugged her body like a wet suit, and George saw again that, while she might be large, she was well-proportioned. She still wore the clunky black shoes with the side strap, although with this outfit the shoes looked fashionably retro.

George was a little relieved that Harris had made him change back into Engineering Dad. It would be overkill for both him and Niagara to be transformed in one day.

"Hello, hello," George said.

"Hey, George," Bev said. "What do you think of the new look?"

"Very aerodynamic," he said. "I like it."

Niagara sat up a little straighter and smoothed her hand over her stomach. "Travis insisted. My other dresses practically fell off when we rode the bike."

It had never occurred to George that bikers wore skintight clothes because of the wind.

"We're going to school today, no?" Massoud asked George.

Bev answered for him. "Unless someone blows it up first."

"Bev and I, we disagree on this project," Massoud said. "Let me spill my thoughts."

George prepared himself to be objective; Bev had previously pointed out that the elegance of Massoud's speech enabled him to win many an argument over Americans.

"I think it's dangerous, not to mention a repeat of past performances," Bev said.

"The danger is much of the point," her husband noted. "Mike was surprised, I think, to see how little an outburst takes. Really, you need a wick, some explosives, and a spark. It frightened him to learn how easy it is to destroy, and with that, I would argue, comes responsibility."

George remembered the rush of splintering Niagara's least ancient radio, even though it had already been classified "DEAD."

Niagara was piecing Massoud's logic together. "By making the bomb, he learned how easy it is to bomb?"

"Yes, that is it," Massoud said. "It is not as if the complexity of the instrument saves us. If a ten-year-old can construct it, anyone can. So the question changes. If everyone can destroy, what makes everyone resist?"

Bev chipped away at a fingernail that had been painted with stripes. "You better hope he resists," she mumbled. Judy had once told George that Bev paid as much for her nails as they paid a cleaning service.

"Washington is not Ethiopia," Massoud said. Though he enunciated "Washington," he pronounced his native country in three fluid syllables. "In Ethiopia, the only danger you face is from the politicians. Here, the politicians are no threat, but the people mean you harm; they will steal your eyes when you are not looking."

"Enough, please," Bev said. "We were talking about my son and his exploding apple."

"Are we going together?" George asked.

"Where?" Niagara said.

Bev stopped chipping away at her nail. "Science fair."

"I would like to be there at twelve-thirty," George said. "Harris doesn't want me to miss a minute."

"I love science fairs," Niagara said.

"It's grade school," Bev said. "I'm a parent and I don't want to go." She wasn't convinced Niagara was really interested. "We may as well get some lunch on the way."

"Lunch?" Niagara said, cupping her ear. "I love lunch."

"You must join us then," Massoud said graciously. Hearing Massoud's invitation, George didn't know why he couldn't have asked her along, especially since she was begging.

In their office, George told Niagara about the surprise Harris was hatching and the clue he kept repeating. George imparted his suspicion that the project had something to do with refrigerators.

"Is he a boy genius or something?" Niagara asked.

"We're not sure." George explained that they didn't really know how smart Harris was. Thus far, he had defied most testing, showing zero to remarkable aptitude depending on the day. George bragged about Harris's reading comprehension, even on the most complex science stories, and he confided his hunch that his son was extraordinary.

"I have a hunch I should believe your hunches."

"I'm not expecting a refrigerator," George said. "Maybe insulation or a thermos."

"Why not expect a refrigerator?"

"Well, for one thing, he's twelve. I was sixteen before I could even build a telegraph."

"You could lie about his age to make both of you feel better. It worked for me."

"When did you lie?"

"When I was six feet tall and doing calculus in eighth grade. Next year, he could say he was sixteen and go to a new school— take it from me, people assume smart kids are immature."

George began a panicked calculation of simple arithmetic. Twenty-eight minus a few years would make Niagara close to the age of his unknown child. Imagining the whereabouts of his and Carol's offspring had become a habit as of yet undone by George's latest information. The train of his thoughts raced ahead of his knowing. He should have investigated Niagara's records on the Internet, where snooping was still the only use anyone at Coldpoint had found for the worldwide linking of mainframes. Had she dropped any clues she might be adopted? George realized that to freely suppose is to put yourself on shaky ground. Paranoia is not much more than an overactive imagination.

Her eyesight, her internal grace crippled by excessive height and self-consciousness—George felt he was witnessing the power of DNA woven from the genes of a curvy, smart-mouthed redhead and himself. And then knowledge overtook him, and with a convulsion of sadness, he remembered he had been released from this worry. Unless the communiqué from George's mother was not authentic—a possibility George rejected—there was no child. For twenty-three years, there had never been a son or daughter as physical evidence of his union with Carol Greyson.

"Are you a little afraid he's smarter than you?" Niagara asked, bringing George back to Harris.

Afraid was the wrong emotion. George had no desire to stunt Harris's mental growth; however, he had expected to retain his intellectual superiority at least until his son graduated from grade school. In the last few days, George had worried that he might not even understand Harris's science-fair project.

"Do you think he's as bright as most adults?"

Niagara's rephrasing the question was a clue to George that he had drifted off rather than respond. "He's certainly smarter than I was at his age," he finally answered.

At eleven-thirty, the four coworkers boarded George's Oldsmobile, and George drove to a nearby sub shop. The mood among the group was more festive than he would have guessed. They dared each other to eat the hot peppers in three bites, then two, then one. They sprinkled each other's food with Tabasco and with salt. Basically, they behaved like the sixth graders they were on their way to observe.

Bev asked, "Are these the kind of lunches you two have been having?"

"God, no," Niagara said. She pulled the zipper of her wet suit up below her chin. "George and I discuss major topics—let's see, there's the weather, the plant, the next refrigerator breakthrough for Mr. Shackelford to veto."

Massoud said, "I hope you'll pardon my saying this, but Shackelford is what we would call, in my country, an ass."

The other three laughed. "Guess what?" Niagara said. "In my country, too."

George had been paying close attention to the clock, and now he hurried them up and loaded them back into the car. As soon as he turned on the engine, gospel music whined through the speakers.

Bev said, "At least turn to some heathen station, would you?"

George hit another preset frequency, and Harris's heavy-metal music rocked the Olds.

"Now hear what you've done," Massoud said. "Does your boy listen to this?"

"Yes," George said and shut the radio off. They got to the school just after twelve-thirty; although there were plenty of parking spaces along the street, George noticed Judy's BMW a few car lengths from the auditorium entrance. She could have walked from their house, unless she was as apprehensive as George about the project. George addressed his group before they entered the grounds. "Harris wants to show me his project himself. So if any of you see it first, steer me the other way and do not even hint at what it is."

"God, I wish Mike would surprise me," Bev said. "Why can't he show how a pulley works?"

Niagara adjusted her dress again, precisely centering the zipper between her breasts. "You guys are making me nervous," she said. She tucked her hair behind her ears, which today were decorated with black rubber hoops.

Inside the small gymnasium, the room tittered with the high-pitched chattering of children. George and Judy visited this room five or six times each year. Besides science fair, there was open house in the fall and spring; the school served as the precinct voting booth as well. Of all these activities, science fair was the one George never missed, and it disappointed him that so few parents would leave their offices to marvel at the displays. Perhaps the event was unimportant to their kids; perhaps the parents had helped or even constructed the project and wanted no more part in it.

George was jittery with anticipated pride. He didn't know if he should face the wall and wait for Harris to tap him on the back, or if he could safely wander among the younger kids' cardboard dioramas populated with plastic army men and farm animals. George stopped at a comparison by brand of paper-towel absorbency, knowing it was probably the entry of a second or third grader. Then in his peripheral vision, he spied Judy practically weaving on her feet.

George caught up to her, bracing her with his strong, brown hands. "I saw it," she said. Her nose was running. "You can't imagine. It's like he's not my child."

"Is it gruesome?" George was suddenly afraid that "You're getting colder" might refer to a cadaver experiment.

"No," Judy said. She pulled a tiny lace handkerchief from her plum-colored purse. "It's stunning. First of all," she blew her nose in tiny puffs, "I never realized how much Harris loves you and how much I love your reflection in him."

George looked with benevolence upon his beautiful wife. This kind of thing had happened to him before, but never with such dramatic impact. Watching Sheridan organize her miniature foodstuffs in her play kitchen, George would see Judy as a six-year-old. Or Harris would comb the hair out of his face, exposing the same flash of light that caught in Judy's eyes. The desire to revel in Judy's admiration for him and his son, amplified by his oath not to peek, made him stop Judy from saying anything more. "Should we wait for Harris?" he asked quietly.

"I know I wasn't supposed to look," Judy confessed. "Technically, I did not promise. I was getting nervous that he had built it up too much. I thought maybe I should start some damage control."

Judy, nimble as a sparrow, looked frail and shaken. Taking the rare opportunity to comfort his wife, George tucked her under his wing and held her close.

"I think he's psychic," she said. "I don't know if I'm just too routine for him, but I swear he has a glimpse of the future. He is a genius."

Rather than ease his mind, Judy's enlightenment rekindled George's paranoia. He concentrated on her being genuinely impressed and moved by Harris's talent; she had even admitted to imposing the ordinary on their extraordinary son. There had been something appealing, George realized, about being Harris's special advocate. In a way, it echoed his relationship with his father, only George hoped the echo was louder in the bond between him and his son.

"What if he's a fat genius?" George asked, testing the waters.

"What if he is?" Judy said. "You'd think I could live with that."

George wondered if he had had anything to do with coming between Harris and Judy. Had he been ignoring a genuine need of Judy's to keep Harris from becoming too strange? There would be a different dynamic if both Judy and George were on the boy's

side. Though he had wanted it for years, George prepared himself
to step over a little and let Judy in.

Up ahead, Harris was dodging among the tables, bolting toward them with his chunky gait. George prayed the boy wouldn't
knock down one of the displays, but seeing his son run the maze
of experiments, he had a glimpse of Judy's agility.

"You guys!" Harris said. "Mrs. Troy let us out late." Judy
averted her bloodshot eyes. "You looked!" he accused her. "Didn't
you?"

Judy wriggled out from George's arm and hugged her son to
her. "I'm sorry," she said. "I haven't said a thing to Daddy. I
know it's your surprise for him."

Harris tried to decide whether he was going to be hurt or
thrilled that his mother was in on the act. When Judy kissed his
nose and said, "You're my little genius," the decision was made
in her favor.

"I'm chomping at the bit here," George said.

Harris took his hand and pulled him along. Judy grabbed
his other hand. "First you have to see Mike's. He's going first."

Harris led them to the side of the gym given over to the
larger kids and exhibits. Massoud and Niagara stood in the back
corner while Bev scolded Mr. Knight, who continued to smirk like
an elf. When he got into earshot, George heard Mr. Knight say,
"I'm just his teacher. I'm not his mother."

"Hi, George," Mike said. "Hi, Judy." He looked a little less
pleased with himself than he had most years. Maybe the delight
of shocking people was wearing off. Or it may have been as Massoud had suspected, that Mike's experiment had become a cau-
tionary tale about responsibility. As usual, George was impressed
with how handsome Mike was. Especially on this day, when Harris
promised to shine and Judy was willing to overlook her son's
doughy demeanor, George tried not to compare Mike's elegant
stature with Harris's earthbound lumpenness.

Mike had drawn a large cutaway view of his firecracker. On
the table there was a box of safety matches, an acrylic dome with
tiny airholes drilled in it, three cored apples, and a half dozen
miniature sticks of dynamite. Mike had decorated each stick like

a race car—"TNT" was written in little flaming letters along the cigarette-size cylinders—and he had painted the apples to resemble globes.

"Niagara?" Judy said, recognizing her across the table.

Niagara shrugged. "I hope you don't mind. I begged Massoud to invite me."

"She loves science fairs," George said.

"It's true," Niagara agreed.

Judy seemed to welcome a larger audience for her son. "Wait until you see Harris's project," she said. George hoped Mike hadn't heard her.

George was still holding Judy by the hand when Mike announced it was time for blast off. Mr. Knight passed out safety goggles to the crowd, primarily made up of sixth-grade boys. George was counting on the teacher to have advised Mike on the requisite amount of gunpowder. Along the fringe were three men with clipboards, a conspicuous panel of judges with whom George had occasionally served. He was relieved not to be judging this year.

Mike donned a pair of oven mitts. Somehow he managed to grip a match, which he unself-consciously lit on the zipper of his jeans. He brought the match to the long fuse of the stick in his left hand, then he waved the match in the air until it went out. He stuffed the dynamite in a miniature earth with as little hurry as Judy stuffed bread crumbs into a red pepper. Mr. Knight, ever alert, stepped on the smoldering match; as soon as Mike placed the apple on the acrylic plate, the science teacher covered it. He latched down the protective dome, then ushered Mike over to join the crowd.

George looked across the table at Niagara, who in only six weeks had become one of the largest presences in his life. She resembled something from a nature reenactment in her tight bumblebee dress, which had come unzipped down to the amber drop at the base of her neck. Millions of years ago, a tiny gnat had rested on a tree trunk, its abdomen full of the blood sucked from dinosaurs. Logy and satiated, the gnat had felt the stickiness of sap on the hairs of its legs, but it could not have envisioned that the amber, the *electron*, would envelop and immobilize it until it was nothing more than a decoration.

Soon enough, Niagara would cease to be George's well-kept secret. She would be leaving him sadder and wiser and susceptible to encasing himself in electricity, though he resolved he would not fossilize. Standing in front of an impending explosion, one hand gripping his son's shoulder and the other holding on to his wife, George was willing to take in whatever came. He hoped the gymnasium would shudder with the blast, that sulfurous fumes would burst through the holes in the plastic dome, sending tiny earth-apple bits hurtling like pebbles against the make-believe sky.

Snaking toward the booby-trapped fruit, the lit fuse burned the paper at the top of the cylinder, then the powder took and ignited the slender stick. Mike's painted apple did explode, but it made a wet, splitting sound, breaking into four pieces that fell away from the ammo. When the potential of the inferno came to nothing louder than a popped cork, George and the sixth graders groaned in disappointment. Bev was obviously pleased; Mike looked a little relieved himself.

George wondered why Mike hadn't used a flammable ball, so that the earth might have ignited in a fiery mass, engulfing miniature people and their pets with apocalyptic panache. The boy should have known that an apple, flesh and juice but for a thin mantle of peel, would extinguish most pyrotechnics. A wad of plastic wrap would have burned brighter. This desire for more of a show seemed a healthy sign to George, a hint that he was past the torpor and sloth of his last few years. He was ready to see Harris's attempt. He was ready to be amazed.

"I'm next," Harris said. "The time has come."

George thought of a gospel tune, "Will You Be Ready When the Time Has Come?" and he prepared himself to be simultaneously humbled and made proud. Harris led his father to a sparse arrangement on a nearby table. A few cassettes were scattered next to Harris's tape recorder, which was hooked up to a stainless-steel canister. The container looked to George like a thermos of some type, though he couldn't imagine what purpose the music might serve. Harris turned a sheet of white poster board over to reveal hand-lettered text and a simple line drawing done in Magic Marker. His sweet, chubby face was grinning in the friendly manner that reminded George of Mrs. Harrison standing in front of her poster-board easel in his beloved Dino Park.

A small crowd assembled at the simple display. George recognized Harris's friend Danny and Danny's mother. When Mr. Knight escorted the three judges over, Harris pointed to the headline on the poster and read it out loud, "The Thermoacoustic Refrigerator—Cooling with Sound."

George tried to take it all in, but the sheer brilliance of it kept tripping him up. His son had built a refrigerator, all right. A refrigerator powered by sound amplification. George had read a few articles on thermoacoustic refrigerators, so he knew Harris had not discovered the technology. The machine was linked to the space shuttle—George couldn't recall if the refrigerator was being tested on the shuttle or if its size and lack of moving parts made it handy for space travel. Harris's machine was not only beyond what any sixth grader could do, beyond what George had ever built in his many years of electrical experimentation, it was beyond what all but a few had imagined to be possible.

"Is that a refrigerator?" one kid asked. "Where does the food go?"

"In Mahoney's mouth," another boy answered.

George glared at the boy, but Harris laughed. Either his son was used to being teased or he had thought the remark was genuinely funny.

"This is a new kind of refrigerator," Harris explained. "It has no moving parts except for a piece of the loudspeaker." He pointed to the cone-shaped end of the silver tube. "I've got carbon-dioxide gas in the tube, and at this end there's a loudspeaker that blasts it with sound." He gestured back toward the wave pattern illustrated on his poster. "It's like kind of hard to explain. The deal is that the sound gets the gas all excited and jumping around, while the sound itself stays in a standing wave. So the gas gets moving to the same frequency as the sound."

"Remember," Mr. Knight interjected, "the faster gas moves, the hotter it gets."

"Oh, yeah," Harris said. "It's really not as complicated as I'm making it."

"You're doing fine," the science teacher said.

He was doing beautifully. George could feel Judy looking at him, but he couldn't take his eyes off his son.

"I've got like this metal plate near the cone part." Harris slid the plate out and showed it to the crowd. "It goes at the thick part of the standing wave, and then all the gas molecules go toward it, bringing the heat away from the other part of the tube. So then the plate absorbs the heat and there is cooled gas throughout the rest of the tube. Get it?"

"Does it work?" Harris's friend Danny asked.

"I'm so glad you asked," Harris said with practiced sarcasm, bringing a laugh from the crowd at the planted question. Harris pointed at George. "I sort of made this for my dad; he invents new stuff for refrigerators to do. He invented the icemaker."

"Cool," several of the kids said, bobbing their heads like pigeons.

One boy said, "I thought they always had icemakers."

George loved hearing that his little addition was part of the children's domestic history.

"I know the thing works if you use Megadeath," Harris said, ejecting a tape from the recorder. "But I thought my dad might want to pick the music for the fair." Mostly to George he said, "I only need like fifteen seconds of sound."

"What have you got here?" George asked. He was amazingly at ease in front of the young crowd. The honored, aged guest whose innovations had been in place as long as these children had been alive, George took his time reviewing his choices. At the head of the swarm, Mr. Knight was grinning, his favoritism for Harris transparent. George wished he had a tape of May-belle Mahoney's speech. What better use for her confession than to drive her grandson's machine? George would have instructed Harris to seal her monologue inside the miniature silver coffin, where it could chill a steak or make ice from here to eternity.

George finally selected a young country singer, mostly for her first name, Iris, and the faraway look in her eyes. "Here's one for you."

Harris popped the tape into his portable stereo. "It's going to be loud," he cautioned the crowd. "But I just need a few seconds." He pressed the play button and crossed his fingers, as a high alto voice without a flourish of affectation sang:

> *Sweet forgiveness, that's what you give to me,*
> *When you hold me close and you say "That's all over."*
> *You don't go looking back*
> *You don't hold the cards to stack*
> *You mean what you say.*

Harris clicked off the machine at the chorus's end. In the abrupt silence, George conscientiously closed his mouth, which had been unhinged by the message of the song. With his mother unavailable on tape, he had stumbled on this carol of pure bigheartedness; absolved nearly to tears, he marveled at what passed for random.

Harris counted to twenty in a steady voice, giving George time to reflect. In those pendulous seconds, George came to understand that his morning pledge to be more present was not nearly enough. He would endeavor to wonder; he would allow himself to err. And if he had a hunch about the next advancement in refrigerator technology or a privileged glimpse into the beyond, more power to him.

When Harris opened the end of the canister, the muffled voice reprised, "You don't hold the cards to stack." He extracted a cluster of plump red grapes and held them out to the crowd. Kids yanked them from the bunch, dropping a few in shock when they felt their chill.

"Cool," they said over and over. "They're like BBs." Boys pelted each other until Mr. Knight stopped them with a look of pained disappointment.

"No ice fights," the teacher said.

Frost crystals crept up along the steel canister. The judges had filled up their comment sheets and were turning the pages over for more room. Judy read behind the shortest judge, barely disguising her actions.

Some gesture of Niagara's caught George's eye. "That's spectacular," she said, looking at George but pointing to the thermoacoustic sensation. "I never would have thought of that."

Poised between embarrassment and immodesty, Harris had been absorbing the crowd's respect. Now, he shone it back on George.

"Could you teach me to build one of these?" George asked. He was sincere, though he also wanted to see more of that crooked smile.

Harris offered the ragged bunch of grapes to his father, who plucked a particularly large orb from the ones remaining. George appreciated how, on its way to being chewed, the grape began instantaneously warming to his body temperature. The rubbery skin resisted the initial pressure of his molars and then burst open to his insistent bite, inviting him to eat of the cool, refreshing fruit.